Viking's

Last

Voyage

VIKING'S LAST VOYAGE

The Lost Greenland Colony
Found and Lost Again

by

Iral C. Nelson

JENAIR PRESS
Richland, Washington

Viking's Last Voyage

ISBN: 978-0-9672904-5-4 (Hardback)
ISBN: 978-0-9672904-4-7 (Paperback)
ISBN: 978-0-9672904-6-1 (Ebook)

Library of Congress Control Number: 2016909958

Cover design by Amanda L. Matthews
http://www.amdesignstudios.net/

JENAIR PRESS
2105 Putnam St,
Richland, Washington 99354-3050
jenairpress@gmail.com

Printed in United States of America

TABLE OF CONTENTS

ACKNOWLEDGMENTS

The encouragement by Alan Aamot to revisit publication of my father's manuscript *Viking's Last Voyage* is gratefully acknowledged. Permission to use the photograph of the Kensington Runestone was kindly granted by Darwin Ohman, grandson of Olof Ohman who unearthed the stone in 1898. Suggestions regarding clarity of content from my daughter Tonja Ann Steel, and the sustained support, as well as the careful reviews of the manuscript by my late wife, Nancy Delores Nelson, are also gratefully acknowledged.

Iral Clair Nelson

FOREWORD

Viking's Last Voyage is a story written by my late father, Iral Conrad Nelson (1900–1994). Based on the finding of the author's collection of papers and notes, the germ of the idea for the story apparently began with reading of *The Riddle of the Kensington Stone* published in *Reader's Digest* November 1948, which was a condensed version of the article published in *The Saturday Evening Post* in August 1948. The carved runic writing on the Kensington Stone is viewed by some to provide solid evidence of Scandinavians in Minnesota in the 14th century.

There appear to be about as many who contend that the Kensington Runestone is authentic, and proof of 14th century pre-Columbian exploration by Scandinavians into the interior of America as those who contend it is a 19th century hoax. While the authenticity of the Kensington Runestone will likely never be settled to everyone's satisfaction, the runic inscription served as an inspiration for his fictional story.

By 1956 he had fleshed out the outline of the story. It was further developed after reading Hjalmar Holand's book *Explorations in America Before Columbus* (Twayne Publishers, NY, 1956). That work appears to have been his only other reference source. However, the reader will likely see some influence from Henry Wadsworth Longfellow's *The Song of Hiawatha*.

In the cited work Holand provided a literal translation of the engraving on the Runestone as follows:

> *8 Goths and 22 Norwegians on exploration journey from Vinland round about the west. We had camp by 2 Skerries* [small rocky islands] *one day's journey north from this stone. We were and fished one day. After we came home found ten of our men red with blood and dead. AVM save from evil.* [On the side of the stone] *have ten men by the sea to look after our ships 14 days journeys from this island. year 1362* (Holand, 166)

By 1964 a draft of the manuscript had been finished and was sent to Einar Hammer, then a Director of the International Headquarters of the Sons of Norway Lodge, for critique. After revision following his suggestions, the manuscript was prepared for publication.

Several attempts were made at acquiring a publisher, with a couple of publishers giving favorable reviews but concluding it did not fit their list. Thus save for "vanity publishers," for which he had neither interest nor resources, he was unsuccessful in its publication. Thereafter he became interested in other matters, and for the most part the manuscript was set aside.

After describing my father's story to my neighbor, himself a novelist, and receiving considerable encouragement toward publishing it, it was decided to retype the manuscript in digital format, and assemble it for publication. *Viking's Last Voyage* was first published as an Ebook in 2016 for Amazon's Kindle reader. Since an Ebook would have been completely foreign to my father it has been edited and reformatted for publication in print form.

Although *Viking's Last Voyage* is fiction, it is suggestive of a "could have been" basis for a 14th-century Scandinavian to have engraved the message as appears on the runestone that was brought to light by Olof Ohman near Kensington, Minnesota in 1898.

Iral Clair Nelson
Richland, WA

PROLOGUE

In the year 986 a Norseman, Erik Thorwaldson (Erik the Red), organized an expedition of Norwegian-Icelander colonists and set sail for the newly discovered land far to the west—Greenland. The new settlement in Greenland thrived, and eventually a second colony was established about two hundred miles to the northwest which was a three or four day's voyage around the island for the sailing vessels of those days. It became known as the Western Settlement of Greenland. (Holand, 24–25)

A few years following Erik the Red's discovery of Greenland, his son, Leif Erikson, took a crew of about thirty men and a lone "Dragon-ship" and ventured farther to the west across the "Great Outer Ocean" to discover the continent we now call North America.

There he established a new colony he called "Vinland," likely situated to the south of L'Anse aux Meadows in Newfoundland, Canada. Butternuts were found in that archaeologically established Pre-Columbian Norse site which apparently do not grow that far north. Although the Vinland location is not known, it would likely need to have lain along the eastern coast between 41 and 50 degrees north latitude—the southernmost for salmon and northern most for grapes, both of which had been mentioned in characterizing Vinland.

After about three hundred years, there came a time when Greenland's Western Settlement no longer prospered. For various reasons, traders from Norway found it increasingly less profitable to extend their voyages beyond the larger Eastern Settlement. Eventually trade with the smaller settlement became practically nonexistent.

However, in the year 1342, at the behest of a Church authority in Bergen, Norway, Father Ivar Bardson of the East Greenland Settlement was outfitted with ships and a company of men and set forth to determine the status of the Western Colony and to render such aid as needed.

But Father Bardson and his men were met with surprise when they reached their destination. A record of the mission reads, in part, as follows:

> ... there are many horses, goats, cows and sheep, all wild, but no people ... . But when they came thither they found no one, neither Christian nor heathen, nothing but some wild sheep and cattle. They took what was needed to feed the men and loaded as many [cows and sheep] as the ships would hold, and then sailed home. (Holand, 124)

Nor did they find anything whatsoever to indicate that the settlers could have been exterminated by the natives nor had they died from disease. All the missionaries could report was the fact the Western Settlement had mysteriously vanished.

Finally when the news reached King Magnus of Norway he was greatly disturbed, not only by the strange disappearance of the colony but with the possibility that its people had also fallen away from Christianity of which King Magnus was at that time an ardent follower.

Although the Christian religion was then some thirteen hundred years old, it was comparatively new to the Scandinavian countries, having been established there some three hundred years before the days of King Magnus. It likely was still considered by some as a departure from the widely held beliefs of their forefathers. And undoubtedly there were circumstances under which dissent groups, or even entire settlements, would abandon Christianity and revert to the worship of their ancestral gods.

The King's religious concern is well envisioned by the wording of the royal order by which he commissioned one Paul Knutson to outfit an expedition in 1354 to search for his missing subjects. It read in part:

> ... for the honor of God and for the sake of our predecessors, who in Greenland established Christianity and maintained it until this time, and we will not let it perish in our days. (Holand, 156)

Although it is reasonably well established that Paul Knutson was commissioned to outfit the expedition, whether he actually led the expedition himself is unknown, however, for present purposes it is assumed that he did.

Viking's Last Voyage is a fictional tale of that expedition which was comprised of a band of 14th century bold, seafaring adventurers from Norway and Sweden—who, although the "Viking Age" had ended roughly three centuries earlier, still considered themselves to be Vikings. The expedition apparently lasted about eight years, but *Viking's Last Voyage* relates only to events that were envisioned to have occurred toward the end of that time.

Except for King Magnus, Paul Knutson, Leif Erickson, Ivar Bardson, Erik Thorwaldson and Olaf Tryggvason, all other characters in *Viking's Last Voyage* are fictitious, and any resemblance to any persons living or dead is purely coincidental.

Native Americans are referred to as Skrellings, which is a simplification of *Skrælings*, after *Skrælingjar,* as used by the Greenlanders for the indigenous peoples, or simply as "Dark-skins."

Iral C. Nelson
Eugene, OR

N.B. The pronunciation of the letter "J" in Norsk is some what like that of the letter "Y, as in Yes" in English.

PART I

THE SAGA OF TORKEL THE WARRIOR

1

ISLAND REFUGE

Again the Skrellings attacked with their nerve-wracking whoops and yells. Fully aware of the likely unfavorable outcome, but with a surge of strength born of desperation and rage, Torkel raised his two-edged sword in the face of the renewed onslaught.

He noted with satisfaction as the blade bounded off the bare skull of the first enemy warrior knocking him senseless, and then on to slice athwart the neck of another. A third soon lost his stone-headed axe. A thrust, another swing, and two more fell. As the two crumbled at his feet, he took a quick backward step to clear the encumbrance to his footing.

But where were his three comrades? At the onset they had stood in a solid group, a little more than a weapon's length from one another. Now he could barely hear their shouts and curses from what seemed a great distance. Yet above the wild and meaningless cries of the enemy he could hear them. He then realized his worst fear was occurring—he was being separated from his companions.

And now another powerful swing with his weapon, but this time the blow was less effective. The old warrior managed to down another of his adversaries, but in the process, he failed to completely fend off a blow from a Skrelling's stone-headed axe and suddenly found his eyesight blurred by a string of perspiration and the blood that flowed from the resulting scalp wound.

Again a step backwards as he wiped his face with the back of his hand and once more gave the great sword an upward swing. But something was amiss. The weapon rose more slowly. Its weight had increased three or fourfold. Torkel felt his knees sagging. The very turf under his feet was sinking.

"Help, comrades. Help—*HELP*," he yelled.

The sound of his own voice awakened him, but it required a moment or two for his mind to grasp the fact that it had all been just a dream. His sword still lay by his side on the grass where he had placed it before falling asleep.

With a feeling of chagrin, Torkel sat up and stole an embarrassed glance at his three companions still awake and reclining by the small campfire on the softness of the late summer grass.

Distinctly they had heard his muffled cry for help and turned and looked in his direction, but there were no remarks. All too fresh in their minds were the events of the last few days—the battle on the lake where six of their comrades were lost to the Skrellings and the tragedy afterwards where another ten were lost. Very well did they realize that Torkel had been reliving those events in a dream—yet transposed to fit their present circumstances.

The old warrior, still on the verge of exhaustion from the earlier struggle and tragedy, and now tonight's dream, staggered to his feet. *"Djevelen koke meg* (The Devil boil me)," he swore softly and strode in the direction of a small thicket which from common usage had become the *uthus* (outhouse) for their temporary encampment.

Taking great, deep breaths of the cool night air to clear his head, he faced in the direction whence they had come. And as was the custom of all seafaring men, he looked skyward and located *Karlsvagn* (the Big Dipper) and the North Star in order to confirm his reckoning of directions.

For a long time he stood there—just gazing northward, listening, remembering and contemplating their future. Then the leader of what had become an ill-fated expedition walked slowly back to the campfire and sat down near his three companions.

More silence; and the younger men, as though possessed with one mind, concluded the silence presaged a lengthy and probably wearisome discourse on recent happenings, but hopefully to be followed by encouraging plans for the future.

Their conclusion was soon proven to be correct.

"*Hør på mig, kamerater mine* (Hear me my comrades). We may well be near the end of our expedition. Whilst we await the setting of the moon so we can leave this place, I must gather my thoughts and speak to you 'The Saga of Torkel the Warrior'—the story of our journeyings—of our fortunes and our misfortunes—that if it so pleases the gods, it be may one day presented to King Magnus, and be told, and retold in our homeland.

"Far away indeed seems our home in the Northland, where the saga began some eight years ago, and where, let us hope, at least one of us might someday yet return. But, should the gods choose not to look upon us more favorably than has been our lot over the last three days, the truth is that very likely we shall never leave this hostile land.

"This strange lake-filled land where the earth and sky have been trampled and flattened by the heels of the gods of olden times—at least as it would appear, if set side by side our homeland where the mountains stand high above the water like a giant warrior, his head and shoulders above the clouds.

"Here we sit this night on a small island refuge in a shallow lake, four weary and straggling survivors of a once-proud band of Vikings. Hiding, as does the hunted beast in full awareness that the huntsman is hard upon the trail and arriving soon. At the most, we are a half-day's flight ahead of the Skrellings, whom we know full well pursue us.

"This day we have spent in resting—and seeking a waterway southward. We have found none. Yet, here we cannot remain. By the dawn they will likely be upon us. And in great numbers, of that we can be certain.

"But should they come not in more than thrice our number, I doubt not in the least that we could slay them all. Our weapons, spears, axes, and our bows and arrows, as we have learned are superior to theirs. But we also have learned, by bitter experience, that they will not be thrice our number when they come; they will be more likely five, or even ten, to one.

"True, we could slay a goodly number. I, who have been called 'Torkel the Wise Warrior,' doubt not that I could take good care of at least a half-dozen of them. Surely that many fell beneath my blade during the battle on the lake. Over fifty winters have I seen in the Northland. And for more than twenty summers did I go forth with the fighting ships; but strong I believe I am as a man half my years.

"And you, Sigurd—and you also, Lars are among my best warriors. Younger men than I, you both are equally skillful with bow, sword, and battle-axe.

"And you, Ivar, although not trained as a warrior, but as a man of learning, have proven your deftness as a spearsman rivaling that of a trained warrior.

"Yes, I doubt not, each of you could slay as many as I— hopefully more. And although a goodly number could we slay, the sad truth remains that by the sheer weight of their numbers they would conquer us.

"And also true—in the tradition of warriors, would it be noble to die fighting. But, equally true would it be foolish.

If we are slain, what then of our appointed task—our orders from King Magnus?

"Who then, will carry the saga of our explorations—the story of the Great New Land of the West—back to our comrades who wait for us by the Great Salt Sea of the North (Hudson Bay), and thence back home to the land of our fathers?

"No. 'Tis no disgrace to flee before one's enemies when there is a purpose in the flight.

"*Ja vel* (Oh well). We shall make the attempt to elude or conquer these hostiles. And, if it pleases the gods, although the odds against us be as one amidst the countless stars above us, perhaps at least one of us might one day return to the homeland ... ."

2

THE RUNESTONE

"But wait. Tell me, Ivar—the task to which I set you early the day before this night to inscribe on a stone a message to be left here on the island—a message which our people will find when they come to the Great New Land of the West.

"And come they will of that I am confident—be it in fifty years or be it in five hundred years. And finding our message, they shall know that their countrymen were the first to come. That it should be their right to lay claim to this new land, which, one day, could well be the new home of the Norsemen and our neighbors the Swedes and Danes.

"You say you have finished the task? Then read to me what you have inscribed. While I learned well the art of fighting, the art of inscribing runes I was content to leave to men of learning.

"Here now ... Lars and Sigurd, lend a hand. Stand the stone erect, here by the fire.

"Now, let us hear the message, Ivar. But wait; you say: 'We were eight Swedes and twenty-two Norwegians.' You inscribed not our names, nor the places of our birth. Do you not think ... but no, it matters not. That is sufficient. The four of us are all from the Northland. Indeed, what matter our names, or places of birth? To he who finds our message, they would mean little. Yes, that is sufficient.

"But time grows short. Read not the rest of the message. Having inscribed it, I trust you also have it well planted in your mind. I bade you inscribe as you thought best—you can relate it to me later when, if it pleases the gods, we have eluded the Skrellings and time presses us not.

"A crafty lot are the Skrellings, but much we have learned of their modes of battle. Well do they know the waterways by which we have fled, and simple it will be for them to follow our trail wherever we found ourselves forced to portage.

"And well do we know that they are not far behind us. Even now, they very likely suspect our hiding place. But I doubt they will attack us this night, judging by what we have learned of their methods of fighting. But certain I am that at the first light of dawn they would be upon us, if we stay here. Unfortunate it is that matters have turned out the way they have. We came not to fight and conquer native inhabitants of this land. Ours was to have been a peaceful mission—a 'journey of exploration' as Ivar called it. It was to be simply an exploration in the hopes of finding the Lost Greenland Colony.

"But now, if my reckoning fails me not, the moon will sink from sight about a half-hour's time before the dawn. In the darkness of that half hour we will make our move and swiftly but with the utmost caution. But before we make our move, I need to relate the saga of our expedition.

"Now, as I have said, for many a year did I go forth on the sea as a Viking leader. Those were the exciting years of my younger days, and before I became a member of the Royal Council, law speaker, and advisor to King Magnus.

"It was in those later years that I earned the name 'Torkel, the Wise Warrior.' So, natural enough it was, that when the King's orders were read to me: ' ... *you are to choose the men who are to go in the Knorr* ... ' that I should carefully choose strong well seasoned fighting men for what could likely be a long perilous journey. And, yes, I made sure they were unmarried men who were not leaving a wife and children.

"And yet, before I begin, let me say this for it too must be well planted in your minds: In truth I tell you, your leader's name is not 'Torkel'—the name by which you have known me. It is 'Paul Knutson,' the so-called 'Christian name' given to me at birth; the name I have used while in the service of King Magnus.

"'Torkel' is my Viking name, and indeed, so long have I chosen to use it, that many of my warrior comrades have never known me by any other. But to King Magnus, I am Paul Knutson. And so, mind you that too must be part of our saga, because the saga must be reported as that coming from Paul Knutson.

"And lest it seem strange that I chose not to use my Christian name in my fighting days, let me say this: for the most part, all of the warriors with whom I sailed the seas, those who fought and lived, and those who fought and died all had names given them at birth by 'Christian' parents.

"Christian names they were, but we used them not. In name only were we followers of the New God of the Christians. In our heart we were still followers of the ancient gods: Odin, Thor, and all the others.

"And why? Very well would you yourselves know the answer; if indeed you would but ponder the question. Well do you know that the business of a warrior is fighting, killing and all that goes with it. Those things which Ivar chooses to call 'evils.'

"And how then, I ask, though this question is foolish for there is no answer. How then shall a warrior follow the teachings of this 'Christian God'—this 'God of Peace,' as Ivar so often calls him. Now ponder this if you will: his followers have a saying—'Love even your enemy'—or some such words. Yes, indeed. Love him, as he comes at you—axe up-raised to split open your skull. Love him, as you thrust your sword deep into his belly.

"*No*—well and good these teachings may be for fishermen and farmers, but for warriors–*Uff.*

"But understand me, Ivar. I speak not these words in disparagement, or in disrespect for your learning. You, I well know, are one of his followers and not a believer in the ancient gods, as are your comrades.

"Though true it is, you have journeyed with us, and you have worked with us, and you have joined with us in fighting our attackers. And so you have sat with us around our campfires, and listened to our talk. And so also have we listened to yours. And often have you spoken of this Christian God and his teachings. But follow him we cannot. No doubt, as you have told us, far and wide have his teachings spread. But I say, and be so kind as to take no offense to my words, there is no room for his teachings among the Vikings.

"But, enough of this sort of talk. Indeed, I intended not to so speak. My purpose was to say that our saga must also be our message to King Magnus that he may know the story of the expedition which he sent forth."

3

THE SAGA UNFOLDS

"So mark my words and heed them well. For thus is the way 'The Saga of Torkel the Warrior' must begin, if any of us live to tell it—

"We had set forth in the 'Knorr,' as fine a ship as ever sailed the seas, and with as fine a crew as ever sailed a Dragon-ship. Thirty men we were, and well chosen for the journey. Fighting men we all were, save one, meaning of course, yourself, Ivar—a scribe and chart maker. And here let me say this: that if it pleases the gods that only one of us should return to the homeland, my hope is that it shall be you as I believe you are the best one to recite our saga.

"Yes, good fortune indeed was mine in choice of both ship and men. Our weapons were of the best, as were our supplies and provisions. King Magnus would not have it otherwise. He is a follower of the Christian God, and indeed it seemed great distress had seized him at reports of the loss of his Greenland colony. Our task it was, to go in search for them. And seek them we did. Two longboats we carried with the Knorr, and on each of these did we carry a small-boat. And these we well used. Anchoring the Knorr at a safe distance in deep water each day when the weather permitted, I would send forth the two long-boats, ten men in each, to search the fjords and inlets for any evidence of the Greenlanders. The small-boats, each of a size to carry four men, we used for going ashore.

"I had said to the King, 'Supposing we find not the Greenlanders?' And he replied, 'If you find them not in Greenland then search elsewhere. Journey first to the abandoned settlement of Leif the Lucky at Vinland in the New Land of the West. And should you find them not there, search elsewhere. But find the lost Colony.'

"And well do I recall how he smote the table with his fist. Then again did he speak more calmly, saying, 'You will take with you a scribe and chart maker, to chart not only your sea journeyings but also to keep detailed record of such explorations inland as you deem necessary for our good. And in this I am determined,' he continued raising his voice almost to a shout, 'neither the abandoned colony of Vinland nor the lost colony of Greenland shall be the end for the Norsemen in the New Land of the West.' And again he smote the table.

"And so did we search for eight years. And so we did fail. We found them not in Greenland. We found them not in Vinland, and we found not a trace of them as we worked our way northward and ever westward around the coast of the New Land of the West.

"And finally late this summer we found ourselves at the inlet of a river (Nelson River) of considerable size, and it flowed northward, into the Salt Sea. Almost certain it is, I said to myself, this river comes from the heart of the new land. If we are to explore the New Land of the West, here is the place to begin.

"And so also, after much counseling, was our course of action finally decided upon.

"The Knorr would be anchored near the river's mouth, and a camp would be established ashore.

"Ten men would be left to look after the ship. Then, with ten men in each of the long-boats; and taking with us in each, one of the small-boats, we would journey southward up the river. One small-boat, of course, would be left for the use of those who would remain at the Knorr's camp.

"For not more than fifteen days would we journey inland, and fifteen days would we allow for our return to the ship. Not more than thirty days could we spare, lest the foul weather of autumn overtake us on our voyage back toward Vinland where we were to winter.

"And now a difficult task—thirty men we were, and thirty wishes there were to be among the chosen twenty to go inland. First, there was Erling Njalson, my second in command. And there was Black Botolf, my good friend from journeys and battles of other years. A quarrelsome one he was and was ever questioning the wisdom of my orders. And there were the two red-haired brothers, Ludolph and Rudolph. They always stayed close to one another, and so much did they look alike I never did learn which name belonged to which. And there was another redhead, Erik the Red, he liked to be called. Always was he bragging that he was a descendant of Erik the Red whose son, Leif, had founded the Vinland colony some three hundred years ago.

"And Hjalmar the Wild Man—now there was a good fighter. A giant of a man he was. He too, had been one of my comrades in years gone by. And there was Big Thor, and Knute—but why name them? Good warriors they all were, and the task of choosing would not be easy. Finally, it was decided to choose by lot. Taking a handful of reeds, I cut twenty pieces about the length of my hand. Ten of these I cut in half thus making twenty short pieces and ten long. Alone, I walked a short distance along the beach, away from the others, and thrust each piece deeply into the sand leaving one end in plain sight.

"But no, this would not do—I must lead the expedition inland, and Ivar the chart maker must accompany me. And also, Erling, my second in command, must remain with the ship. Thus thinking, I discarded three of the reeds—one long and two of the short. Then calling the other twenty-seven, I bid each man to choose a reed and pull it from the sand. Those pulling the short reeds were to go inland. Those with the long were to remain with the ship. Thus would the choice be left to the gods.

"And so were the lots drawn. And so there were ten unhappy faces—those who stood ruefully viewing the long reed-sections in their hands, and Erling, who was not included in the drawing.

"Botolf, the quarrelsome one, at once commenced to question the wisdom of my decision as to the drawing. 'Why,' he asked, 'should not Erling have been permitted to draw with the others? To be sure, he is your second in command—but the ship will remain at anchor and needs not a commander—'

"Waiting not for him to finish, I silenced him by saying 'The duty of the second in command shall always be to look after the ship in the absence of its commander.' And Erling, though saddened, nodded agreement to my words.

"And so it was that the next day, the two long-boats with fair weather and sails well filled by a brisk north wind moved southward into a river of considerable size and the New Land of the West.

"For four days did the gods favor us with fair weather and a following wind—nor did the course of the river change but little. Ever did it flow north or northeastward as we sailed against the current, but strong enough was the North wind; seldom did we need to make use of the oars.

"Neither had we seen any sign of the Skrellings, of whom we had seen so many at the place of the abandoned Vinland Colony. Perhaps it was, as I recall thinking, that there are no native people in this part of the new land. Nor did it matter greatly. Never had they given us a great deal of trouble at our Vinland camp, save for now and again helping themselves to one of our livestock, and quite certain it seemed, that they would not give us much trouble here, if, indeed we were to encounter any.

"But yet it was our habit as warriors of other years, if for no other reason, to ever hold our weapons in readiness and to set sentries whenever we went ashore to rest or make camp for the night.

"And so neared the end of the fourth day, when the swifter flow of the water and a portage around a waterfall told us we were nearing its headwaters. And now did we have use for the oars, but not for long. As evening approached, we entered a small lake and were welcomed to quiet water once more.

"This lake, so we discovered the following day, was the beginning of a chain of narrow lakes finally opening into what proved to be an inland sea (Lake Winnipeg) of tremendous length. In a general north-and-south direction it seemed to lie. And for three days did we follow its eastern shore with the north wind again serving us well.

"At the extreme southern end of the great body of fresh water by a stroke of good fortune we discovered another fine stream of goodly size (Red River of the North, boundary between Minnesota and the Dakotas). It flowed northward, emptying into the inland sea. This new river we followed southward for a full three days. And along its banks, we now discovered signs of human habitation. An abandoned yet smoldering campfire we first found. And later, a half-day's journey southward, an arrow. At an upright angle it stood, in the soft earth at the water's edge. Of rather crude workmanship it proved to be; its point being fashioned from stone, much like the flint we used with fire steel, although the shaft had been well formed. And at once we recalled the stone-pointed weapons we had often seen carried by the Skrellings near our Vinland camp.

"No doubt the arrow had been loosed from a canoe, and aimed at wild game on shore. But why, we asked ourselves, had not the bowman tarried long enough to retrieve it?

"But no more than had we pondered the question until we had our answer. It was you, Sigurd—was it not?—who first spied the Skrelling boat about to disappear from sight around the bend upstream it was—its two oarsmen fleeing it seemed in great haste.

"And, of a sudden as though we were of one mind, and for what reason we knew not, we found ourselves seized with a powerful urge to set out in pursuit.

"Not that we bore the slightest malice toward them. In truth, no violence would I have been permitted on our part. A friendly pursuit it was, born of idle curiosity, if naught else—and the excitement of the chase spurred us on.

"We shouted greetings to the Dark-skins, urging them to hold up, but it seemed they shared not our enthusiasm for a friendly encounter.

"In desperation, it appeared, were they wielding their paddles. And whether we were to succeed in overtaking them was yet an unanswered question when, suddenly veering toward the right bank of the river, they ran their craft aground, leaped out and vanished into the trees and undergrowth.

"Landing hurriedly alongside their boat, we again shouted after them but received no reply save for the soft echo of our own voices from among the trees. And being mindful of the possibility of an ambush by their comrades, we refrained from attempting to go further.

"A light and cleverly fashioned craft their canoe proved to be. And sorely tempted were we by a desire to tow it away. Black Botolf, I recall, argued that since they had abandoned it, 'twould be no wrong in our laying claim to it.' But I said, 'No,' as we were not at odds with the Dark-skins, our trespassing upon their hunting grounds might well be reason enough to stir hostility without making off with their belongings.

"And so ended our first encounter with the Skrellings in this land. I ordered a small packet of food to be left in their canoe as a token of friendship, and once more were our two long-boats headed against the rather slow current of the river—southward into what we now well knew was the land of the Skrellings.

"Nightfall of the tenth day since we left the ship found us camped near where a smaller stream (Buffalo River in west central Minnesota) entered into the larger one (Red River) from a southeasterly direction.

"And now, of a sudden, did my mind seize upon an interesting speculation. Very possible it is, I said to myself, that by following this smaller stream in an easterly direction, we might perchance, discover a waterway back to Vinland. And if, in truth, we were to meet with such good fortune I would proceed in that direction with one of the long-boats. The other, would be sent back to the Knorr, so that our comrades there might know of my change in plans.

"And the more I turned it over in my mind, the more reasonable did it seem. But, no—ten days had we used of our allotted fifteen for our journey inland. Unlikely it was that another five days would carry us far enough to the eastward to establish any certainty of a return route in that direction. Perhaps it would only be a waste of time.

"But that night, I slept not well—the thought kept returning to my mind again and again. And in the morning, I announced my decision—we would turn to the southeastward with the smaller stream.

"My friend Black Botolf questioned the wisdom of my choice, but seemed at a loss to put forth a good reason. He grumbled to himself as he walked away to gather fuel for the morning's campfire. Returning shortly with a supply of wood, he found his comrades taking to the plan with enthusiasm, and said no more against it.

"But disappointing the new route proved to be. For two days did we ply the oars against the current, with no wind to aid us. At one stretch were we forced around rapids. And now, twelve days had we used of our allotted fifteen.

"Scouting to the southeastward, we finally discovered what could be another waterway—but which had to be reached by a short portage—and a more difficult one it proved to be. This course we decided to take, and on the morning of the thirteenth day we set forth upon what was to be the most strenuous part of our journey.

"Midafternoon found us at the second portage and a troublesome one it too proved to be. Not only were we beset with boulders and the steepness of the land, but here we encountered our first signs of hostilities. A small band of Skrelling warriors it was.

"They followed us at a safe distance, shouting what seemed to be threats and defiance. Occasionally with a great shout, they would surge toward us and loose several arrows in our direction, as though they were about to launch an attack, but at the same time holding their distance so that their arrows fell short.

"Reasoning that they were merely attempting to frighten us to the point of abandoning the portage and turning back, I gave the order to pay them no heed. And at this, Black Botolf, the quarrelsome one, argued that instead, they would reason that we feared them. Perhaps he was right. You will recall, comrades, that he asked permission to take half our crew and advance against them.

'Certain I am,' he argued, 'that they will retreat before us, and give us no more trouble.' This I pondered for a moment. But on second thought I considered the risk to the expedition, if Botolf's plan were not to go as he envisioned, and I said, 'No.'

"The Skrellings, after a final great clamor and motions in our direction, finally quieted themselves and disappeared into the forest.

"Had there been a larger band of them, possibly they might have attacked, but not knowing when more of them might arrive on the scene, I ordered haste in the final reaches of the portage, and we were finally able to float our boats in a small lake.

"Again loading our supplies and weapons into the boats, I bade the oarsmen pull out into deeper water before settling to rest from the struggle of the portage.

"And from here, we observed a small outlet connecting with what appeared to be a larger body of water a short distance away to the South.

"It was now nearing the end of the day—and after a short rest and deeming it prudent to move farther away from the scene of the unfriendly acts of the Skrellings, we decided to move on into the waterway we sighted.

"And this lake, in turn, we found to be connected, by another shallow stretch of water at its southern end, to a yet larger body of water almost of a size to be called a small inland sea (Big Cormorant Lake).

"And here was it our good fortune to discover two skerries (rocky islands, too small for habitation) rising from the water near the northwest shore. Lacking a means of anchoring in deep water, and questioning the wisdom of spending the night ashore, these rocks would prove a convenient means of mooring for the night. This I made known, and immediately my friend, Black Botolf, uttered a few words which I recognized as the beginning of a protest against this added precaution. But I silenced him with a look and gesture, gave the order to pull alongside, and assigned two men the task of wielding the drilling tools and preparing the holes for our anchor bolts.

"And now, having secured the boats to the mooring rocks, and after the evening meal was finished, I called for a council—should we push onward toward the southeast? Or, was the time now at hand to prepare for the return to the ship, and to our comrades awaiting us there? You, Lars and Sigurd, I recall, counseled wisely on this. But listen, I would not. No—the thought again returned to my mind. Certainly, it seemed that another day would bring us upon a waterway back toward Vinland. I argued to push forward for two more days.

"True, we had encountered hostility as we worked our way southward. But only a small band of Skrellings they were—most likely a hunting party, coming upon us accidentally. No, we did not fear them. We would simply avoid engaging them in combat. In truth, certain it seemed that they lacked the courage to attack.

"Also true it was, the waterways were no longer what we had hoped for. The streams were rocky and the portages had grown more difficult—and had been the cause of considerably more grumbling than usual.

"But no, we must push onward. Surely there must be a sea to the southeastward. And equally certain it seemed, we must soon come on a stream bearing in that direction. Unlikely it seemed that this new land could be much larger than our own homeland.

"And so it was finally decided. For two more days would we journey southeastwardly to find a shorter route to the sea. That decision was one which I, who have been called 'the Wise Warrior,' was destined to greatly regret.

"And now, even as we talked, there appeared on the shore, but a short distance to the east from us, three Skrelling women who watched us from across the water and no doubt with great curiosity. Certainly, no sign of hostility this was. And also certain it was that if the Skrelling warriors at the portage had, in truth, planned to give us trouble, their women would not be allowed to come near. No doubt there was a hunting camp in the woodland to the eastward.

"It was then that I bid Ivar take the small-boat and row over to them, alone, despite the clamor of some of the men who wished to accompany him, some of them begging earnestly for the privilege.

"But I said, 'No,' this was to be a gesture of friendship. One man might well approach them, but three or four would no doubt frighten them into flight—or arouse anger of their men, who very likely were not far away.

"And so we sat there in the two long-boats, and having now decided upon our course for the next two days, we fell to discussing the return journey and the possibility of discovering a shortcut westward to the great stream we had followed for several days on our journey to the southward.

"The sun was now down and darkness was approaching, when it came to my mind that Ivar was yet on the shore with the Skrelling women. At this moment, one of the younger men in the other boat shouted across the water, *'Ho, Ivar, Hvordan går det* (How is it going)?' whereupon there followed further shouts and joking remarks.

"This saved me the trouble of hailing him myself which I was about to do with no little impatience at the loitering. This he no doubt expected, and now made haste to return.

"You reported, I recall, Ivar, that they seemed friendly, but that there also seemed a feeling of apprehension among them which you had sensed, despite your inability to understand their words and gestures. And a strange thing too, was your discovery that the women each carried a bow and quiver of arrows. Do you suppose, comrades, that in this strange land, the women also serve as warriors? But no, certain it seems that their weapons were for the hunting of waterfowl and such—and no doubt, for self-protection against wild animals, or unfriendly people.

"And now, amid much grumbling at the inconvenience of it, we prepared to spend the night in the boats. Fairly safe it seemed at least, anchored thusly offshore but still remembering the signs of hostility at the portage, as a precaution I appointed six men to take shifts at watching throughout the night.

"Weary to a point of near exhaustion we were from the toil of the day's journey, and the added struggle of the portage. The younger men soon tired of chiding Ivar about his visit with the Skrelling women—and soon all was quiet for the night.

"And so we awoke, with the first light of dawn on the fourteenth day of our journey southward into this great unknown New Land of the West. It was yet quite dark, and a heavy morning fog lay over the water, betokening the coming of another fair day. I decided to set out at once and to follow closely the northeastern and eastern shore while awaiting the broadening of daylight and the lifting of the fog. We would then seek a convenient spot to land for the morning meal. And this, so I reasoned, would take us well beyond the Skrelling camp which, no doubt, lay near where we had anchored for the night.

"Stiff and sore we were, from the labor of yesterday's portages, and from sleeping cramped in the boats. And while the grumbling, tempered somewhat by the prospect of a morning meal, came quite freely as I gave the order to man the oars, we soon found ourselves pushing forward into the gloom of the early-morning mists—and to what destiny we knew not."

4

UNHEEDED WARNING

"But daylight had come on apace, and scarcely had our mooring place vanished behind us and we had rounded a little point of land, where the deepest of the water allowed us to follow close ashore, when there through the fog we beheld a lone Skrelling warrior. Standing near the water's edge he was, as though awaiting our coming. Appearing out of the mists so suddenly, he seemed like a ghost .

"He raised his hand in a gesture which said, 'Stop, I wish to speak.' Raising my own hand in a sign of friendship, I bid the oarsman to stop the boats and hold steady about two boat-lengths from the shore.

"The apparition there on the shore seemed to be an ancient warrior, very likely a chief or other leader among his people. Large he was—for what we had seen among the Skrellings—and a powerful man no doubt he had been in his younger days. He carried no weapon, but straight and unsmiling he stood, as though to command our attention.

"At length he spoke, uttering strange sounding words of which we knew not the meaning, and making signs and gestures with his hands.

"First, he pointed toward the south, in the direction we were journeying. Then holding his hand flatwise, with the palm downward, he motioned as though to present a picture of a giant, moving his hand in a great circle, over the lakes and forests. And then with his right hand, he pointed toward his own chest. Folding his arms, he waited a moment. And again the old warrior made similar motions, save that at the end he pointed toward our boats, then, turning slowly, his stretched his arm in a motion to the north.

"I knew not the meaning; and at once made a sign which said, 'I understand not.' As I made this gesture, there appeared, out of the nowhere of fog and forest, a Skrelling woman who stopped and stood silently behind the old warrior. I doubt he knew of her presence. Probably one of his wives, or, more likely, one of his daughters. Young she was, and pleasing to the eye, as she stood there, clad in what would likely be considered finery among her people.

"A murmur commenced to arise from both our boats—with undertones of surprise and pleasure—and I quickly ordered, 'Silence.'

"And facing the Skrelling, again I motioned, 'I understand not.'

"And again he repeated his strange utterances and sign-talk, and looking beyond him, I observed the woman repeating his gestures, as though trying to add stress to his message.

"And this time I understood full well his meaning as plainly as though he had spoken in the language of our own Northland.

"He was saying: 'To the south lies our land. Go you now back to your land to the north.'

"And this time, I spoke a falsehood when I again gave answer by signs, 'I understand not.'

"At this, the young woman, sorely vexed at our apparent stupidity, raised her hands to her face as though weeping and vanished into the mist and fog and forest.

"Once again the old chief commenced, and this time more urgently, it seemed, to repeat his order, warning, or whatever, but I waited not for him to finish. An act of cowardice it would seem, to heed his message and turn back. And with a show of impatience I bade the oarsmen bring the boat around and again head southward.

"The old Skrelling, with arms folded, stood glaring after us and was soon lost to view in the dense fog.

"There was no breeze stirring, but the sky was commencing to lighten overhead, and the fog would vanish with the sunrise, or soon after. Almost at once did we encounter shallow water and rushes or reeds to hamper our headway and changing our course toward deeper water, I ordered the oarsmen to take a leisurely gait in a generally southward direction, while awaiting lifting of the fog.

"A silence came over our comrades; some no doubt pondering the old Skrelling's message, warning, or call-it-what-you-will. And some of them were very likely thinking more about the Skrelling woman.

"But well do I recall pondering the suddenness of the silence. There was a strangeness about it—a strangeness that seemed to hang in the air like the mist hovering over the water. Like the mist whose very stillness seemed to echo the old Skrelling's words, 'Go back—Go back now.'

"But not for long did I ponder—for suddenly directly across our course we beheld through the lifting fog what was, to say the very least, a truly alarming sight—great numbers of Skrelling boats. It was as though they awaited our coming.

"They held their silence as we drew nearer. There was no question as to the reason for their presence. They were there to turn us back. And in my comrades' faces, I could see the old battle tension rising.

"It was then obvious that this was the meaning of the old chief's warning.

"At length the silence was quietly broken by Black Botolf the quarrelsome one. 'Think you that we can yet make friends with the Dark-skins, friend Torkel?' To which I replied, 'Make friends, perhaps not, but avoid combat, yes I think we shall.'"

"He answered, 'Great are my doubts, my friend. And I say this: We should strike them and have done with it.'

"'I am yet giving the orders on this expedition,' I replied in anger. And, facing the Skrellings, I arose to my feet and, although I expected it to be futile, gave them the sign that said, 'Peace and friendship.'

"They returned not the greeting. And as we came into range, I observed their bowmen stringing their bows and selecting arrows, and I ordered the oarsmen to stop the boats and to hold steady.

"No. There was no doubting their intentions. They were there to simply turn us back so I reasoned. And, judging by their number full well did I realize that we had little choice in the matter.

"No. We came not for the purpose of fighting the Dark-skins. Fighting was not in our plans. Thus, it would be no dishonor to turn back and head northward.

"Perhaps without thinking, it was that I leveled my gaze back in the direction whence we came. And what I observed in the near distance to the northward brought a sudden change to the whole affair.

"And in the next instant, it dawned upon me. No—their plan was not to turn us back. Now there appeared fully as many boats behind us as there were fronting us— their plan was to attack and totally destroy us.

"No. There was no such choice as turning back. But, yet was I unwilling to engage them in combat—for the reason I have already given—and now, it was obvious that we were hopelessly outnumbered.

"Waiting not for further orders, my comrades guessing what my next order might be were making haste to ready their shields and to don their leathern armor and helmets. Next a great shout arose from the nearer Skrelling boats. And a scattering flight of arrows sped toward us.

"But more of a warning it seemed, as most of them sang harmlessly over our heads.

"Again arising to my feet, I once again gave the sign which meant 'friendship'—useless though I expected the gesture to be. Then turning to the oarsmen, I ordered them to bring the boats around; reasoning that the Skrellings would understand, at least, that we intended not to attempt to force our way through their lines. In truth, the attempt would have been doomed to failure before it commenced.

"As our boats swung broadside to the Skrellings, Black Botolf, kneeling with bow and arrow in readiness, turned and questioned me loudly, 'Now, friend Torkel?' And again turning on him in anger I shouted, 'NO, I will give the orders.'

"I doubted not but what the Skrellings, hearing this exchange of shouts, took it to be our signal to attack. Again they raised a great clamor—and another flight of arrows engulfed us. But this time, they were in earnest. No longer were they aiming over our heads. 'Si ... it ... Si ... it,' said the arrows as they sped past our ears. 'Tok ... Tok,' they said as they were stopped by our shields and the thickness of our heavy leathern armor.

"Black Botolf lowered his shield, raised himself on one knee and drew his bow. He looked up at me as though impatiently awaiting my order. And in that very instant—'Si ... it ... klup'—a Skrelling arrow struck him through the neck. Falling backward, his own arrow sailed skyward as he crumpled to the boat's bottom—the arrow had gone half its length through his throat.

"Kneeling beside him, I grasped the arrow and breaking it in half, drew it through in order to bind the wound. But no, it was of no use. The missile had severed a vital blood vessel. Bleeding profusely, he died without making a sound.

"My quarrelsome friend, Black Botolf, would never question the wisdom of my orders again.

"Black sorrow and then red anger boiled up in my heart as I took to my battle stance. '*Drepe dem, kamerater mine* (Slay them, my comrades). *DREPE DEM*,' I roared.

"Shields lowered, our arrows were sped on their way. The battle was on.

"There were good bowmen among the Skrellings, but ours were better. And our metal-tipped arrows were far better than their points fashioned from stone. Their half-naked bodies made excellent targets, and many were our arrows that found their mark.

"And our shields and leathern armor served us well. It stopped their arrows, although they often came with such force as to knock a man down if he had failed to brace himself for such a blow. It soon appeared that unless an arrow should find an unprotected spot, as with my friend, Black Botolf, their weapons were to have little effect.

"Again and again did my warriors draw their bows with deadly aim. And with each flight of arrows, ten or twelve Skrellings died, flinging their arms upward and toppling into the water.

"We took heart at the prospect of an easy victory. Certainly, it seemed, their leaders would soon observe that they were no match for us and call off the attack.

"But on they came. For each one we killed, ten more seemed to take his place. The lake seemed filled with Skrelling boats—and bodies. With wild shouts and screams they seemed to summon such courage and recklessness as to entirely lose fear of our weapons. Their leader seemed to care not how many were slain. And closer and yet closer did

they crowd in upon us, as though to improve the effec-
tiveness of their arrows. And more and more of them fell as
our comrades drew their bows at closer range.

"But still they came. The fog vanished entirely as midmorning neared and the sun's heat beat down. Yet, still
they came.

"But now, at last—and rather suddenly—things commenced to take a different turn. Their leaders seemed to be
taking council among themselves. Perhaps they had gotten
their fill of fighting. Their arrows came in smaller flights.
Then they ceased altogether as they drew back out of range.

"Glad indeed we were to get this unexpected rest. We
had lost but one man. Two more had suffered wounds, but
not seriously. Still able and willing to fight, they were.

"But our rest was not to be for long, as we soon learned.
No— by no means had the Dark-skins so soon wearied of
the fight. They had only changed their plan of attack. For
now we observed that their light boats were withdrawing,
and they were bringing in a large number of heavier craft,
some almost the size of our own. And they had entirely
abandoned their bows and arrows; they were coming at us
with sturdier weapons, spears, and battle-axes.

"But great was the surprise we had in store for them.
They knew not that we too, were well supplied with the
same type of weapons: spears and battle-axes—to say
nothing of our shields and the heavy swords some of us
preferred for hand-to-hand fighting.

"And once again were the Dark-skins to learn that our
weapons were superior to theirs. And another thing they
were about to learn: that hand-to-hand combat was more
to our liking than was fighting at a distance with arrows.

"As the Skrellings closed in toward us, I quickly gave
the order to lash the two boats together, thus to prevent
their driving us apart. And also, to provide the more steady

footing we would need to better wield our heavier weapons. Those not occupied with the task continued to loose their arrows into the mass of Skrellings.

"I glanced in the direction of our comrades in the other boat and was about to shout the order to change weapons, but there was no need. Already had they discerned what was to come next. Hjalmar the Wild Man carefully laid aside his bow and arrows, and taking his great two edged sword, he spat—first in the palm of one hand, then the other—then seizing the weapon with both hands, he raised it to striking position and flexed his elbows twice before lowering the point of the blade to rest on the boat's railing awaiting the first Skrelling to taste its blade.

"And you, Lars, I observed handing Ivar a spear with your right hand as you reached for your battle-axe with the left. And full well did your gestures tell me you were bestowing upon him a brief tutoring in its use.

"And now, again summoning their courage with frightful yelling, our attackers came at us from both sides—not heading their boats directly toward us, but by forming two great 'millwheels' of perhaps thirty boats each, in a solid mass, as though they would grind our craft between them. In this manner, they would be in motion as they drew alongside to lay at us with axe and spear as their boats rubbed sides with ours. And a clever bit of planning this was; it meant that our warriors would be pressed by fresh adversaries constantly, thus would we gain little, if any time to rest between encounters.

But yet, with our boats lashed together, side-by-side, we had but two sides to defend, instead of four, and thus, unless we were to lose several men, we were of sufficient numbers so that two or three men could, now and then, drop out of the fight for a short rest. And now they were upon us.

"But too late did the Skrellings, in the first few boats to engage us—too late did they learn that we depended not alone upon the bows and arrows we had used until now. Good fighters they were, but their stone-headed axes and spears were no match for the sharp metal points and keen blades we now wielded against them.

"And still they came at us. And so did we cut them down. With swinging blades and quick spear thrusts we felled them as they came.

"But yet, we ourselves were to soon learn that it was not by any odds to be an easy battle. I observed one of the men in the other boat to crumble under a blow to the helmet from a Skrelling's axe.

"And you, Sigurd. The Dark-skin weapon that reached you in the same manner but a few moments later—I saw you go down on one knee from the blow. Had it not been for your good helmet, certainly would he have split your skull. And, too, had it not been for the thrust to the Skrelling's belly from Ivar's spear, a second blow would have caught you athwart the neck before you could get up.

"No—it was not to be an easy battle.

"Midday had now passed, and still they came. We slaughtered them and yet they still came. For every boat that was beaten out of the millwheel attack, it seemed as though two more arrived to take its place.

"And we cursed them as they came at us. And we cursed them as they died; some cursing in the name of the ancient gods, and some calling upon the God of the Christians to damn them.

"And some, like you, Lars, cursing in the peculiar manner of our Northern tribesmen from the Lofotens, not calling upon the gods—but upon the Devil: 'Kan Djevelen la deg ta advarsel (May the Devil let you take warning),' you shouted to the young Skrelling who raised his axe the instant one of their boats, bearing two warriors, touched sides with ours. *'DJEVELEN KOKE MEG.* (THE DEVIL BOIL ME),' you roared as your own battle-axe swung through the air opening his belly like a butchered ox. And his body fell with its upper part hanging over the railing of our boat while his companion made haste to pull away.

"Hooking your foot under his middle, you rolled the Dark-skin back and into the water. *Uff.*

"Until now we had lost only but one man in our boat, Black Botolf, who died in the first flight of Skrelling arrows. But the other boat was not faring so well. Despite the fury and confusion of the battle, I could well discern that they had suffered some losses. Whether killed or lying wounded, I could not make out, but, of their ten men, I could count only seven up and still fighting.

"But yet, they were holding their own in repelling the attackers. There again, stood Hjalmar the Wild Man, so called by his comrades because in battle he seemed to be the equal of three good fighters. A swordsman he was and there was none better.

"'*Kommer til helvete* (Come [go] to Hell),' he would warn them brandishing his heavy double-edged sword as they approached within its reach.

"And in the fury of the encounter, he had a curious habit of grasping the weapon with both hands. Wielding it thus, in what looked like an awkward manner; its blows seemed to become a continuous whirling motion—slanting downward from left to right, and again upward from right to left. And many were the Dark-skins who died before they could manage a single blow of an axe, or thrust of a spear in his direction. Yes, to be sure, good fighters we had in both boats, but now with some of our comrades showing signs of weariness—and the literally hundreds of enemy craft awaiting their turn at the encounter, I was suddenly struck with the realization that this could not go on. If we were to remain alive, something must be done and done without delay.

"But what could we do, but keep up the fight? Certainly, there was no other choice. Men fighting for their lives must either kill or be killed, if the gods choose not to come to their aid.

"Thus were my thoughts running when suddenly I felt the faint freshness of a breeze coming from the south. Perhaps it would strengthen. It was a slim hope, but grasping at the possibility, I ordered two men to drop their weapons and rig the mast and sail. And following my shouts and gestures the men in Hjalmar's boat did likewise.

"No small feat, it proved to be, in the turmoil of the struggle. But well did the task finally succeed, despite the difficulties encountered.

"The Skrellings seemed to hesitate at the sight of the sails. Perhaps it was that they had never seen the like before. And, for a moment did I hope that the spectacle as of our boats suddenly spreading their wings might strike them with fear and superstition.

"But no. Not for long did the sight interrupt their attack. And now they observed, as even did we that the breeze had strengthened slightly, and our boats commenced to move slowly up the lake in a northerly direction.

"This gave us a small advantage. Now the Dark-skins were forced to make more use of their oars, while encountering us, and to keep their boats in motion along with ours.

"But the outlook was still far from bright. Suppose we were to continue thusly, drifting before the south breeze, until we are driven ashore at the northern end of the lake whence we came. What then? Hopelessly outnumbered we were, and if driven ashore we certainly would be in no better position that we now found ourselves. No, ours was not a bright outlook by any manner of means. Perhaps, I was saying to myself—perhaps Odin will yet come to our aid, or perchance even the Christian God. But no—he is the God of peace—and we are Vikings.

"Thus were my thoughts when of a sudden, a rumble of thunder rolled down from the northwest. And loud enough it was to be well heard above the tumult of the struggle.

"The Skrellings also heard it. I observed some of them turning their faces to look skyward.

"A fierce black cloud was indeed fast approaching. And odd it was, that it was coming upon us from the northwest—against the southern breeze. This I have sometimes observed, when storms approach at sea, but never have I seen the like on land.

"And now, once more did the attack bear down upon us with renewed fury. The Skrellings in haste, hoping as it seemed, to finish the battle before the arrival of the storm which even now had commenced to darken the sun, pressed in more strongly than ever, and from all sides.

"And again there was Hjalmar the Wild Man near the bow of his boat wielding the great sword with such lightning strokes one could scarcely follow the blade. But well could I see Dark-skins going down, like grain before a farmer's sickle in the middle of fall harvest.

"This was good. But yet it was not good. For indeed, with such fury as he was now swinging, his comrades must keep their distance for fear of stumbling into the path of his sword. Now were they forced to stand too close in the other end of the boat. Yes, too crowded they were to properly handle their weapons. Neither dared they to make room by taking shifts at fighting, being too hard pressed as they now were, to lower their weapons even for a moment. And our own boat was faring but little better. Now were the attackers pressing in upon us with eagerness and the expectation of victory.

"And now, as though by a prearranged signal, two light boats with one warrior in each dashed in toward the ends of our boats.

"Instantly did I discern their purpose. At the stern end, one of the Dark-skins swerving an instant before his boat would have crashed against ours raised his axe with lightning like movement and severed the thong that bound our boats together. And he was off and away in a flash. The other warrior, however, fared not so well at the bow end. As he raised his axe, a quick spear thrust succeeded in staying the blow that would have separated our boats entirely. But the Skrelling, carrying with him a bad wound in the chest, managed to escape.

"A wild shout and a sudden onslaught from the attackers, and one of the men in the other boat crumpled and fell. I opened my mouth to shout an order, but no sound came forth, for in that instant I observed two more men go down, almost at the same time. And at once, a great wave of screaming and struggling Skrellings poured over the stern end of Hjalmar's boat.

"Indeed, certain I was, that the Skrellings were even struggling among themselves, as though there were two, possibly three different groups of them, each fighting to get the prize they believed now to be within their grasp.

"And as they swarmed over it, Hjalmar's boat commenced to settle at one end and rise at the other tugging at the remaining thong that bound the two boats together.

"What happened next, I can scarcely say—so quickly did things happen. Men, both ours and our attackers, were struggling hand-to-hand in the boat and in the water— some still fighting as they sank. And Hjalmar the Wild Man was still swinging his great sword while in the bow, in which he stood, rose high as the other end went under.

"By now the melee in the water had caused the two boats to swing apart at the stern, until they stood almost at right angles with one another. And as Hjalmar's long-boat commenced to sink, with a wild leap his right foot found our boat's railing and turning in the instant he reached solid footing in the boat's bottom, he severed the remaining line connecting the two at the bow with a deft flick of his sword. And again turning, in a flash he dispatched a Skrelling with axe raised to strike at Herjolf as he struggled to reach up and grasp the rail.

"And in that instant it was; the other boat plunged beneath the waves leaving only a struggling mass of heads, arms, and weapons showing above the surface.

"Quickly did I scan the scene for more survivors. But I saw only two—the two red-headed brothers, Ludolph and Rudolph, were striving desperately to reach our boat.

"Close behind them followed a young Skrelling, and a good swimmer he was. Now he raised his axe for a blow, but too late did he discover that he was well within a spear's length from us. Oskar the Tall One, it was, finished him with a thrust of his spear.

"At my feet, another thrashed toward us through the water, axe dangling from a leathern thong about his shoulder. Reaching up, he seized the boat's railing with both hands. As he pulled himself up I kicked him in the face, and he fell back and sank.

"Now with the survivors from Hjalmar's boat in ours were we faced with the difficulty of being too crowded for close fighting. And the Skrellings, encouraged by their success and eager to finish us ahead of the storm, were screaming and shouting as though they had lost all sense of fear, came at us in a solid mass from all directions. 'Now it is almost the end,' I recall saying to myself, for it appeared that all of us were about to die fighting.

"True, we would take a great toll in Skrelling lives, but now we could no more stop them than we could halt the approaching storm cloud. Now would they overwhelm us with the sheer weight of their number, and our boat would meet the same fate as had the other boat—unless possibly, but no, there were no more possibilities. This was surely the end.

"Just then, with a terrible crash, a bolt of lightning split the storm cloud. A moment of dead calm, and the storm struck with all its fury.

"In an instant did the south breeze give way to the giant from the north. Then came the downpour, and the crackle and roar of lightning and thunder. Wind and still more wind—again the like of which I had never seen on land.

"Great waves leaped up, tossing the Skrelling boats like dry leaves. And again the blast of the wind tore at our sail with such force, I feared the mast could not bear the strain.

"But hold it did—and almost before we were aware of having commenced to make headway, were we slowly crashing headlong through the mass of Skrelling boats.

"Little time had I to see how the Dark-skins fared at the hands of the storm gods, but certain I was that many of their boats were overturned. Indeed, so concerned were the Skrellings with the task of keeping afloat, they seemed to forget the battle entirely. But no, this was not wholly true either. For as we finally broke free of the hindrance of their boats, there came a full half dozen of their more sturdy craft—with all hands wielding the oars with mighty strokes in an attempt to overtake us. But our own oarsmen, bending to the task with all their strength, and the wind, tearing at our sail, steadily increased our headway, ever widening the stretch of water between us and our pursuers.

Yet the lightning still crackled and crashed around us and appeared at times to strike the water between us and the pursuing Skrellings.

"And down lashed the rain, slanting with the wind, and lowering the storm cloud until it almost rode the tops of the surging waves.

"One by one did the Skrelling boats seem to abandon the pursuit, until at last I observed a lone canoe riding the wavetops as though manned with great determination. But soon, it too was lost to view in the downpour and darkness of the storm.

"And so we fled—and so ended this day's battle with the Skrellings.

"The storm gods had come to our aid and had served us well. But now, having finished that task, they seemed to turn against us. Now they unleashed the storm with yet greater fury. The giant waves threatened to engulf us. There was no shore to be seen in any direction. There was nothing but the howling of the wind and the rain that seemed to beat down heavier with each crash and roar of thunder.

"I counted the men in the boat. Fourteen, we were, too much weight for a boat built for not more than ten. And ten we had in each boat before the battle. Six men had we lost. Yes, fourteen were too many for the size of the craft in a storm such as this.

"There was the small-boat bobbing along behind at the end of its line and half filled with water. Well did we finally manage to draw it alongside and empty it, reasoning that perhaps one man might climb into it, thus to lighten the load in the long-boat. But no—too great were the waves, for its low sides, even to bear the weight of one man.

"In the confusion of the battle I had forgotten about Black Botolf whose body was still lying there in the boat's bottom. Yes, to lighten the load, it must be thrown out. I gave the order, and looked in another direction as my good friend's body rolled into the water.

"Someone picked up his sword and tossed it after him as he sank.

"Yes, five men besides Botolf had we lost. But there was no time now to neither grieve over the loss, nor ask if anyone had observed how they died, whether by weapons of our attackers, or by drowning when Hjalmar's boat was lost. After all it mattered not how they died. Our task now was to fight the storm that was upon us.

"And so we fought it. Finally the wind slackened, the rain did likewise, and we won. The storm cloud rumbled and growled ahead of us, off and away into the southeast, complaining, so it seemed, at our having survived its fury. And before us, in the distance, could we well make out a shore line. And the sky lightened and, though the sun was yet hidden, we reckoned that this dreadful day was nearing its end.

"Wet and wearied from the rigors of the day we were. And now, our comrades began to recall that we had not eaten since last evening, and a great hunger seized us despite the recollections yet so fresh in our minds.

"Taking heart at the prospect of food, now that the storm had passed on beyond us and we were nearing shore, the crew took to the oars again with vigor.

"But shallow and marshy the water became and there was no choice but to anchor in deeper water and make use of the small-boat sending it ashore with four men, one to return and take three more, and so on until all fourteen were on land.

"And this night, surely would it be safe to establish a camp and sleep ashore. The Skrellings we had left far behind. Certain it was that they could not have followed us in the storm. No doubt most of them had landed before the full fury of the storm gods was upon them. And, if they followed us into the heart of the storm with boats much lighter than ours, surely they had perished. Yes, this night we could rest safely.

"Nightfall was upon us ere we had prepared and eaten our meal. Weary to the bone we were and eager for sleep, yet plans for the next day were to be made and I called for a council.

"And so it was decided. You, Lars and Sigurd, were to arise early before dawn and set out on foot to scout the island to the southward for a waterway, and to return by midmorning.

"Ivar and I would take the small-boat and go out to the long-boat, where we would sleep until about an hour before sunrise. Upon arising, we would take the small-boat and the fishing nets and row to deeper water in the direction whence the storm had carried us. We would try for a catch or two of fish, and we also would return to the camp by midmorning.

"The remaining ten of our comrades would sleep ashore, taking shifts at sentry duty through the night, one man to the left and another to the right of the camp. Small need though it seemed to post sentries.

"The storm had carried us fast and far. The Skrellings, so I reckoned, would need a good half day if not more in which to overtake us, if indeed they had the heart to follow us and attack again after seeing so many of their warriors fall before our weapons. No, fairly certain it seemed, that they would give us no more trouble—at least for this night.

"And so we slept. And so the coming of dawn found the two of us, Ivar and me, out on the lake in the small-boat, as we had planned at last night's council. The lake was calm after yesterday's storm, and again a heavy fog lay over the water as signs of daylight showed toward the east. Dawn was upon us as we lowered our nets in the midst of water, fog and silence. Now would we settle down to our task. No need for haste, and indeed would it be almost impossible to find our way back to the long-boat and our camp before the lifting of the fog which would surely be shortly after sunrise. Time enough would we have to take a catch or two of fish, and then to return to camp for our morning meal.

"Yes, the time now certainly was at hand to make plans for turning northward toward our ship and our companions who were waiting for us by the Salt Sea. Six men had we lost in an unwanted battle with the Skrellings. And but for the storm gods, we very well could have met the same fate. We could not risk another such battle.

"Yet we must first find another waterway to the south. We dare not return northward at once. We must circle this hostile region and then turn back north toward the Salt Sea. So ran my thoughts as we lowered the nets and sat in silence—a silence that lay heavily upon us, not unlike the fog that engulfed us."

"And then, suddenly, as though shattered by a blow from a giant war club, the silence was broken. There was sound. And there was no mistaking its meaning as it reached our ears from far over the water—shouts, curses, and screams—and the clash of weapons in hand-to-hand fighting. Our camp was being attacked.

"Waiting not to even raise the nets, we made all haste in the direction of the sound. Nor did we speak a single word to one another.

"With all our strength did we ply the oars but, as it seemed, could make little headway. The very fog appeared to hamper the forward motion of the boat—fighting to hold us back. And now, it seemed that we must have covered at least half the distance, but the sound still came as though from afar. And then, abruptly, no sound at all. No sound, save the dashing of our own oars.

"For a moment did we cease rowing—to strain our ears toward the wall of fog, whence had come the sound. There was nothing but silence—a deep chilling silence. 'Perhaps my wits were fooling me,' I said to myself. Perhaps I had not heard sound at all. Turning to Ivar, I was about to ask if indeed, he too had heard sounds of battle in the distance. He answered my question before I could ask it, 'Yes, I heard it, but no longer hear it,' was his soft reply.

"And again wielding the oars, we pushed onward again with all our strength. But without the sound to guide us, we could only guess our course in the whiteness of the fog. And then, after what seemed a great while, there was the long-boat riding at anchor to our left. We were somewhat off course to the right. Angling sharply to the left we soon reached the reeds and rushes near the shore. Again did we stop and listen—and again the silence.

"Still further off to the right we found ourselves as we stepped ashore. The tops of the trees near the camp loomed up thru the fog to the eastward.

"And as we ran toward the camp, I was seized with a frightful feeling. A fight had taken place. Of that there was no question. But where were the shouts of victory? Why no sounds at all?

"And then, almost at once were we upon the scene and my questions were answered. Fallen warriors— bloody and dead—and more silence. The battle had been short and terrible. Our comrades had been greatly outnumbered and were overwhelmed. By stealth had the enemy approached. They had attacked while our comrades slept. There had been no time for putting on helmets and armor—barely time enough to grasp their weapons. One man had died without even rising to his feet.

"The sentry stationed to the left, whence the trampled grass told us that they had come, had been struck down from behind. The one to the right, aroused by the sound of the attack, had rushed to meet the same fate as the others.

"Quickly did I count the bodies—eight, nine, ten. No one survived. But surrounding the gruesome heaps, I waited not to count, but there were at least thirty dead Skrellings. Certain it was that the attackers had numbered twice that number.

"And there by the water's edge I beheld a comrade who surely had been the last to go down. With his back to the water, had he beaten them off to the bitter end. Around him lay Skrelling bodies piled one atop the other, half-dozen at least. And as I gazed—my wits not able to grasp what my eyes were seeing—his hand moved. I ran to him. It was Hjalmar the Wild Man.

"Right hand still grasping his great sword, he moved as though to raise his body on his left elbow. He was attempting to speak as I knelt beside him. '*Skrellings ... i ... hundrevis* (Skrellings ... in ... the hundreds),' he groaned, and rolled forward on his face in the trampled grass, mud, and blood.

"I rolled him over, and, placing my ear against his chest I listened for a heartbeat, but there was none.

"I arose to my feet, staggering over the dead Skrellings, to observe you, Sigurd, with Lars not far behind, returning in great haste. You had also heard the sound of battle from afar. I stood for a while, my wits in a terrible tangle of grief and anger—I knew not what to do. There stood Lars and Sigurd puffing from the exertion of their haste, white of face and cursing the Skrellings between breaths. And Ivar, sickened at the sight, turned way to retch violently.

"And then, the sudden thought, 'something must be done.' Where were the survivors of the attackers? Why had they disappeared as soon as the battle was over? And when would they return? Certain it seemed they would return. Whether it is their custom to bury their dead, I knew not, but surely would they return to salvage the weapons of their fallen warriors—as well as those of our comrades.

"And there was the long-boat—the Skrellings must have been aware of its lying somewhere out there in the fog. And a valuable prize it would be. No doubt their leaders were, even now, saying to themselves, why hasten? We have slain them all. When we have eaten and are rested, and the fog has lifted will we return at our leisure to do what we must, and claim the spoils.

"Yes, almost certain it seemed, that they had retired to their camp which must be close at hand to rest, care for their wounded, and await the lifting of the fog. By the action of the fog must we reckon the time of their return, and already was it breaking overhead. Whatever was to be done must be done without delay. And the urgency of the task before us served to somewhat settle our wits.

"No. There would not be time enough to bury our dead. But loath we were to leave them lying as food for the wild beasts and birds. It was you, Lars, who now thought of the long-boat. 'It is of no more use to us,' you said. True, the four of us could handle it in calm weather, but certain it is, we could never portage it. To what better use can we put it than to use it as a funeral boat for our fallen companions?

"And so we set to work moving the bodies out to the long-boat two at a shift. Five trips did we make with the small-boat, and on the fifth trip did we carry the bodies of the two red-haired brothers, Ludolph and Rudolph, who were always together.

"Then one last trip ashore to bring live embers from the campfire, and an armful of pitch wood. The fog was now lifting fast, and we knew our time was growing short. As

Ivar and I set out for this last trip, I bade Lars and Sigurd move away from the scene and to the westward along the shore, reasoning that the Skrelling camp lay in the opposite direction. Later we would meet a point well away from this terrible spot.

"With the last of our dead comrades placed in the long-boat, five in each end, and salvaging what supplies and weapons we could, we kindled a good sized fire in the center of the funeral-boat and pulled it a short distance out to deeper water. Waiting only for Ivar to say a few words to the Christian God urging him to accept the spirits of our dead, we now hurried back to meet our companions.

5

TAKING FLIGHT

"A simple matter would it be for the four of us to carry the small-boat when necessary, and now our flight to the southward was on. And as we turned our backs to the lake—the sun was breaking through the fog.

"At once we moved into an area of tall grasses, bushes, and small trees—and none too soon.

"For now, from the direction of our ill-fated camp, came many voices, and then, what sounded like shouts of confusion and dismay. The Skrellings had returned and found our dead companions gone.

"And then, almost at once, another great outcry—they had discovered the long-boat burning out on the water.

"Great excitement and fear must have seized them, so we judged, but we waited not to listen to their clamor. Now did our lives depend upon the task of putting as much distance as possible between us and the Skrellings.

"Time would we now need, if the gods would but give us of it. And, of a sudden, did time seem to become a thing of great value. How much of it would the gods choose to give us? So ran my thoughts as we hastened southward, and were soon out of range of the sounds of commotion on the lakeshore.

"And would the Skrellings, fearful that the gods had carried away our fallen comrades, and perhaps fearful for their own safety, make haste to leave the scene of the battle? Would they wait to bury their own dead? No doubt they had boats near their camp. Would they have the courage to go out to the burning long-boat, if indeed they had time enough to reach it before it sank?

"Or, would their leaders wisely say, 'No. This could not be the doings of the gods. Surely there must be survivors.' And their next question, 'Where are the survivors?' Then the search for our track, and the trampled grass would soon betray us.

"Thus were my thoughts running as we then reached a marsh. Shallow indeed it was, but the heavy downpour of yesterday had deepened it to where it floated the small-boat easily. Eagerly did we grasp the oars and again the thought, if only enough time.

"And another thought, if indeed the Skrellings were to seek our path of escape, no doubt they first would come upon the track leading directly away from the camp where you two, Lars and Sigurd, had walked southward to seek a waterway in the early morning. Perhaps they would follow it and thus be misled. But then, too, perhaps the crafty demons could discern that the same track led back again to the camp. Then surely would they commence to seek another track and just as surely would they find it.

"Soon the marsh led to a small stream, hardly more than a boats length in width, but a welcome sight it was, as it appeared to flow almost directly southward. The left bank of the stream, where it emerged from the marsh, was a low ridge of dry ground topped with oak trees.

"And as we passed, almost brushing their lower branches, a great flock of large raven-like birds arose from the treetops with a terrible clamor in fright at the sight of us. No doubt we were disturbing their nesting grounds. And so loud a din did they raise with their excited cawing, that we were struck with fear lest the Skrellings, back at the lake, would also hear and guess its meaning.

"For not more than two hundred boat lengths, so I judged, did the stream continue before it widened into a rather shallow lake of irregular shape. Marshy it was near the shore, but with quite an expanse of open water farther out. One arm of the lake seemed to lie off toward the west—another smaller arm to the southeast, while the main body stretched away southward. And this seemed a bit of good fortune. There were now three different routes from which to choose and the possibility that our pursuers, if indeed we were being followed, might guess the wrong route. Without hesitation we took the route that appeared to lead southward—and once more plied the oars with all our strength.

"And once more I said to myself, 'If the gods will but choose to give us enough of that strange thing we call time. If they would give us a sufficient stretch of that something that we can neither see nor feel, that something that never travels at an even gait, but somehow passes now too slowly, and now too fleetingly. So quickly do the long years of the future become the short years of the past.'

"Thus my thoughts wandered without purpose as we crossed the first open stretch of water and neared the point of marshy shore forming an angle between the main body and the west arm of the lake. Here was what could be our last opportunity to change our course and turn westward. But no—I would hold to my plan to press onward to the south for at least two more days, before turning toward the west, where certainly must lay the great river we had followed after leaving the inland sea on our journey southward—the same route we must attempt to use if we were to reach where we left our ship and companions on the Salt Sea far to the north. Certainly would it be unwise to attempt to turn westward immediately through this hostile land in which we now found ourselves. No, if we were to escape, we must first move southward for a day, or perhaps two days.

"We had no more than passed beyond that point of land when from far behind us we heard the indistinct but unmistakable sound of the frightened cawing of the birds. There was no mistaking the meaning of the sound. These evil birds had betrayed us and told the Skrellings that we had passed that way in our flight. They were now passing the same grove of oaks—and the nesting birds now were telling us as plainly as though they were calling out to us in our own language that we were being followed.

"Very unlikely, it seemed, that these birds accustomed to the prowling of the wild animals of the countryside, would set up such a clamor except at the unusual sight of a group of humans.

"Now we were again faced with a troublesome situation. Soon the Skrellings would reach the lake following the course of the small stream and before we could reach the far shore to the south. We could not risk being seen. Abruptly we turned the small-boat into the rushes along the shore near the point of land. Here must we either take to the land and carry the boat, or hide ourselves on shore and hope our pursuers would pass by without discovering our path.

"If they were to pass us by on toward to the south, we would refloat the boat in the west arm of the lake. And likewise, if they choose to turn westward, would we turn southward. These two possibilities gave us encouragement.

"Carrying the boat a short distance ashore, we walked to a slight rise of ground where we could conceal ourselves in the tall grass and bushes and observe the point where we had entered the lake from the small stream.

"And so we waited and were to about to judge that the birds had falsely informed us, when there appeared a

Skrelling canoe in the haze and distance across the water.
A lone warrior the canoe carried, but he seemed in no haste
to take to the open water. Certain it seemed he was awaiting the coming of his comrades.

"And so again did we wait, and so did we watch. And
did we listen for the clamoring birds who would tell us that
the Skrelling's companions would soon arrive to join him.

"And finally, for what seemed no good reason, the lone
warrior moved his canoe a short distance along the shore,
to the westward from the mouth of the stream and concealed himself and the canoe in the rushes or went ashore;
we could not make out which at so a great a distance. Very
likely his plan was similar to ours, to lie in hiding and
watch for movements either in the rushes or out in the
water.

"So now my reasoning ran thusly: since if the Skrelling
had gone ashore, he must be expecting to wait for some
time for his comrades. Now, so it seemed, were we wasting
time by waiting.

"Moving with great caution toward the higher ground
to the west, I surveyed the lay of the lake to the southward.
And here again, good fortune was ours. By carrying the
boat a considerable distance across the point of land, we
could refloat it in the south arm of the lake at a point out of
sight of the spot where the Skrelling lay in hiding. Then, by
holding a course southward, as close to the west shore as
possible, we could reach the south end of the lake without
being seen.

"Surely, as soon as the lone warrior's comrades arrived,
they would take to the open water and head for this same
point of land where they could survey the entire south arm
of the lake. And yet we must take the chance. And so, once
again, the gods came to our aid giving us time enough to
reach the south shore. And, turning to look over the water

we observed no pursuers. Perhaps we had outwitted the Skrellings—at least for the moment.

"Observing no immediate prospect of a further water route, we now pushed through the reeds and rushes and stepped ashore once more to rest and find a place of concealment for the boat.

"And now again were we met with a misfortune in one way, but a benefit in another. We had no more than set foot on land when a vast flock of waterfowl, alarmed at the sight of us, took to the air with almost as great a clamor as had the other birds earlier in the day. They first circled in confusion, and then took a course to the northward flying low over the water.

"Their flight led them directly toward the point of land whence we came. We observed them rising higher to clear the point, and at the moment they appeared to be over the spot where we had lain in hiding, they suddenly veered off to the right in fright, no doubt, at something they saw on the ground.

"So now, once again were the wild fowl of the air betraying us. But by the same token they were betraying our pursuers. The Skrelling warrior that was concealed from our sight by the point of land had likely covered the width of the lake's west arm, and was now without a doubt following our path where we crossed over to the south arm of the lake. If that is the case, he is close upon us.

"And now, another question arose. Was it only the lone warrior following us? Or had his companions now overtaken him, and would they in turn be making a great effort to overtake us? We waited not to learn the answer. And, raising the boat to our shoulders, we set forth on foot with all haste.

"And so we fled. The day wore on, and we still fled, stopping only for a short rest now and then when fatigue threatened to halt us.

"Once, while resting, we discussed the wisdom of lying in ambush and attempting to slay at least enough of them to put their survivors to flight. But no—we knew not their strength in numbers. The probability was, judging by the number that must have attacked our camp by the lake, that we could expect a band of forty, perhaps more. The odds against its being a smaller band were far too great.

"And so we pushed onward; it was our only hope for survival. The sun sank in the west and the twilight turned to darkness. The moon appeared over the treetops to the east, and still we fled—now carrying the boat on our shoulders, and now again floating it in a marsh, or once again plying the oars on open water.

"At last, near morning, so I judged by the position of the moon, we reached what appeared to be a rather large but shallow lake. And by chance it was, that nearing its south shore we came upon a small island. Here, I said to myself, would be an excellent place to halt for a much-needed rest, a rest we must have or soon perish from exhaustion.

"Here would we seek a hiding place among the bushes and tall grasses and rest for at least a full day. Here would we be able to keep watch across the water to the north for our pursuers in case we, perchance, had misjudged the progress of their pursuit.

"By traveling almost the whole of the previous night, certain it seems that we have left the Dark-skins far behind; I doubt they would attempt to follow our path in the darkness. Yes, here did we seem safe to stop for a rest, and to set about the task of seeking a further waterway to take us to the Salt Sea.

"And so here on the island have we spent the day resting and here will we leave our mark—our runes, engraved on stone.

"*Ja vel*—in truth I say, 'Torkel' has talked long, and grows weary of talking, even as he has grown weary of fighting and fleeing. *Gammel og mett av dage* (old and full of days) indeed he feels—and in the need of a good rest.

"And so, again must I say, as I said in the beginning, thus must our saga be told. And, if it so pleases the gods that one of us may live to tell the tale—to him I must leave the task of supplying the ending.

"But enough now—enough of the deeds of the past. Now we must again look to the future, and lay our plans.

"The sun is well below the horizon. In a few moments we shall have darkness—then to move quickly on until just before the first light of dawn.

"You, Lars and Sigurd, I trust you have the small-boat in readiness with provisions and weapons.

"We shall take toward the woodland on the south shore following the open water, and that as quietly as will our oars permit, yet holding as closely to the rushes in the marsh as possible.

"Ashore will we bury the greater part of the provisions and, overturning the boat, we will sink it in shallow water; weighing it down with stones to hold it in place.

"We will then journey southward taking with us what provisions and weapons we can carry on our backs. After a day's journey, we will rest a full day, if by then we have not found a waterway. If perchance we come upon a waterway the first, or even the second day, then two days will we take for resting. And then, with stealth and caution, will we attempt to return and retrieve the small-boat and our provisions. Certain I am that by then, they will either be upon us, or they will have abandoned the pursuit.

"For no less than two days will we move southward, thence in a great circle to avoid, if possible, meeting the tribes who attacked us. And thence move northward again towards where our comrades await us by the Salt Sea.

"And here again, comrades, comes the troublesome thought—should we fail to return to the ship, our companions who wait for us there, are but ten of the thirty who set forth in the Knorr to sail her back to Vinland and thence to the homeland. If they perchance meet with foul weather at sea ... .

"But back to our plans. Possible it is that we may encounter friendly Skrelling tribes to the south. But, upon this we cannot depend. Best it will be if we avoid them at all costs. However, if we are attacked, let us not be fearful. If they outnumber us by not more than three to one, certain I am that we can slay them all.

"Should we encounter a larger number, we shall first make signs of peace in the hope that they be not of the band that pursue us.

"But if it appears that we must fight, mind you, strike not until I give the signal. Lars, you will take your stand to my left, being certain that you allow enough space to properly wield your axe. And you, Sigurd, will stand to my right as we face them.

"Ivar, you will stand slightly behind and to the right and use your spear. But take care not to waste your strength on wild thrusts. Your task will be to watch for double attacks—where two enemy weapons may be raised against one of us at the same instant. But watch closely, as his arm goes upward a quick thrust to the belly, halfway through his body will be sufficient and instantly make ready for the next one.

"And one thing more, Ivar, if the battle goes against us, if you observe that we must fight to the death—you yourself must be the judge—you are to abandon your comrades and attempt to escape. This I command you to do. You are young and fleet-of-foot, and there is the possibility that you can escape and make it back to the Salt Sea ... if it so pleases the gods.

"But, the moon is down, we must be off. Kindle the fire more brightly now, Lars, thus to beguile them should they be watching across the water. Beguile them to think we will yet be on the island. But not too brightly, lest they suspect the ruse—there, that should be sufficient.

"And you, Sigurd, go you and—

"Hark, comrades, hear you not—the frogs in the marsh to the north of us. Something has disturbed them, and they have stopped their croaking.

"But wait. It could scarcely be the Skrellings—'tis not their nature to attack in darkness. Would they not make camp at a safe distance, and await the dawn? Yet, we know not—

"And now hear you not that sound as of the sides of boats rubbing against the rushes near the shore?

"Lay hold of your weapons, comrades. Crouch here in the bushes away from the firelight. This time they shall not surprise us. Move not, nor make any sound, until they are well into the firelight. I will give the signal.

"There—something moves on the shore, or so it appeared when the fire blazed brightly in the breeze. There again—they come. Steady now, comrades. They know not rightly where to look for us. Await my signal now, mind you.

"But how is this? They hasten not to attack. If they do attack at night they could rush into the firelight, shouting and beating the bushes in attempt to frighten us into betraying our hiding place. Something is amiss.

"Ah, there—look sharply—almost exactly toward where we concealed the boat in the rushes. In truth now, did I see something move. And a Skrelling warrior, I'll wager. Yet his comrades hold back in the darkness, as though they would hesitate to enter the fire light. But again he moves, and again does he hesitate. I understand not ... .

"But hold on. By the gods—now it comes to my mind. Now do I understand their plan. Lead us to hold our attention to one, perhaps two or three warriors while half their number circle to the rear of us, and, then to strike from two sides. And a goodly number there must be that they thus divide into two attacking groups.

"Far outnumbered we certainly are, comrades. And certain it is—

"But no. We are Vikings and we shall fight as we have never fought before. And, though small comfort it be, let us make certain that there will be a goodly number of Skrelling bodies to cobble our path to Valhalla.

"By the beard of Thor, then, let them come. 'Torkel the Warrior' welcomes the Dark-skins to his sword. The first beneath my blade shall be for Black Botolf, and the second for Hjalmar the Wild Man. The third—

"But see. Again something moves in the rushes toward us, but slowly, as though. ... Perhaps, in a moment—again I say, mind you: make no movement until I give the signal. Steady now. Wait—

"Ivar, DOWN. *DOWN, YOU FOOL*! What? He heeds not my command. He leaps forward to face them alone. He has gone berserk.

"*DREPE DEM (SLAY THEM)—OR IT'S ON TO VALHALLA.*"

PART II

THE LEGEND OF THE MANDANS

6

INTRODUCTION

To the eastward from the river,
Eastward from the Great North River,
In the land of lake and forest,
Dwelt the tribes of the Ojibwahs.

Mighty nation; the Ojibwahs,
Mighty hunters, mighty warriors.
Jealous of their hunting forests,
Jealous of their lakes and meadows.

Tribes from nations to the southward,
Sometimes moving north in Summer,
Moving north for better hunting,
Felt the wrath of the Ojibwahs.

Met their fate in fierce encounter
With the strong and mighty warriors,
Who claimed the land of lake and forest,
Hunting grounds of the Ojibwahs.

Westward from the Great North River
Lay the land of the Dakotahs
Land of prairies and of meadows,
Land of prairie fowl and bison.

And the tribes of the Dakotahs,
They themselves a mighty nation,
Rivals of the great Ojibwahs,
Sometimes met with them in battle.

Sometimes tribes from the Dakotahs,
Faring forth in hunting parties,
Fearing not their mighty neighbors,
Dared to cross the Great North River.

Dared to venture to the eastward,
Hunting grounds of the Ojibwahs.
Often thus began the quarrel,
Began the battle and the bloodshed.

Likewise sometimes the Ojibwahs,
Roving westward crossed the river
In search of the mighty Bison;
In the Autumn hunting season.

And once again was heard the war cry.
Once again the painted warriors
Fought and bled upon the meadows,
Fought and died along the river.

Thus it was; the Great North River
Became the boundary between them,
Dividing line between two nations:
The Ojibwahs and Dakotahs.

And so it was for many summers,
There was peace along the river;
So strong had grown the rival nations,
That neither cared to fight the other.

Then one day a band of strangers,
Coming on the Great North River
To the land of the Ojibwahs.
Strangers were they from the north.

Strange their canoes and their weapons,
Strange their faces and their language.
So odd they seemed, that the Ojibwahs
Stood in wonder as they watched them:

Watched the strange men from the north,
Watched and wondered at their coming,
Wondered what might be their purpose,
Wondered: were they friend or foe?

7

BLACK EAGLE'S PLANS

For two days now had the Ojibwah scouts watched the coming of the strangers from the north. In secrecy had they watched them, trying never to allow themselves to be seen by the newcomers. Early each morning a messenger had been sent back to the camp of Black Eagle, the war chief of the Ojibwah nation.

And the second day the message had been the same as the day before: "Yes, there were but two canoes. Large canoes they are, each carrying ten strangers. Each evening do they make camp on the river's bank, and at dawn, again are they wielding their paddles and pushing southward."

But now came the evening of the third day and a different message. The strangers had left the Great North River, by way of the River of Pezheekee the Bison (Buffalo River), a smaller stream that flowed from a southeasterly direction. They were now moving up this stream toward the very heart of the Ojibwah stronghold.

Black Eagle was perturbed to say the least. Not that he feared this handful of strangers. He could send out a war party to wipe them out without any great difficulty. But still, he was cautious. News travels fast, and he had other and greater plans which could well be upset by a minor battle with these newcomers. No, he could not risk a battle, and the news that could spread despite all precautions.

And yet, if they were to continue their present course, he would well be forced to annihilate them. They could very well be enemy spies. And he would take no chances: they must not learn of the great war camp on the western shore of the Lake of the Bird-of-Magic (Big Cormorant Lake).

Dismissing the messenger, the young war chief turned on his heel and strode in the direction of the lodge of old Grey Hawk, Great Chief of the Ojibwah nation.

Waiting not to greet the old chief at his doorway, as was customary, and in an attitude of irritation he demanded, "What think you now, Foster-father, those meddlesome strangers from the north—'harmless strangers' as you called them?

"They are not merely 'passing through on the river,' as you thought. They have left the river and are moving toward our war camp by the very route I shall use in my planned march against the Dakotahs.

"Where they are going and for what purpose I know not." He raised his voice almost to a shout, "But this I do know, Foster-father: if they discover our war camp they shall not live to carry the news back to the Dakotahs."

The old chief raised his hand as though to calm the younger man, but the prospect of being interrupted only served to excite him the more.

"Hear my words, Foster-father," he stormed, "ever since I was a small boy—since my father was killed in the war with the Dakotas fifteen summers ago—have I lived for nothing else but to make ready to avenge his death.

"Now I am war chief of our nation. Since early spring have I been gathering the warriors from all our tribes to my secret war-camp. Seven days hence is the appointed time to commence our march against them."

As he paused for breath, Chief Grey Hawk said calmly, "Foster-son, well do I understand the feeling for revenge in your heart. Forget not that your father was also my younger brother. But for myself, the years have mellowed my thirst for revenge. And forget not that in the great war of fifteen summers ago, it was we who made war against the Dakotahs; they did not attack us. We could not well blame them for defending themselves. Why then, should we seek revenge? Why then do you not abandon this wild plan to conquer our neighbors to the west?"

"Why indeed," Black Eagle blazed, "let the sun abandon its rising and setting, let summers and the winters abandon their coming and going. But I shall not abandon my plan to conquer those hated Dakotahs."

Old Chief Grey Hawk studied the bear-skin rug at his feet for a moment, and then, "Let us think calmly upon this thing, Foster-son. Supposing now, that you are marching against them and you have twice the number of warriors we had fifteen summers ago. But supposing, and no doubt they do, they have twice as many as before. And, as before, they have the advantage of fighting on their own familiar ground. Could not the outcome be the same as it was in the other Great War? Could we not lose half our warriors, and again be driven back across the river?"

"No, Foster-father," came the angry reply, "the outcome could not be the same. This time we shall take them by surprise. We move down the River of Pezheekee the Bison under cover of darkness. We cross the Great North River at sunrise, and we are well into their territory before they know we are coming. Straight west will we march for a full day. Then half our forces will swing northward, the other half southward, thus to split their nation asunder, and finish them before their friends, the Mandans, can come to their aid."

The old man nodded as though in agreement, and said, "A well laid plan, Foster-son. Yes indeed, a well laid plan. But forget not; always do things arise for which you have no plans. That we learned fifteen summers ago."

"That I well know," the war chief grated, "well and long have I talked with the old warriors who fought them before, and talked with them of things for which there were no plans. And one of those things, one which I have been told could well have been the cause of our defeat was the taking of captives.

"How can warriors fight, if they must at the same time be looking after their captive women and children. This time there shall be a better plan. This time we shall take no captives. This time we shall kill any of their women and children who encumber us."

He turned his back to the old chief and angrily strode off in the direction of his war camp.

For a long time Chief Grey Hawk sat there shocked and saddened with the realization that this son of his brother, this young madman could do just what he said. Nor was it within his power to prevent what he felt would be a suicidal war with the Dakotah nation. Too well entrenched in his power and influence was this nephew whom he had adopted as his own following the disastrous campaign he himself had led against the Dakotahs fifteen years ago—the "Great War" he had launched and lived to regret.

And then, there was the problem of these strangers from the North. That they would soon reach the Lake of the Bird-of-Magic and discover Black Eagle's war camp, the old chief had no doubt. But, equally certain was he, that it was merely by chance that they had taken this route, and they could not be spies for the Dakotah nation, as his foster-son had insisted.

All this summer there had been talk of secret plans being laid by Black Eagle. But, even as the warriors of the tribes had begun arriving and setting camp on the lakeshore, Grey Hawk had brushed aside as utterly impossible the idea that his nephew was seriously considering an invasion of the land of the Dakotas. Surely, he told himself, it was only a plan on the part of Black Eagle to boastfully parade his newly gained power and authority.

But now he was not so sure.

* * * * * * * *

Chief Grey Hawk saw no more of his nephew for two days. Black Eagle had established his headquarters a short distance around the curve of the lakeshore near the war camp. And, of late he had for the most part avoided the old chief.

And then, at dusk of the second day, he saw his nephew approaching in what appeared to be great haste and agitation. Black Eagle did not enter the lodge, but stood in the doorway as though expecting to stay but a short time.

"They have arrived," he announced irritably, but with an unexpected calmness that startled the old chief.

"I sent a band of warriors to the portage to threaten the Northerners and attempt to turn them back, but they paid no heed. They have anchored their canoes to the rocks near the north shore, but they have not yet discovered the war camp." He was controlling his voice with great effort.

"Foster-father, I already told you that those spies from the north shall not discover my war camp. Already have my warriors gone out—two hundred war canoes and four hundred warriors shall lie in wait for them in the morning."

The old chief stared at him in disbelief, unwilling to admit in his mind, the realization that his nephew spoke the truth.

"I am saddened, Foster-son," he finally said, "if this is to be your course, I cannot stop you. But this I still say that they are but harmless strangers passing through. They know nothing of your plans to attack the Dakotahs. I doubt that they even understand our language.

"But grant me one favor, Foster-son. Let me talk to the strangers in the morning as they leave their anchorage. Certain I am, that I can persuade them to turn back."

"Talk to them if you wish," Black Eagle growled. "But again I say, they shall not live to carry the news of our war camp back to our enemies. Five days hence do we secretly begin our march against the Dakotahs over the portage and down the River of Pezheekee the Bison."

Again his voice was rising in anger, "Six days hence we cross the Great North River—at sunrise. And there will be five hundred dead Dakotahs before they can assemble their warriors."

With a short, horizontal movement of his right hand, a gesture of finality, he turned to leave. Then suddenly, as though with an after thought, he turned and again faced old Grey Hawk.

"One more thing I have to say, Foster-father. When we have finished with the Dakotahs, and I return from the war there shall be a wedding." Something like a smile came over his face, "Your foster-daughter shall become my wife."

A moment of stunned silence, and then, "No, Foster-son, she shall not," the old chief objected. "Both you and the maiden are my adopted children. You have grown up together as brother and sister. Brothers and sisters cannot marry. No, Foster-son, you must seek a wife elsewhere."

"Foster-father," the young man snapped, his voice again rising in anger, "you know, and I know the girl is not my sister. Always have you deceived her by calling her 'Daughter.' But well do I know that the girl is not your daughter. She was taken captive in the Great War as a small child, and so young she remembers it not."

"For the most part," the old man agreed, "you speak the truth in this. But it is not to deceive her that I call her 'Daughter.' It is for another reason, but you would not understand," he ended suddenly and sadly.

And then, as though in desperation, he continued, "But, would it not be wise, Foster-son, again I say, to think more calmly about this as well as your other plans? Always is it possible that there may be wiser courses to follow.

"First, let me ask, does the maiden take kindly to your proposal?"

Again with a look which could have been intended as a smile, "In truth, Foster-father, I have said nothing to her about my plans. But what matters it? That which I desire is what I shall have. And possible it is," he added, "that you speak the truth when you say 'there may be wiser courses to follow.' But I care not about 'wiser courses.'

"And now hear you these words, Foster-father." He again raised his voice as though greatly irritated at the old chief's attitude. "Three things do I desire, and three things I shall have. First: I shall have the death of those spies from the north. Second: I shall have one thousand dead Dakotahs in revenge for my father's death. Third: I shall have your foster-daughter as my wife, whether she likes it or not. I have spoken."

And again he turned and stalked away into the growing darkness.

A terrible feeling seized the old chief. Not since that day of anguish fifteen summers ago, had he felt so heavy a crush of utter failure, defeat, and regret.

That was the day his once-proud warriors, or what was left of them, had been beaten back across the river, thus ending his ill-advised campaign against the Dakotahs. That was the day the messenger brought the sad tidings that his younger brother was one of the warriors left lying somewhere out there in the grasslands. And that was the day his friend and life-long companion, Red Fox, coming in the dusk of evening in a simple even perhaps childish effort to assuage the grief of a friend, brought him a little captive Dakotah child.

A beautiful child she was, and somehow, he knew not how or why, as the years passed and the child grew, she had become a living symbol of a deep and growing determination—never again should the Ojibwah nation wage war against its neighbors to the west.

And now, for the last several winters, as he had sat by the fire in his lodge, awaiting the coming of spring, old Chief Grey Hawk had told himself again and again: In the Moon-of-the-new-leaves, I shall journey to the land of the Dakotahs. I shall take the child back to her people as a promise of everlasting peace between our nations. And each summer he would say to himself, "No, I cannot part with the child now. I must wait until another summer."

And now, it was too late.

* * * * * * * *

Two years ago, it was, at the Great Council of all the Ojibwah tribes, the question had been raised. The question Chief Grey Hawk well knew he must face sooner or later. He was growing old. That he could not deny. For so many years he had been the Great Chief of the nation that none but the oldest men of the tribes could remember when there was any other.

Yes, the tribal chiefs had agreed, Grey Hawk was a good and wise Great Chief and right it was that he should so continue until his death.

But, should there not be a war chief for the Ojibwah nation—a younger man, around whom the warriors of all the tribes could rally in case of war? To this, Grey Hawk had readily agreed. And at the time proud indeed he was, to approve of their choice: his young nephew, his foster-son, Black Eagle.

But, he knew not that depth and blackness of the hatred in the young man's heart toward the tribes of the Dakotahs.

Now it was too late.

As though in a stupor the old chief stood for a long time, looking and gazing without seeing into the growing darkness of the night. And then, seemingly bent with the great burden of his remorse he stepped quietly into the doorway of his darkened lodge.

8

OLD GREY HAWK'S DAUGHTER

The young Ojibwah maiden, daughter of the Great Chief of the nation, returned later than was her custom to her father's lodge. Returning from a most delightful stroll along the lakeshore in the cool of the evening, she stepped through the rear entrance to her private quarters and at once recognized the sound of her brother's voice. He was speaking to her father with what seemed a forced calmness to cover a feeling of great irritation.

Through this thin wall of woven willow branches and buffalo robes, she heard him and told herself it was wrong to listen to words not intended for her ears. She would pay no heed. Of late, she had been hearing talk of great plans and boasts by her brother, but surely nothing would come of them.

As far back into early childhood as she could remember, Black Eagle had always been the quarrelsome, overbearing older brother, always determined to win, in all their childish contests of strength or dexterity. Always he was the winner, by fair means, or otherwise.

But well did she recall, only a year ago, it was, at a council of the younger men and women of the Ojibwah tribes she had bested her brother in a contest. There had been a special event for both men and women—target practice at close range with bow and arrow—a contest not of strength, but of skill. She had taken top honors—several points ahead of her brother. But afterwards, seeing him sulk in sullen resentment for two days, she almost regretted having won the match.

The older brother—Black Eagle—always the winner.

And now, this evening, perturbed perhaps by some minor frustration, he was standing out there disputing some triviality with her father—a not uncommon occurrence of late.

Only in recent days had she been aware of what seemed to be a growing animosity on her brother's part, something akin to an attitude of disrespect toward her father—an attitude which ordinarily would not be tolerated among her people.

She would pay them no heed, she told herself.

Besides, she had at the moment other and more pleasant thoughts to be savored. A dream to be dreamed while earlier events of the evening were yet fresh in her youthful mind. All too soon would the delightful evening be something to be remembered as a yesterday, or a last month, or a last year.

For several days now, there had been rumors in the village—rumors of the coming of some sort of "strange men from the north." No one seemed to know when they would arrive, nor why.

And then, suddenly that evening, almost unbelievably it seemed, they were there—out there on the lake.

Two large canoes—strange looking canoes manned by odd-looking, hairy-faced strangers. And the sound of their voices coming clearly across the water were human voices, to be sure, but with words less meaningful than the sounds made by animals of the forest and birds of the air.

But there was one notable exception, she told herself, was the laughter of the strange men from the north. As though in some sort of irresistible fascination, the young maiden and her two companions had stood there on the lakeshore watching and listening. And still fascinated had they stood as one of the strangers, having climbed into a small canoe, turned it in their direction and paddled swiftly toward them.

True, there had been an impulse to take flight as the canoe drew near, but just as suddenly had it given way to a stronger force that held them spellbound. Perhaps it was the smile of the young man who had raised his hand in a gesture of friendship.

And a fair-haired, handsome stranger he was. He had blue eyes, fair skin, and a short, slightly reddish beard. He was like nothing she had ever seen.

Then again had he smiled and spoken, again that strange meaningless chatter, or was it meaningless? Had not she observed that his words, his gestures, and his smile were directed for the most part toward her rather than to her two companions.

And had it not been to her that when leaving he had handed a parting gift, a gaily painted arrow, feathered in red and with such a strange point? And had she not felt a sort of sadness when he paddled away back toward his comrades?

But no—it had not been sadness, exactly. It had been some other strange sort of feeling as though she must, she knew not how, nor where, nor when; she must see that "Fair-haired One" again.

And now at home in her father's lodge, with the friendly darkness of evening closing in upon her, the young maiden lay alone on her soft pallet of pine boughs and furs—alone with a dream.

Then suddenly—from the direction of the front entrance of her lodge, where her father and brother stood talking—came an outburst of angry words. Terrible words they were. Words not intended for her ears. She tried not to listen, tried to pretend she had not heard them, even that they had not even been spoken. But no—it was of no use to pretend. She had heard her brother's words—and her dream was shattered.

And so the young Ojibwah maiden wept as have maidens since the beginning of time at the shattering of the fragile dreams of youth.

* * * * * * * *

In the heavy fog of early morning old Chief Grey Hawk walked in silence toward the lakeshore. A rather simple matter it would be it seemed. Yes, he would speak to these strangers from the north. In sign language he would talk to them. He would tell them; yes, he would make them understand that they needed to turn back.

And as he walked he was aware, though he understood not how, that he was being followed. Perhaps his ear had caught the faint sound of footsteps in the dewy grass. Or it could have been something akin to an animal instinct born of a lifetime in the wilderness that was his home.

Yes, he knew without turning to look, but he pretended not to know. He suspected the maiden's reason for following him—but somehow, could not bring himself to send her back.

But, of another thing, old Chief Grey Hawk was not aware, despite the wisdom of age and experience. He knew nothing of the native stubbornness of the Northmen.

And now the attempt was over, and he had failed. Abruptly had they turned their boats away from him and out over the fog shrouded lake toward the south, and toward certain death.

He stood and watched them disappear into the whiteness of the fog. They had spurned his well meant warning, and his first reaction was a feeling of resentment. But immediately it gave way to a deep sadness, as he pictured in his mind the fate that awaited the Northerners.

Turning to retrace his steps, he noted absently that his foster-daughter had gone on ahead. But no—a few steps from the lakeshore, seated on the mossy trunk of a fallen tree, he found her bent over and in tears.

"You need not tell me why you weep my daughter," he said, and sat down beside her. "I failed," he added sadly.

"I know," she replied softly, "but blame not yourself, Father. I was watching, and I know they understood your message—but they chose to heed it not."

She rose, rather impatiently, took two steps and then stopped as her foster-father again spoke, "I beg a favor of you, that you will not be angry with me."

The young woman returned to her seat beside him and said, "No, Father. I am not angry. You have always been so kind." She hesitated as though choosing her words carefully, and then said, "Last night I ... I learned I am but a foster-daughter. But you are the only father I have ever known. You shall always be my father."

She then continued, "I also heard about Black Eagle's war against the Dakotahs. And I don't believe the strangers are spies, and I *will not* be his wife."

One small gesture of emotion she made. She put her hand on the old man's shoulders for a moment. And then suddenly said, "But the time for weeping is past. I must go." Leaping to her feet she ran toward her lodge.

Startled, the old chief rose as though to follow her and then sank back down again on the log. She is no longer a child, he said to himself, she is a woman. And who is there who understands the thoughts of a woman in tears?

Again he rose and walked slowly, retracing his way back to the lodge. I must send for Wauwona (Always speaks softly), wife of my old friend, Red Fox, he mused. For years has she been like a mother to the maiden; yes, I will have old Wauwona talk to her.

But when he reached the lodge, his foster-daughter was not there.

* * * * * * * *

Almost out of breath, the young woman was when she came in sight of the lodge of her foster-brother, Black Eagle, who was near the war camp. She had run all the way.

And while she ran, the girl had turned it over in her mind, again and again, what she would say to him. She would convince him that the strangers from the north meant no harm, and that it would be a great wrong to attack and slay them in cold blood. Yes, she would convince him. She must convince him.

She saw him step out through the doorway as she drew near. She called a greeting to him and forced a smile half expecting a smile in return. But no—he was surly and stubborn faced.

"What brings you here?" he demanded, but waited not for a reply. He knew full well the reason for her coming. "I have no time to talk," he went on, "already are my warriors out on the lake waiting only for lifting of the fog. I must go now to see that they do well their task."

"Then it is not too late—" she began, desperately searching his face for some sign of human compassion.

"Not too late for what?" he snapped, "To recall the orders I have given my warriors? Well do I know, without

asking that your father succeeded not in his attempt to turn
the Northerners back. They have scorned his warning.

"Now let them suffer the result of their scorn," he
ended, as though seeking to justify his course.

"And what is this report that my messenger brings me
this morning, just before you arrived, that you had met and
talked with one of the strangers last evening?" he demanded, his attitude turning to one approaching jealous
rage.

"You need not attempt to deceive me with lies, and you
saw him as handsome and looked upon him with favor." he
shouted.

"Very well then," he raged. "Now hear you these words:
ere the sun of noon rides high, our task will be finished,
and he shall be handsome no longer."

And as the young Ojibwah war chief turned toward the
lakeshore, the girl reached out a hand toward him, instinctively, as though she might yet detain him, might yet
reason with this madman who had once been her brother.
She touched his arm as he turned, but he ignored her and
stalked away.

* * * * * * * *

When old Chief Gray Hawk's daughter reached her foster-
father's lodge he was gone. And she was glad, in a way
—almost certain she was that he would question her as to
where she had been, and what had happened. Not that it
was a thing to be ashamed of, certainly, but the talking
would take time, time she could not well spare.

And she had lost no time in returning from the fruitless
attempt to reason with Black Eagle. At first, her steps had

been slow, her limbs heavy as stone it seemed. Then faster as her strength commenced to return, and the dim outline of a plan had commenced to form in her mind.

And with the plan came determination, and with the determination came more strength until at last she had found herself running as she neared her lodge.

And now, once more, the maiden stood in the familiar shelter of the place she had called home. But, of a sudden, there was a strangeness about it, as though it were no longer her home. Her heart it seemed was elsewhere.

And the plan? Suddenly she realized that, in truth, the plan was only a blind, unreasoning resolution. Somehow, yet she had not the remotest idea of the means, but somehow she must forestall Black Eagle's warriors' assault upon the strangers from the north.

I must stop them, her mind kept saying, the 'Fair-haired One' must not die.

"... waiting only the lifting of the fog ... ," she remembered and recited Black Eagle's cruel words. No. There was no time to lose.

Without thinking, but acting upon impulse, the maiden seized her hunting bow and slung the quiver of arrows over her shoulder. Grasping an empty deer-skin bag, she quickly tossed in a few articles of provisions and started toward the doorway. Halfway there, she stopped, turned, and picked up another bag containing a few of her personal belongings, though she gave no thought as to why.

And again she ran. This time in the direction of the nearest shore of the lake where lay her own light canoe. Floating the canoe, she climbed in and grasped the paddle, and then, swiftly and silently, old Grey Hawk's daughter disappeared into the great white blanket of fog.

Meanwhile the old chief returning in company with his friends, Red Fox and Wauwona, stepped into the doorway of his daughter's personal quarters, glanced quickly around the room and read the story in missing articles. His daughter had gone, perhaps never to return.

* * * * * * * * *

The maiden finally rested her paddle across the canoe, and looked and listened. It was growing lighter overhead as though the sun was about to break through the fog. Yes, even now the fog was lifting. Certainly, she told herself, she must be nearing the area where the encounter would soon take place.

There was a strange silence over the water—that deep, foreboding silence that almost foretells certain tragedy.

Then she saw it, and her heart sank—hundreds of canoes now closing into a great circle. And yet she knew, though she could not distinguish them at such a distance, that the two canoes of the strangers from the north would be at the center.

And the thought struck her, "Why would Black Eagle send such a great, formidable force to wipe out the small handful of strangers?" Then she realized the truth. He was taking no chances of there being any survivors.

"When the sun of noon rides high," she again remembered his words, "our task will be finished." She shuddered, and a feeling of illness came over her. She must do something. But first she must think, and think fast.

But there was no time to think. The distant sound of wild shouts cut short her thoughts. The attack was on.

In a frenzy of desperation the young woman seized the paddle and drove the canoe forward. Without thinking, without reasoning, a wild, insane compulsion it was as though single-handed she would scatter the warriors and stop the assault.

Reaching the outer rim of the gathering circle, she singled out a canoe manned by a lone warrior, probably the leader of the near sector of the attackers. He sat in open-mouthed astonishment as she approached, and then finding his voice, he shouted, "Go back, young woman. Go back now."

Ignoring his command, she came on, and stopped a canoe's length from him.

"I am Chief Grey Hawk's daughter," she shouted, "you are to stop the attack. Pass these words along at once."

For an encouraging few moments he hesitated. And then, "You speak not the truth. Black Eagle, our war chief, passed by here but a few moments ago. He said nothing about our halting the attack."

Other canoes were crowding in close—their occupants curious to hear what was being said, and surprised to find a young woman in their midst.

"Go back now, I say," he repeated, "before your belly stops a stray arrow," he added, as though to bring reason to her mind.

Ignoring him, she screamed, "Call and stop the attack." She seized her bow and set an arrow. "Do as I say now. Pass my words, or I shall kill you."

She raised the weapon to shooting position and drew the bowstring. But in that instant, a tall warrior, his own canoe almost rubbing sides with hers, reached with a spear and struck the arrow forcing it downward.

"Seize her and bind her," the first warrior shouted.

And unfriendly faces closed in from all sides. Almost instantly strong hands were upon her, and her hands were securely bound behind her back.

And so she had failed in an attempt which had she been thinking rationally would have recognized as one doomed to failure from the outset.

For what seemed like an eternity, the young maiden sat there in her canoe drifting in the water, silently, helpless, and listening to the distant sounds of the battle. Listening, and dreading, but yet hoping. And there was some small measure of hope, so she reasoned, for so long as the sound continued there was yet the possibility, however small, that the Northerners might somehow break away and escape.

The warriors who bound her had long since moved on toward the center of the ever growing circle of war canoes. The sun of noon was now riding high over the scene of the battle, and by the sounds she heard she realized, with a feeling of renewed hope that her brother's prediction of "finishing the task by noon" had not materialized.

And so the early afternoon hours wore on. There was no breeze, barely the faintest wafting of a warm air current from the south, and the sun's heat was stifling. The thought of sitting there helplessly became unbearable. If only she could free herself from the thongs that bound her hands, she kept thinking, there might be something she could do. She knew not what but, there must be something.

Another small group of canoes, a half-dozen or so, appearing to the westward hurried to join in the excitement of the battle. No doubt they would pass by without so much as a glance in her direction. But yet, there was an inkling of a possibility.

As the lead canoe approached within calling distance, she shouted loudly for help. The warrior halted his paddle in mid-stroke, raised it above the water's surface as though arrested by indecision, and then, with impatient paddle strokes, changed his course and came toward her.

"I am bound," she called as he drew near, "come and loose me."

"Who are you, and who caused you to be bound?" the warrior demanded, as he pulled his canoe alongside.

"I am Chief Grey Hawk's daughter. Those strangers from the north are the cause of my being bound." The half-truth was an intended deception. A deception born of necessity, however the strangers were in a way, the cause.

"So," the warrior scowled, "they would even carry away our women as captives." Then he quickly added, "It shall be my pleasure to split their skulls for this."

"You are most kind," the maiden managed to say and forced a smile as the warrior quickly loosed the thongs.

But, when he was gone, she pondered his distressing remark, and again the feeling of illness seized her.

But now a new surge of hope arose as she heard the distant rumble of thunder in the northwest. If only the storm would be swift enough in its coming and severe enough. Well did the young woman know that even a moderate storm could put an end to the battle.

And the storm was not long in coming. Soon the early-afternoon sun was hidden. And now there was the rolling and churning of angry black clouds almost directly over-head. And the distant roar of the wind, and for a few moments, the sound arriving ahead of its cause. Then it struck with all its fury. Already she could see the lighter canoes scattering; warriors heading for the safety of the nearest shore.

But the young woman, compelled by some force stronger than fear of the tempest, turned her canoe in the direction of where she well knew the boats of the strangers from the north must lie. Angling slightly with the wind and taking full advantage of its power she pushed forward with all her strength.

And now, through the driving wind and rain, with a cry of delight she saw it. One of the strange-looking canoes she had seen anchored near the north shore last evening—its sail stretched taut in the wind as it broke through the maze of war canoes.

Another wild impulse seized her. She would follow the strangers. She would overtake them. Too far away the canoe was to distinguish the faces of its crew, but somehow she knew it could not be otherwise, the 'Fair-haired One' was one of its occupants.

Skillful as any man at handling a light canoe, she turned and set out in swift pursuit of the Northerners' canoe.

But a losing game it proved to be. Their canoe with full sail and paddles manned to the limit, was soon lost to sight in the downpour of the wind driven rain. No. To overtake them now was obviously an impossibility. Nothing remained but to change her course and make for shore.

For a fleeting moment there was a feeling of panic when she realized the narrow margin by which she had missed being caught in the storm with her hands bound behind her and unable to protect herself.

She was overjoyed that the strangers had escaped, yet deep was the feeling of disappointment that she had been unable to overtake them in their flight. But, as old Chief Grey Hawk's daughter neared the shore, once again was she able to reason clearly and already a new plan was forming in her mind.

9

BLACK EAGLE AFTER THE STORM

Black Eagle stood on the lakeshore drenched with rain and in a sullen rage at the unexpected outcome of the attack on the Northerners. Another half-hour of fighting and the victory surely would have been his. Success would have been within his grasp had they not eluded him by the aid of the storm. He cursed the storm cloud violently as it rolled away into the southeast with its distant rumbling and growling seeming to mock his anger.

True, his warriors had slain a few of them and sank one of their canoes. But his losses in men had been at least five to one. Black Eagle had reckoned without knowledge of the fury and skill of the Northerners in battle.

Nor did it improve his frame of mind when Running Wolf, his chief henchman, reminded Black Eagle that he had failed to heed his advice: that he should have attacked them at the portage rather than out on the lake.

Perhaps somewhat less of a radical this Running Wolf was—less impulsive and more of the shrewd, level-headed type. And he knew, so he thought, how far he could go in criticizing the war chief, even when Black Eagle was in a mood such as that in which he now found him.

This time, he had almost gone too far. But Black Eagle just glowered at him and said nothing. Well did he realize Running Wolf had spoken the truth.

And now to make matters worse, even as he was assembling his leaders on the lakeshore for a council to consider his next move, the news was spreading. Both in the village and in the war camp was it spreading; old Chief Grey Hawk's daughter was missing. And, as the news spread so spread the rumors. It was generally agreed that the strangers from the north had carried her away. There were several among the warriors who remembered seeing the maiden floating, bound and helpless in a canoe. And at the time it seemed that in the excitement of battle they had not given her so much as a second thought. But now, certain they were, that this could have been the work of none other than the Northerners.

Nor did Black Eagle's warriors who bound her dare admit to their act. To them, their very lives would well depend upon their silence. Well did they know the fate that had befallen the maiden. It could not have been otherwise. Her canoe had overturned in the storm, and unable to free her hands from behind her back, she had drowned.

Neither did the warrior who had loosed her bonds come forth with any enlightenment on the matter. Very likely it was, that the unfortunate fellow had been silenced forever by a blow from a Northerner's battle-axe.

Black Eagle alone it was who guessed the truth, but for the moment chose to keep it to himself. His "woman," as he had of late referred to her, had followed the strangers of her own free will. And he was furious to say the least.

Matters had now taken an unexpected turn. At first, Black Eagle's only interest in the total annihilation of the Northerners had been his unalterable conviction that their purpose was to spy upon his preparation for war with the Dakotahs—for a war that was to be won by an early dawn surprise attack. But now—now there was the added personal incentive calling for the death of the strangers. Now, his woman had likely fallen in love with one of them. Either that or they had taken her by force. Either way there was only one solution: Follow them. Overtake them and kill them.

"I want two hundred of the strongest warriors," he shouted to Running Wolf.

"We shall follow them after nightfall. We know the direction the storm has carried them. We know most likely where they will land. We shall take a course well to the left of their landing. Almost certain it is that they will camp to rest after the strain of today's battle. .

"We shall approach their camp this night by stealth. And with the dawn, we shall fall upon them. This time we shall not fail."

* * * * * * * *

And with the dawn they did not fail. On the south shore of the Lake of-the-Bird-of-Magic, Black Eagle made good his boast.

Taken by surprise, the Northerners had fought as they had never fought before. Attacked even while they slept and the battle was soon over. Being outnumbered twenty to one, the result could not have been otherwise.

Black Eagle was in high spirits as he surveyed the scene of the battle despite the fact that the victory had cost him the lives of perhaps fifty of his best warriors. He had made amends, so to speak, for the failure of yesterday. He had accomplished his mission and was highly pleased with himself.

But the exultation of his triumph was short lived. Now he found himself deeply disturbed by the fact that they found no trace of the missing daughter of Chief Grey Hawk. This could have but one or possibly two meanings. If the

Northerners had made off with her, willingly or otherwise, either they had slain her, or much more likely, there were survivors of this morning's battle. Some of them had escaped and taken her with them. No, now there was no doubt about it he assured himself.

"Yes, some of them escaped of that I am certain," he declared, "When we have rested and eaten, we shall return. It should be an easy matter to find their track. What think you, friend Running Wolf?"

"Here lay ten of them slain," he replied. "If there were survivors, they certainly could not number more than three or four at the most," Running Wolf estimated. But he seemed not inclined to offer any further suggestions. Perhaps it was that he would as soon have let the matter drop and returned to the war camp.

"We shall find their track. We shall follow them," Black Eagle declared, ignoring his friends apparent lack of enthusiasm. "We shall overtake them. I will take ten light canoes and twenty warriors and follow them."

And then, forgetting his earlier intention to say nothing of his conjectures regarding the missing maiden, he continued, his voice rising in anger, "We shall overtake them—they shall not escape. Then if we find the maiden bound and helpless, we will free her. But if we find she has followed them willingly, I shall split her skull."

And the insane fury of his leader's jealous rage so astonished Running Wolf that he stood speechless for a few moments. And then, thinking it wise to change the subject of conversation, he reminded the young war chief of their plans for marching against the Dakotahs, "Three days hence, Black Eagle, is the appointed time to commence our march. If we are to follow the survivors of this morning's battle, and no doubt they will be making great haste, it could well cost us two days to overtake them. We could well be delayed in commencing our march. It could be bad luck," he ended cautiously.

But, if he thought to dissuade Black Eagle from wasting time by following the escaped Northerners, he was soon to think otherwise.

"There shall be no delay," the war chief ordered, "already I have said: I shall take twenty warriors and follow them. You, Running Wolf, shall return with the others to the war camp.

"If I have not returned by the appointed day, you shall lead the march. Almost certain it is that the Northerners have fled southward, or possibly, westward toward the Great North River. When I and my companions have finished with them it will be a simple matter to travel northward on the river. And it could be our good fortune to reach the River of the Pezheekee the Bison in time to join you in the crossing.

"But mind you, Running Wolf," he continued with a new outburst, "you are not to await my coming. You are to cross the river as planned, striking straight to the westward from the crossing. And I shall overtake you, if not the first day, then surely the second. And there shall be a thousand dead Dakotahs before we turn our steps homeward."

* * * * * * * *

But when Black Eagle and his warriors returned to the scene of the massacre later that morning to tend to their dead and seek the track of the fleeing survivors, they were met with an astonishing sight. They had left the dead warriors from the north lying where they fell, and now their bodies and weapons had mysteriously disappeared.

Then suddenly far out on the lake they beheld what appeared to be a flaming canoe, now almost burned to the waterline. A superstitious fear seized them. But Black Eagle and Running Wolf were not to be stopped by vague apprehensions, or fears of the unknown.

Leaping into a canoe, they made great haste in the direction of the burning boat. But too late—halfway there, they saw it settle at one end, and plunge beneath the surface.

To the warriors watching from the shore, the canoe and the fire appeared to vanish as if by magic. And a great, slender ghost of smoke moved skyward in the stillness of the morning air.

There was some delay but no great difficulty in locating the path the survivors had left in the tall grass. Black Eagle and his twenty picked warriors were soon on their way in pursuit of the fleeing Northerners. And the other warriors headed by Running Wolf were wielding their paddles back in the direction of the war camp.

But the mysterious disappearance of the ten dead Northerners had its effect particularly upon the twenty warriors chosen to accompany Black Eagle in the pursuit of the survivors. Something strange and unearthly had taken place. And, aside from the driving force of their leader, there was little to encourage them to make any great haste in overtaking the strangers.

And Running Wolf, second-in-command to the Ojibwah war chief, pondered long and hard the whole unexplainable mystery of the coming of the strangers. Could it be possible, he finally wondered, if the spirits of their dead could somehow, bring bad luck to the coming expedition against the Dakotahs? Perhaps it had been a grave mistake to slay them. And now it disturbed him further to think that such a question should even enter his thoughts. Finally, as his armada of war canoes neared the war camp Running Wolf shrugged his shoulders and dismissed the matter from his mind. But at last, when the day came to assume command of the Ojibwah army and commence the great march over the portage and down the River of Pezheekee the Bison, Running Wolf was aware of a growing feeling of apprehension.

His friend, Black Eagle, had seen fit to set out upon what now seemed the pointless pursuit of three or perhaps four strangers. Strangers who almost certainly knew nothing of the coming campaign against the Dakotahs.

And what proof was there, that the Northerners had carried away Black Eagle's woman? Absolutely none, he told himself. And then, too, even if it were true that the maiden had followed them of her own choice, what would be gained if Black Eagle were to "split her skull," as he had threatened?

And if Black Eagle should fail in his plan to make the rendezvous for the river crossing, he asked himself, what then? Running Wolf had no doubt as to his own ability to lead the Ojibwah warriors in a successful campaign. But shrewd enough he was to acknowledge the possibility of failure, and if he were to fail, it would be his failure.

On the other hand with victory crowning Running Wolf's efforts, Black Eagle would, of course, reach the battlefield in time to reap the harvest of glory.

"It is not good, no matter which way it goes," Running Wolf said aloud to himself, as he reached the summit of the portage and looked back at the vast throng of warriors toiling up the slope, carrying canoes, weapons, and supplies on their backs.

But he was pleased, when upon reaching the Pezheekee, to find due to the recent heavy rains, that it was swift and deep. Ordinarily shallow and rocky, the stream was now in perfect condition to carry the war canoes safely and swiftly to its confluence with the Great North River.

Time enough there would be, he reckoned, for a good rest, while awaiting the appointed time for the river crossing and the invasion of the land of the Dakotahs.

And, for the moment at least, he found his attitude changing to one of optimism. He would perform his assigned task, and let the results take care of themselves.

And yet, despite his new optimism, Running Wolf could not shake off the feeling, unreasonable though it must be, that the spirits of the slain Northerners might yet give him trouble.

* * * * * * * *

Black Eagle and his warriors followed the survivors' track for the rest of the day and toward evening the track played out at water's edge—the survivors had taken to the water again. Black Eagle then told his warriors that they would rest until just before dawn and then split up and begin a search of all of the nearby shore and islands. If the survivors were found, they were not to call out, but were only to mark where the survivors were camped, and return to where they now were no later than when the sun was two hands in the sky. When they had discovered the survivors' camp they would move into positions surrounding the survivors at a distance, and on his call of the raucous crow would attack at dawn of the next day and slay them all.

10

IVAR GONE BERSERK

Ivar had gone berserk that night. At least that was the word Torkel used, half jokingly, in describing it later. Perhaps it was not so in the strict literal sense of the word. But, in truth, it was something closer to it than he ever cared to admit afterwards.

He remembered seeing one of his comrades, Thorvald Hammer, it was, in the fury of the life-and-death struggle that fearful day on the lake, tore off his helmet and armor, frothed at the mouth, and howled like an enraged animal. He had then swung his battle-axe at the attackers with such reckless and insane fury that he had to be forcibly restrained by his companions.

"Berserk," Torkel had called it. And now crouched here in the darkness, and as it turned out, both literally and proverbially, in the darkness that precedes the dawn, Ivar had in a sense, gone "berserk."

For the greater part of the night, they had sat around the campfire, Ivar and his three companions: Torkel, the leader of the ill-fated expedition, and Lars Nielson and Sigurd Vogge, the other two survivors.

Since about noon of the previous day they had rested, hiding there on the little island and saving their strength for what they well knew would be a continuation of the flight, or fight, for their lives. So they had felt no great need to sleep as they sat there listening to Torkel's recounting of the happenings of the past few weeks, and the past few days in particular. "It must be well planted in your minds," he had urged, "as the 'Saga' of the expedition—as the Saga which shall be told and retold in our homeland." "If, perchance," he had added, "one of us should ever live to retell it."

The moon had sunk in the west. And at the moment, it seemed to Ivar that the prospects of "living to retell the Saga" were indeed remote and as black as the night itself.

And then out of the dark silence they had heard sounds, faint but unmistakable. Sounds that could have but one meaning: the Skrellings were coming. Torkel had miscalculated the distance by which they were leading their pursuers and misjudged the margin of their safety.

Too late now for flight—too late now to reach the boat, which, unfortunately, lay beached in the very direction whence came the sound. Barely time enough to grasp their weapons and leap for the darkness outside the ring of the campfire's glow—and wait.

And to Ivar the waiting—after a few moments that seemed like hours—became unbearable. Although he had become skilled in the use of bow and arrow, he was not a warrior, as were his companions. He was the scribe and chart maker for the expedition. And, in marked contrast with his pagan comrades, he was "a follower of the New God of Christians," as Torkel had so often referred to Him, sometimes chafingly, and yet again with an attitude of respect for his religious belief.

And here in the darkness, awaiting what could very well be the final struggle to the death, the awful experience of recent days pressed upon his mind like a nightmare.

First, there had been the terrible battle on the lake—an unwanted battle and one certainly not of their choosing. For apparently no reason at all, the Skrelling horde, in both small and large boats, had surrounded them. Outnumbered by at least twenty to one, they had fought desperately and almost hopelessly for their lives.

Never before had he, this "man of learning," as Torkel had called him, fought with a weapon. Although for some reason he was not permitted to use his bow and arrow, with the first hand-to-hand onslaught he had seized a spear and marveled to himself that he was able to use it so effectively. Surprised indeed, he had been at the ease with which he could sink the sharp metal point into a living human body. There was no time to ponder the matter—it was simply a matter of "kill or be killed." Although afterwards, the very thought had made him rather ill.

Yes, a rather simple matter it had seemed. A skillful parry of the blow from the Skrelling's axe, a quick thrust, and it was finished—for the moment.

But more had come—and more, and more—like a vast swarm of locusts, they had come. And then finally, the soul-sickening feeling of utter hopelessness fell over him.

Then there was the great storm that had put an end to the struggle—the storm almost as frightful as the battle itself. It had saved their lives to be sure only to carry them to the far shore of the lake to the tragedy of the massacre —the blood, death, and silence. He shuddered violently at the thought.

And then, there had been the flight of the four survivors. Pushing through the marshes—desperately rowing across the open water and carrying the boat where there was no water to float it. No time to rest—always pushing onward—and onward to where they knew not. All day and far into the night they had fled—pursued, and hunted like animals.

And by no means the least of his dismal reminiscences, was a deep, sad feeling as of something lost forever. Like the loss of some golden opportunity never to be regained.

There were the three Skrelling maidens there on the lakeshore that wonderful evening. Already it seemed so long ago—so long ago and far away. It could have happened in another world. Or perhaps it never happened at all. Perhaps what now seemed like a recollection was only a gleam of light in the blackness of this terrible dream.

But no, it had been real enough, Ivar reassured himself. Yes, there were three of them. And a most pleasant picture it was as they stood there, side by side, on the shore. Ah, but the one in the center.

Somehow, she was different—the "One-in-the-Center," as he had since named her in his mind. Slightly taller of stature, she was, than her two companions. Her hair was perhaps a shade lighter and her skin noticeably fairer.

And he had talked with her, so he told himself, even though her language was foreign to him. Not, of course, in words to be heard and understood, as words usually are. Somehow, there was no need for spoken words. Yet they had talked by some means. By some mysterious means beyond human comprehension, they had exchanged their thoughts—their favorable impressions of one another.

And it had been delightful—delightful beyond words.

To Ivar it had been an event such as no human being had ever before experienced, or could experience. But of course older and wiser heads have a word for it—a word to describe the reckless emotions of "Youth."

And well did he remember having been rudely jolted back to his senses by a shouted taunt from one of his comrades across the water, "Ho, Ivar, how is it going?"

But, even as the flush of embarrassment had reddened his neck and face, another thought, a rather distressing one, had suddenly entered his mind: Now he must leave her. Then, should there not be some token by which perhaps she might remember him after he was gone?

Despite the fact of his Christian upbringing, the young man had always had a certain flair for superstition and magic. From his leathern arrow-quiver, he had brought forth what he called his "Good Luck" arrow. A special arrow it was—the shaft colorfully decorated in blue and white and with red feathering. This particular arrow was to be reserved—to be used only in case all others should fail to hit the mark.

Yes, this would serve very appropriately as the parting token. And he remembered now in the minutest detail how she had held the arrow admiringly in both hands, and gingerly testing the sharpness of its strange point with the tip of her finger.

And then, she had looked up at him and smiled. He returned her smile, and speechless he strode back to the small-boat and rowed swiftly away.

But, as events turned out much to his surprise, Ivar had seen the maiden again the following morning. She had been with the old Skrelling who warned the Norsemen, in sign language, that they must go no farther southward—the warning they chose to ignore. But only for a few moments had he seen her. She had made the same gestures as the old Skrelling, then turned and fled.

Truly like a dream she was, but now the dream was gone. No, he would never see her again.

Ah, but now there was something moving out there in the darkness and of that he was certain. This was no time for reminiscing. Whatever it was it was moving through the tall reeds and rushes along the water's edge. Not much longer to wait, Ivar told himself. And somehow, he was glad in a way. It would soon be over, one way or another.

And no one, not even Torkel the Wise Warrior, could predict the outcome of the impending struggle. Ivar heard him mutter, "If they be not more than thrice our number—" But he had not finished the sentence. It was as though he had said: "Since we are so few, if we are out-numbered by more than three to one, the chances are we will be ... we are finished."

"Finished." The word flashed through Ivar's mind, and he realized at once that he had only used it because it seemed less frightful than "slaughtered."

And again came the disturbing thought: the maiden, "The-One-in-the-Center," gone forever. Never would he—

But now, suddenly, his thoughts, if one could describe the workings of the mind of a young man faced with certain and violent death, they went back to the evening before.

He glanced in the direction of the campfire. There it stood: the flat stone on which he had inscribed the message. Torkel had ordered it; a message to be left there on the island. For the benefit of future explorers, Torkel had explained—if there should ever be any.

The greater part of the day and evening Ivar had spent, working on the inscription. A rather brief record it was; perhaps more in the nature of a warning to other venturers into the Great Land of the West; in case, as Torkel had also explained, he and the other survivors were overtaken and slain by the Skrellings.

A possibility, it had seemed at the time, but now ... .

With great care and pride in his skill he calculated the number of words he could place on the flat side of the stone. He then planned the inscription and formed the letters with as much precision as his present physical condition would permit. But toward the end of the message, with the task nearly completed, he decided, to insert a plea to the Christian God for protection—for himself and his companions. By so doing, he had run short of space, and found it necessary to inscribe the final wording along one edge of the stone. Afterwards, he had felt displeased with himself for thus having unbalanced the artistry of his work.

But it made no difference now. Now the stone stood there over beyond the campfire like a tombstone, Ivar said to himself.

At too great a distance it stood to read the inscription, but well did he remember every word. "We were eight Swedes and twenty-two Norwegians on a journey of exploration," it commenced. In his mind he recited the words, but stopped abruptly when he came to the appeal for Divine Protection. He was seized with an overwhelming surge of disappointment and resentment.

His Christian God had failed him. Scorned his plea and left him and his companions to be slaughtered like animals by these inhuman devils called Skrellings.

So, Torkel had spoken the truth when he had declared, "There is no room for Him among the Vikings." Then let the Skrellings have Him and good riddance.

A cold chill ran down his spine.

And there stood the stone, as though to mock him with his own words. The words he had engraved upon it—the futile plea for Help from Above.

A sudden gust of the night breeze and the campfire blazed brightly, for an instant lighting up the face of the stone. As though it were now a living thing he cursed it in the name of the Norse god, Thor.

And having thus given vent to his anger, the young man's thoughts took a different turn. Now, in his mind, he pictured himself as the sole survivor of the impending struggle. For what reason he knew not. There was no reason and no purpose in the thought, but in his imagination, his three companions would be killed. It would be a terrific struggle, to be sure. But in the end, he would hurl his spear through the heart of the last Skrelling. Yes, he would be the sole survivor. Of that he was certain. And, when it was over, he would bury his companions there on the island. The Skrelling bodies he would leave lying where they fell. Let the wild animals pick their bones.

Thus he would set forth alone to find his way back to the ship. But no—one more thing he would do before leaving the island. He would kick over the stone and deface the inscription—the words he had so carefully engraved. He would obliterate forever the futile appeal for the divine help that never came.

And a sudden unreasoning anger came over him. Let the Skrellings come, and the sooner the better. And it mattered not how many. No longer was he the Christian "man of learning." He was a warrior and a killer lusting for blood. Had not Torkel complimented him upon his skill as a spearsman after the battle on the lake?

He tightened his grip on the trusty spear and made a short, thrusting motion in the direction of whence came the sound. Let them come, and the sooner the better.

The blood pounded through the vessels in his temples as he strained to resist the urge to leap up and defy the Skrellings to come out and fight.

Ivar strained his eyes in the direction of the rushes along the shore. Yes. Something was moving there in the darkness, moving as though with great stealth and caution—a Skrelling, or more likely a number of skrellings. Of that there was no longer doubt.

He heard Torkel's half-muttered, half-whispered command, "Steady now, comrades, and await my signal. mind you."

A startled night-bird called loudly from a nearby thicket and almost instantly, as though in alarmed reply, from out in the marsh to the north came the cry of a loon. Not unlike a human cry, it was. High-pitched, piercing sound like the blood-curdling scream of a maniac—and Ivar went berserk. Like a wild animal at bay, he leaped to his feet. Distinctly he heard Torkel's order: "Down, Ivar. You fool!" But he paid no heed. Well did he know, but cared not, that to disobey the command of an authority created by King Magnus himself was to invite the death penalty. But no matter, he cared not.

Uttering a terrible sound that was half a sob, and half a cry of rage, the young man dashed toward the moving object, raising his spear to thrusting position as he ran.

But halfway there he stopped, as though suddenly turned to stone and stared. And the thought struck him: he had lost his wits entirely, now he was utterly insane. And well he could have been, for as he gazed in disbelief, the Skrelling warrior—there in the half-light between the campfire's glow and the darkness—was transformed into the figure of a woman—a Skrelling maiden.

"The One-in-the-Center," Ivar cried aloud, but heard not his own words, as he dropped the spear and ran toward her. He sought to take her in his arms, but recoiling she stepped backward—such behavior was unknown among her people. But with the invitation of Ivar's outstretched arms and smile, she relented. And he held her, for what must have seemed a long time to his three companions.

"By the beard of Thor," Torkel exclaimed when he had recovered somewhat from the let down from the battle that was not going to take place, "The maiden who was with the old warrior that morning before the battle. And now, if I mistake not, the lone canoe that has been following us."

11

TORKEL'S DILEMMA

Torkel the Wise Warrior had now somewhat recovered from his astonishment at finding his little group of fugitives faced by a lone Skrelling maiden, rather than by the immediate prospect of death at the hands of a large band of Skrelling warriors.

But the Norsemen had been keyed for a fight. And the suddenness of the let down left them in a rather unusual frame of mind. Certainly, with the odds they were expecting against them it could not have been a feeling of disappointment. And neither was it entirely a feeling of relief. It could have been somewhere in between, some mental process which left him in what might be described as a rather petulant mood.

The harassed leader of the unfortunate venture was not to be beguiled by what appeared to be a deep feeling of affection on the part of the maiden toward one of his men. It could be a crafty bit of strategy as old as the art of warfare itself. He would take no chances, he told himself firmly, muttering a curse under his breath.

Immediately, and rather gruffly he dispatched Lars and Sigurd to circle the little island on foot in opposite directions to look and listen for signs of the approaching enemy. Then, turning toward the young couple, he demanded, rather roughly, "What think you, Ivar? Is this young woman sincere, or are we to think otherwise?"

Ivar's face reddened as thoughts raced through his head. "I think," he finally said, "that she comes to warn us and to aid us in our escape—she is attempting to tell us something."

"Yes, but what?" Torkel asked rather suspiciously.

Gesturing rather aimlessly at first it seemed, and speaking in her own strange language, the young woman stepped closer to the campfire that the Norsemen might better observe her motions, and hopefully better understand their meaning—at least so Ivar reasoned. But Torkel was not unaware of the possibility that they were being skillfully enticed into the firelight.

Now she extended her right arm, pointing toward the north for a moment in the direction whence both she and the four fugitives had reached the island. Then, with both hands she pantomimed the motions of paddling a canoe.

"Very well," Torkel interrupted, "she comes from the north in a canoe. But I like it not. She could well be holding our attention thus while her warriors approach by stealth." He shifted his feet and glanced around uneasily at the same time slipping his hand slightly on the hilt of the sword, subconsciously no doubt, as though to improve his grip upon it.

"But wait, comrade Torkel," Ivar urged, "there is more to come. She speaks further."

The girl now raised three fingers of her left hand, and then, with her right index finger, pointed to the three fingers, each in turn. Then she pointed in turn to Torkel, Ivar, and herself.

"Do you not see?" Ivar exulted, "Each finger represents a person. Now let us see—"

But the maiden did not wait for him to finish. Using both hands, she raised all ten fingers twice, and then instantly followed with the raising of one finger. Again pointing northward, she gestured as though rowing a boat. Except this time the motions were made more earnestly.

"Well do I now understand." Torkel said. "She is saying there are twenty-one warriors coming in pursuit of us. But yet, this I do not understand: she makes no move toward urging us to leave in haste. She seems not greatly excited. One would think—"

But once again she was gesturing. And now the assignment seemed more difficult. She extended her right arm toward the east, flexing her wrist so the open hand was held at right-angles to the arm. She then extended her left arm likewise, and placed the left hand over the other. Alternating thusly, left had over right, right over left, she continued as though measuring the sky from the horizon to the zenith.

"This has no meaning, so far as I can tell," Torkel complained. "Again, I say, I like it not. It could well be her plan, thus to—but yet, she has in truth told us twenty-one warriors follow us. What think you, Ivar?" he ended in what seemed, to his young companion, a rather unusual combination of suspicion and confusion.

"Nor do I understand it," Ivar admitted, "but let us not betray our failure to understand lest she despair of her attempts. See. She now repeats the same motions—hand over hand."

Having once more measured the heavens with her hands, the Skrelling maiden again told them in sign language, "Twenty-one warriors are coming in boats."And once more, she measured the sky. But this time, she measured: right, left, right, left, and then stopped.

"Now I understand," Ivar announced, "She is measuring time by the sun's distance above the horizon. Had it been daylight, we would have understood her at once.

"See, comrade Torkel. Again she makes the measurement—one, two, three, and four. Do you suppose—yes, certain it is—she is estimating the time of the arrival of our pursuers."

"Very likely," Torkel agreed, "but would you say this means four hours from now, or four hours from sunrise?

"But it matters not," he continued, not waiting for Ivar's reply, "in either case, if the maiden speaks the truth, we are leading them by a fair margin of time—by a better margin than I had hoped. At least they will not be upon us with the dawn as I expected.

"And yet, we must not tarry. I have an uneasy feeling, and again I say, and ponder this if you will: supposing she speaks not the truth. Do you think—"

But he left the question unfinished. And, had it been daylight, Torkel would certainly have noticed Ivar's face reddened with displeasure at the attitude of suspicion toward the girl.

The sound of hurried footsteps brought him around with a start, as Lars and Sigurd stepped out of the darkness. "No sign of the Skrellings," Lars reported, "There is but one canoe on the shore, a light one, of a size to carry but one person. We could neither see nor hear her followers. Possible it is they—"

"She brings no followers," Ivar interrupted. "She comes but to warn us, and to tell us we are four hours ahead of our pursuers."

"So it appears." Torkel said, by way of apprising Lars and Sigurd of what he and Ivar had learned from the Skrelling maiden during their absence. "We gather that there are twenty-one warriors following us, and we have but a four-hour lead."

"But we are squandering time, comrades. To the boat," the old Viking commanded.

And then, as an after thought, "But what about the maiden, Ivar? I presume she will attempt to follow us?"

"I presume so," Ivar agreed, his face reddening with embarrassment.

And Torkel's silence for the next few moments told Ivar more plainly than words that the old warrior was not pleased with the prospect of the Skrelling maiden joining their group. And yet, to his great relief, that same silence told him Torkel was hesitating to raise an objection. Fully expecting his relief to be short lived he stood breathlessly enduring the suspense, but the older man said nothing further on the matter.

As Lars and Sigurd turned toward the boat, Torkel said, "I trust that the boat is in readiness with weapons and what provisions we have left."

There was another short silence. And then Torkel turned to the maiden, and with gestures told her, "We are now ready to leave," speaking the words aloud at the same time, as though he had forgotten that she could not understand them.

Whether or not she understood, the young woman turned toward where she had left her boat, and walked briskly in that direction.

But Ivar had one more thing to do before leaving the island. As Torkel turned to follow Lars and Sigurd, he stepped quickly back to the dying campfire to look one more time at the message he had engraved on the stone. But he did not kick it over, as he had resolved to do less than a half-hour before. Instead, he knelt before it and ran his fingers reverently over those special words he had inscribed near the end of the message: "Mother of Christ, save us from evil." Then he hurried back to join his companions.

As previously planned, the four Norsemen steered toward the south, and nearest shore. And, although this had not been in their plans, the Skrelling maiden followed in her light canoe.

Pushing through the rushes at the waters edge, they dragged the boat ashore just as the first hint of dawn was tempering the darkness of the eastern sky.

Torkel had planned to abandon the boat, after unloading their weapons and provisions, and to conceal it by sinking it in the shallow water near the shore—then to set out on foot to seek another waterway to the south.

But now, to the astonishment of the Norsemen, the Skrelling maiden was attempting to tell them something by signs and gesturing which could mean nothing but a vigorous protest against their plans.

Finally, she turned to her own boat, and pushed it back into the water, then made motions as though urging the Norsemen to do likewise.

"Now what think you, Ivar?" Torkel asked, somewhat impatiently. "Are we to abandon our own plans—to follow this strange young woman? Again I say I like it not."

And for another hesitating moment Ivar stood in silence at a loss for words with which to make reply. Plain enough it was that the Skrelling maiden was desperately attempting to convince the Norsemen that they should follow her, but why?

Why had she not tried to dissuade them when they left the island and turned southward? Why wait until they had landed?

For an instant too long Ivar hesitated in attempting a reply to Torkel's query. And now, there was a distinct tone of displeasure in the old Viking's voice as he turned to address the same question to his other two companions.

And now, Ivar's felt a flush of resentment. It was not all that uncommon for their leader to ask his advice even though, often as not, the matter under discussion would have already been settled in the old warrior's mind. In most instances, the asking was but a formality.

But this time, as far as Ivar was concerned, the implication was, that under the circumstances—the presence of the Skrelling maiden and all—Torkel was doubting the younger man's ability to reason clearly, and he was turning to his other companions for advice.

"I would say—" Lars began rather cautiously, and immediately felt relieved when Ivar stepped forward and interrupted.

"Comrade Torkel," the young man said, controlling his voice with a noticeable effort, "you asked me a question. Please be so kind as to allow me to reply. You are the leader of this expedition, if it yet pleases you to call it an expedition, and your comrades have no choice but to follow your plans. Yet, I doubt not but what Lars and Sigurd will agree—"

"But that answers not my question," Torkel broke in rather heatedly. He sensed the rising resentment in the young man's voice. And another thing he had sensed as plainly as the first: young Ivar was about to declare that he would refuse to abandon the Skrelling maiden—come what may. And, as leader of the expedition, Torkel would now be forced to make an unpleasant decision. And again he "liked it not."

"Again I ask," he began, but he changed the question slightly and said, "Do you deem it wise to abandon our well laid plans? But hold on," he continued hurriedly, "you need not make reply to my question. Now it comes to me that there is only one answer so far as you, Ivar, are concerned, so you need not give it.

"Instead," he went on, "you shall have your choice, though plain it appears that you have already chosen. Very well then—you are now freed from your bondage to the expedition. Lars, Sigurd, and I shall carry forward as planned toward such fate as the gods may choose.

"You are free to remain with the maiden," he ended. And Ivar was almost certain he detected a note of sadness tempering the older man's displeasure.

There was another moment of silence. A bird chirped softly in the wood to the southward from where they were standing as though to remind them that the dawn was at hand. That they could ill afford to waste time. Time—that could mean the difference between life and death.

Then the old Viking extended his hand to the younger man and said, "And may the Norse gods and the New God of the Christians preserve you and the Skrelling maiden."

Ivar groped for words, and finding none, managed to substitute a thin smile, despite the strange feeling of tightness in his throat.

Torkel then turned to face his other two companions, both of whom stood in astonished silence. "We shall now—" he began, but checked his words and again turned to gaze for what seemed a long time in the direction of the young woman, who had stepped into her canoe and sat there in the dim light of the early dawn silently watching the Norsemen.

Again there was a long, drawn-out silence broken finally by the call of an owl somewhere in the trees off to the left. "Whooo ... hoo ... oo ... ooo," almost like a friendly voice it seemed.

Torkel straightened, and gazed for a moment in the direction of the sound. What took place in the old Viking's mind was forever to remain a mystery so far as his three companions were concerned. He glanced once more toward the Skrelling maiden, and then suddenly and to the other's amazement, the older man stooped, and laying hold of the boat beckoned Ivar to lend a hand refloating it.

Torkel then addressed a single word to Lars and Sigurd, "Come."

And before Ivar had sufficiently recovered his composure to fully realize what was happening the four Norsemen were again wielding their oars—this time in the wake of the Skrelling maiden's light canoe.

The girl led them back in the direction of the island, whence they had come; carefully, so it seemed, to retrace the exact path they had made through the rushes in the shallow water near the shore. As they cleared the reeds and reached deeper water, she abruptly turned her canoe directly westward bypassing the island.

Torkel and his three companions followed in silence. She set a rather swift pace with her light canoe, but the Norsemen, their four oars sweeping in perfect rhythm easily kept pace with her.

And to Ivar, the task seemed strangely effortless.

For a long time no one spoke. There was no sound, save the rippling of the water complaining, it seemed, at finding itself disturbed in its early morning slumber with each stroke of oar and paddle.

Finally, as they once more neared the shore far to the west from their first landing, Torkel broke the silence, with suddenness and cheerfulness that startled the others, "I say, comrades. In truth I say a genius at strategies the young woman is. I have been turning it over in my mind. She lets us make a landing on the south shore only for the purpose of leaving our path, and then the marks of our landing thus to beguile our pursuers.

"Our flight has been ever southward," he continued, "and they may well expect us to continue in the same direction, so they will first look for our track on the south shore. And finding it, the Skrellings could well spend an hour or so in learning of their mistake."

"I had the same thought," Ivar said, highly pleased with the change in Torkel's attitude. "But I thought not mention it for fear of ridicule," he added with a short laugh.

He had expected his remark to lead toward light hearted banter and general good cheer, but Torkel again became silent.

But from that moment on, Torkel the Wise Warrior seemed content to allow the young woman to serve as their guide. And Ivar, needless to say, was more than pleased with the arrangement.

And so the four Norsemen and their guide pushed westward. They found no great expanse of water— nothing indeed that could be called a good waterway. But the Skrelling maiden seemed to possess a natural instinct for finding small lakes, marshes and streams, and the fugitives found their portages to be rather few, and usually of short duration.

Sunrise found them at what seemed a comfortable distance to the westward from their previous campsite on the island.

The Norsemen had, by now, become accustomed to the task of shouldering the small-boat between waterways. And they marveled at the ease with which their young guide could sling her belongings over her shoulder, turn the light canoe bottom side up, and hoist it over her back. Cleverly fashioned from the bark of the birch tree the canoe was light but sturdy. On the water it seemed to float like a dry leaf.

By midafternoon a feeling of weariness was coming over the fugitives when at last they came to a fair sized stream. It seemed to bear in a west-northwesterly direction. And a pleasant surprise it proved to be. Here was an opportunity to make real headway in their flight.

A surge of new hope and relief possessed the Norsemen as they once again took to their oars with renewed vigor. Now and again the young woman turned to glance back at her followers with an encouraging smile.

But to Ivar, there was something more to her smile than mere encouragement. It held some magic that gave him a strange feeling, as though he could follow in the wake of that little canoe forever. There was some enchantment that even caused him to forget that he and his companions were fleeing from almost certain death.

The sun was low in the western sky when finally Torkel again broke the silence and said, "Observe, comrades, the stream widens, and becomes of greater depth and the maiden wields her paddle more vigorously."

And then, suddenly, even as he spoke, there burst into view another stream—a great river of considerable width.

"Again observe," Torkel almost shouted, "the current is to the northward. Certain I am, comrades, that we have come upon the great river which we followed southward into the New Land of the West."

And he had no more than made his observation when there was the sound of alarm from their young guide, as she suddenly pointed in the direction of the opposite shore.

"Skrellings," Torkel groaned, as though weary of the very word. "Skrellings pursuing us and Skrellings before us. Three I observe, but very likely there are more in hiding."

But even before he had finished speaking, Torkel was observing the young woman's gestures. She was saying, as plainly as though she had spoken the words, "I shall take care of this matter." And immediately she set forth across the river.

Ivar had a sudden impulse to insist that the girl should not be allowed to face this new danger alone. "Comrade Torkel—" he began, but instantly checked his words as he strove to convince himself that the young woman could indeed cope with the situation.

And yet, despite his efforts, the words came, subconsciously mimicking Torkel's often used expression, "I like it not."

Had the truth been known, Ivar would have admitted to himself at least another concern besides that of the safety of their young guide

"Only three of them," Torkel repeated, ignoring Ivar's remark, "and I judge by their gait that they are younger men, not much more than boys. But observe—they carry bows and arrows.

"Yet I see no great cause for alarm," he continued. "Observe also the maiden stops at a prudent distance. And, possible it is they may not even be of the tribes who attacked us—but they are enemies until proven otherwise."

There was a cautious shout, no doubt some sort of greeting from the girl, and the Skrellings on the shore replied. One of them made a beckoning motion as though inviting her to come ashore, but she made no move to do so. Then came gestures and the sound of voices. The Norsemen guessed that they themselves were the subject of the conversation.

"I see no canoes on the shore," Torkel said, "and likely they are afoot."

"And that being the case," Ivar added, "there could well be a camp nearby."

Torkel ignored the suggestion. And presently, the shouting across the water seemed to take on a tone of alarm and excitement; the three young Skrellings alternately addressing the maiden and chattering among themselves. There seemed no doubt but what she was attempting to persuade them that it would be unwise to engender hostility.

Finally, the young woman raised her voice in what could have been both urgency and impatience. And, without another word, the three turned abruptly away from the river and fled as though their very lives depended on their haste.

"Well," Torkel exclaimed, "it appears that we have won the skirmish without a single blow. And judging by their haste, I would wager that these three, at least, will give us no trouble."

"Yet one never knows what to expect of these Dark-skins," Ivar added, speaking more to himself that to his companions. "Their haste, no doubt, means fear of us, but it also could very well mean eagerness to convey to their warriors the news of our coming." Torkel and his other two comrades nodded in agreement.

They watched the Skrellings disappear into the trees and thickets to the West, while the girl turned her canoe back across the river. As she drew near, Ivar looked for the familiar smile of encouragement, but there was none.

Torkel and his companions fully expected, now that the way had been cleared, that their guide would lead them either directly across the river or downstream to the north. But instead, she turned southward. "Now what think you?" the old Viking asked absently, as though not really expecting an answer. And then, after a moment's hesitation, he conjectured, "It grows late in the day and we need rest. Perhaps she seeks a suitable campsite for the night."

At some distance upstream to the southward from where the fugitives first encountered the river there appeared, along the west bank, a long strip of land which in years gone by could have been a long low island near the shore. Now it was connected with the west bank toward the lower end by a narrow marshy area perhaps twenty paces in width. A thick growth of trees covered the ancient island with heavy underbrush giving way to a grassy strip along the water's edge.

Reaching a point opposite the upper end of the wooded peninsula, their guide stopped and studied the terrain for some little time, then turned her canoe in that direction.

"Well, comrade Torkel, here is our campsite," Ivar said as they followed her toward the shore.

"And I could do with a good rest," Torkel admitted. And then, as though ever mindful of the reason for their flight, he added, "Of one thing I am fairly certain. We are now, either a good half-day ahead of the Skrellings, or they are about to overtake us. If the maiden spoke the truth this morning that we were four hours ahead of them, it is simply a question of whether we are gaining, or are they."

Ivar made no reply. He had hoped to hear Torkel predict that, after today's flight, their pursuers would never be able to overtake them. He was to be disappointed.

And so they made camp there in the shelter of the trees. The Norsemen were tired and hunger was commencing to gnaw at their stomachs.

Then much to their astonishment and delight, the Skrelling maiden proved her worth, not only as a guide, but as a traveling companion. From the soft rich soil along the river's bank she gathered edible wild roots to supplement their dwindling supply of dried fish and barley meal. She showed the men where to search for the fresh-laid eggs of waterfowl and prairie chicken. Torkel struck sparks with his flint and fire steel and quickly kindled a campfire. And presently, almost as if by magic—a small meal was ready. A meal such as they had not enjoyed for many a day.

The evening meal and an hour's rest put new cheer into the hearts of the fugitives, as they sat around the campfire. Ivar and the Skrelling maiden were now attempting, with little or no success, but with obvious pleasure, to converse in sign language.

Lars and Sigurd amused themselves by pretending to offer their assistance. "And now she asks ... ," Sigurd grinned, "now she asks: are you a Norwegian or a Swede?"

Ivar laughed at their remarks but would rather have gotten along without their help.

Torkel sat silently and absently whittling a twig, fashioning it in the shape of a spearhead. Had his companions been watching him they would have been able to predict a forthcoming decision.

Finally he spoke, "I like not, comrades, to put an end to your merriment. But hear you these words: Almost certain I am that the Skrelling warriors have by no means abandoned the chase. And, it stands to reason that we cannot flee from our pursuers forever. Possible it is that today we may have improved the margin by which we lead them, but what about tomorrow and the next day? They are familiar with the lay of the land, while the strangeness of the land fights against us.

"Certain I am also, that had it not been for the Skrelling maiden, we would have long since been overtaken.

"We must have rest, and when I say rest, I mean more rest than a single night affords. And, if we push onward without rest, exhaustion will soon stop us before many days have passed.

"True, it is possible they may have abandoned their pursuit, or may abandon it shortly. But this we know not.

"There is but one answer, comrades, and that is to prepare to make a stand against them. This night we shall rest, but taking turns at sentry duty to guard against a surprise attack. And, in the morning we shall make preparations to make our stand."

The old Viking paused—as though waiting comments, but none forthcoming, he continued, "If this maiden speaks the truth, the Skrellings are twenty-one in number. That is odds of five to one against us.

"You will say that in our present condition these odds make victory impossible." He glanced sharply at his three companions each in turn. "*Ja Vel*, then must we attempt the impossible. With our bows and arrows, and the help of the gods, we should fell four, perhaps five of them as they approach. That will leave sixteen, or four to one.

"And with those odds I would say a victory could be barely possible. Even in our state of fatigue we could handle a three-to-one attack. But four-to-one—and then too, if one of us should go down early in the fight ....

Torkel fell silent and pretended to study the result of his woodcarving. But Ivar guessed that the old warrior was turning some new thought over in his mind.

And then: "Do you suppose, comrades, that by some means or other, we could entice them to make their attack on the river? You will recall the day of the battle on the lake they were no match for us—man for man—in fighting on the water. We were twenty men that day, and surely we must have slain a hundred—perhaps more.

"But no. I doubt if we could thus mislead them. They learned their lesson that day. No, they will not give us the opportunity to choose the place of battle.

"Ah, but I spoke without thinking," he continued, "—we have only the small-boat, and it would be near useless as a platform for fighting."

Torkel's companions, who had all sat silently while he spoke, now nodded their heads to indicate agreement to his conclusions.

There was another silence. And again Ivar predicted to himself a new turn in the old warrior's train of thought. He had an uneasy feeling that the Skrelling maiden would be the next subject of conversation. And he had surmised correctly.

"But what of the maiden, Ivar?" he asked, and then continued, "She must not be allowed near the fighting. The bow and arrows she no doubt carries for self-protection, and very likely she is well schooled in their use. Do you suppose she would feel driven to join us in the battle?

"But no. It must not be permitted," he answered his own question. "But can you explain this to her? Can you convince her that she must stay away from the fighting? Sad indeed would it be to have the maiden killed by her own people should the battle go against us."

Ivar sat silently gazing at the ground. He had no ready answers. There were none, so far as he was concerned. And the girl, perhaps sensing the gist of the discussion, moved closer to the young man, and looked searchingly into Torkel's face, as though trying desperately to understand his words.

"I had the feeling," Torkel continued, "this morning when we left the island—that we should have left the maiden behind. But I had not the heart to so order, nor a plan to make the necessity of it clear."

"Perhaps," Ivar said, without looking at the older man. "Perhaps it would have been better."

And now, he almost wished they had. But, deep in his own mind, Ivar realized full well that he could not, and would not abandon her for Torkel, or anyone else.

A strange feeling, something like an illness came over him. But it soon passed, as the old Viking abruptly ended the discussion.

"It grows dark, and we are tired. In the morning when we are somewhat refreshed we shall be able to think more clearly. But for now, we must rest. I will take the first watch, Lars the second, then Sigurd. Ivar will take the last—from two hours before dawn until broad daylight."

And the silence of the night soon settled over the camp.

12

IVAR ON SENTRY

Ivar's turn at sentry duty that night was to be "from two hours before the dawn until broad daylight." For the greater part of the night he had slept, yet he was wide awake when Sigurd, having finished his shift, came to awaken him.

For a long time he had been pondering the far too many things he had experienced in the past few days. There, in the comfortable cover of the darkness, he had even commenced to feel reasonably certain, despite Torkel's rather pessimistic attitude, that he and his companions had eluded their pursuers. He also began to wonder whether or not the things which had taken place really happened at all. Perhaps he would awake and find it had all been but a dream.

But no—here was Sigurd, and here it was his turn at sentry duty. No, it was no dream. Over here to the right he could hear the snores of "old Torkel the Wise Warrior," and of his other companion, Lars. And over there to the left behind a screen of bushes, though he heard nothing from that direction, he could imagine the Skrelling maiden sleeping soundly, yet no doubt, with subconscious alertness.

He stretched and yawned as he arose to his feet—and then remembering his spear, picked it up. In the darkness and in a strange country there is always a comfort in having one's hand on a trusted weapon. Walking slowly through the shadows of the campfire away from the camp he took his stand that he judged to be about halfway between it and the river's edge.

And so Ivar stood his watch, now pacing quietly back and forth, and then stopping to look and listen in the direction of the river, or to lean for a while upon the shaft of his spear. Scattering clouds moved eastward with a high air current, now and again blotting out the light of an almost full moon that hung low in the western sky.

But, willing though he was to take his turn as sentry, the task now commenced to seem rather unnecessary or tedious, to say the least. And he now found himself waiting rather impatiently, for the coming of daylight—daylight and return to the "The One-in-the-Center."

And again the feeling of disappointment that had come over him last evening when Torkel announced his decision that here would be the place to wait and to make a stand against their pursuers.

Ivar had hoped that they would continue their flight. Continue it, if need be, until the Skrelling warriors would finally abandon the chase. To him, this seemed the only reasonable course. And now he was sorry he had hesitated to so say anything, although at the same time, he told himself he would have failed to convince the stubborn old Viking.

True, as Torkel had declared, they could not flee from the Skrellings "forever." And yet, we have been moving steadily, so did it not stand to reason that we are gaining in the race? True our pursuers must have set out soon after the massacre. But, had not the maiden estimated our initial lead as about four hours? Surely we are gaining. Then why, in the name of reason, should we halt our flight and await the arrival of the Skrellings? "Make a stand against them," as Torkel had called it.

Could it be possible that the old warrior possessed some instinct that told him the Skrellings were about to overtake them? Surely that was impossible, Ivar told himself. Even if so, why stand by and wait—for a struggle in which the odds against them would be far too great? True, they might be fortunate enough to overcome their attackers, but it would certainly be a miracle. On the other hand ... .

And so it went, the thoughts whirling through his mind in a great jumble of confusion that finally gave way to a sort of unreasoning resentment.

Barely twenty-four hours ago, Ivar reminded himself, in the before-dawn darkness of yesterday, the young maiden, "The One-in-the-Center," had come to him out of the night at a moment when he was sure he had lost her. And now, within the next twenty-four hours, the chances were, he would again lose her, this time forever. The chances were, in truth, that they would both be dead.

And the thought of his death, somehow, seemed of minor importance. But the thought of the death of the maiden—at the hands of her own people—and the vengeance behind the blow that would snuff out her life was intolerable.

With a violent effort the young man thrust these thoughts aside, suddenly fearing he would lose his mental balance if they continued unchecked.

It must be almost dawn, he finally said to himself, half aloud, as though to deliberately turn his mind into another channel of thought. Already the moon has sunk from sight. Why not stroll down to the river. After all, if we are yet being followed, which I doubt, the Skrellings would come from that direction.

There was a grassy margin between the trees and the river, perhaps six to twelve paces in width, and as Ivar stepped into the open, he instinctively scanned the river and the opposite shore, first to the right, then to the left.

And then suddenly, a short distance downstream to the north on the other side of the river, he saw, or thought he saw, a faint glow as from a small and well concealed campfire. Almost instantly it vanished.

Surely, he told himself, it was only the workings of his imagination. But yet, he was almost certain he had seen a glimmer off there across the water.

For a long time, he stood and watched. Perhaps it would appear again. But no—by now, the moon had sunk well below the western horizon, and there was nothing but the blackness of the trees on the far side of the river.

Very likely it was nothing, he finally told himself, and yet, I cannot dismiss it from my mind. But also, I cannot return to the camp with what, in all probability, would be a false alarm.

Yes, he must have a closer look. He would walk northward following close to the water's edge and away from the tall grass and bushes, to a point about opposite where he thought he had seen the glow.

An excellent path it made where the level of the river had receded in recent months leaving a narrow strip of almost bare ground. And not more than fifty paces had he covered walking slowly and silently on the smooth soft earth next to the water more by feeling his way with his feet rather than seeing, when suddenly, he found the path obstructed by a fallen tree. A giant cottonwood it was—no doubt uprooted by the great storm that day of the battle on the lake. Its topmost branches extended for several yards out into the water.

Ivar picked his way carefully through the maze of leaves and branches. And then as he again stepped out onto better footing, something loomed up in the darkness before his face. Two more steps and he would have stumbled into physical contact with a fearsome object, man or beast, he knew not which. But in the next instant came the realization: he was face-to-face with a Skrelling warrior.

The Skrelling had just beached his canoe, and straightened from the task at the instant Ivar stepped from among the branches. They were almost at arm's length before either was aware of the other's presence.

There was no time to take stock of the situation, much less to raise the spear, which he was holding, walking-stick-wise, in his right hand. In fact, he was instinctively aware that he was too close to his adversary even to bring the weapon into position for a thrust. No, the spear was a useless encumbrance at such close quarters.

But he was also instantly aware of a slight advantage: the fact that he was standing against the black background of the fallen tree, while the warrior was silhouetted against the faint glow in the eastern sky.

He dropped the spear and twice with a surge of lightning-like reflex action the muscles of his right arm directed the Norseman's hand toward the familiar feel of the knife at his belt. And twice did his fingers close upon emptiness before his mind could grasp the truth; the weapon had been left lying on the grass where he had been sleeping.

Caught by equal surprise, the Skrelling hesitated for a split second before swinging his axe high for a blow. And in the instant the axe descended, the Norseman leaped at his antagonist; making a lusty swing with his fist. But it was with little effect. He had misjudged the distance in the darkness, and his hand barely reached the Skrelling's face.

But, in hurling his body toward the warrior as the blow descended, he had caused the heavy stone blade to miss his head by perhaps an inch, and the arm carrying the

Skrelling's stone axe came down with a numbing thud across his shoulder.

With his right arm, Ivar pinioned the Skrelling's left while he tried desperately, but unsuccessfully, to seize the axe handle with his other hand as his opponent again swung the weapon upward. Failing in this, he managed to grasp the warrior's wrist, thus to prevent his attempt to back away to permit another blow.

And Ivar knew full well that his only hope, for the moment at least, was to hold on in this manner. To hold his body close to that of his opponent and to give him no opportunity to step back for another swing with the axe. Yes, he must hold on, and try desperately to think.

And so they fought in the before-dawn darkness by the water's edge. Strong men they both were with the advantage of weight, if any, on the side of the Skrelling. They strained, and they struggled, and they sweat, each exerting himself to the utmost—the Skrelling to free himself to where he could use his weapon, and the Norseman to hold his grip on his arm.

For a fleeting moment Ivar considered the possibility of releasing his hold and attempting to retrieve the spear. But no—he would no more than turn and stoop when his attacker with a single leap and a long reach would land the fatal blow from behind.

He thought of shouting for help. The distance between the scene of the struggle and the camp was not too great. And, very possible it was that some of his companions could be awake—even at this early hour. Strangely enough, he remembered Torkel's half-joking command of last evening: "In the morning we must rise *før djevelen blir støvlene på* (before the Devil gets his boots on)." At the time, the expression had seemed rather appropriate.

He drew a quick, deep breath and opened his mouth to shout, but so taut was every nerve and muscle in his body, he could utter not a sound.

And now, another thought. If only he could force his opponent backward into shallow water at the river's edge and the uncertain footing. A chance slip of a foot and he was certain he could force the Skrelling to the ground, and perhaps seize the axe handle and wrench it from the other man's grip.

Ivar took a half step backward and with a mighty surge flung his weight against his opponent's body. But the attempt was doomed to failure. He forced the Skrelling back but a single step—a step that lacked a full span of reaching the water.

And once again they were deadlocked. The stench of their mingling perspiration filed the air. Also filling the air was the short, deep-throated growls of the Skrelling—they could have been curses—and the Norseman's sounds, also without meaning. They were not unlike the sounds of struggling animals. Ivar Kristenson, the young "man of learning," fighting for his life.

The Skrelling, meanwhile, had maintained his position of holding the axe at arm's length, high above his head, despite Ivar's grip upon his wrist, as though aware that the struggle could well go against him, should the Northerner succeed in an attempt to wrest it from him. Perhaps, also, it was in order to have the weapon in position for a blow the instant he might make good his attempt to break away.

Then of a sudden, Ivar's opponent ceased his frantic attempts to free himself. And by instinct, more than by reason, the Norseman sensed that the other man was planning some sort of quick surprise movement.

The next instant it came. Loosening his grip on the axe handle, the Skrelling let it slip through his hand by its own weight, and instantly gripped it again as the heavy stone axe head reached his hand. Jerking his arm downward at the same split second, and breaking Ivar's hold upon his wrist, he swung the flat side of the axe head forcefully against the side of the Norseman's head.

Ivar did not remember falling. But in the next instant he realized that he was lying on the ground stunned almost to the point of unconsciousness. Through what appeared as a round opening in the blackness that was closing in upon his mind, he was aware of the dark outline of his attacker against the growing light in the eastern sky.

And then—GET UP—LEAP TO YOUR FEET. His mind was shouting orders to his body as though it were that of a different person.

He's coming at you. Leap to your feet. UP. *UP*—no, it's too late. Raise your foot. Kick him in the groin as he lunges forward. Raise your foot—raise it. RAISE IT.

But Ivar's legs were made of stone. His foot budged not an inch. As though in a dream, he saw the axe against the sky swing upward over the Skrelling's head.

The warrior, weapon poised for the blow, seemed to straighten and hesitate for an instant, as though he would savor the moment of triumph, before stepping forward to bury the axe head in his fallen opponent's brain.

So this is the way it ended, the young Norseman's half-conscious mind was again speaking, as though of a happening that had already taken place. This is how it ... ended ... ended ... .

But the blow never came.

Although Ivar didn't see it happen, the Skrelling's body seemed to jerk violently, and the weapon fell from his hand. For a moment he seemed to balance in an upright position—then he fell to the ground backwards, full length at the water's edge.

Ivar distinctly heard the thud as his attacker's body struck the ground. Then his mind gave up its struggle to cling to consciousness, and the blackness closed in.

* * * * * * * *

Meanwhile back at camp Torkel the Wise Warrior awoke with a start that brought him to a bolt-upright sitting position. Instinctively his right hand sought the haft of the ever pre-sent weapon, the trusty sword that was never more than an arm's length distant, night or day.

What had awakened him, he knew not. It could have been the startled call of a night bird. Or the strident sounds of a cricket close alongside his ear. Or, at least the old warrior did not overlook the possibility that it could have been the faint whisper of footsteps on the grassy carpeting of the campsite.

Or, it could even have been an unexplainable warning of danger. A warning brought to his subconscious mind by that mysterious means known only as "animal instinct."

Torkel did not rise to his feet, but sat there weapon in hand gazing into the darkness and listening. If indeed a sound had roused him, likely it was that it would occur again. But no, save for the little night sounds familiar to all whose sleeping place is the friendly turf, nothing reached the old warrior's ears but silence.

The moon had sunk behind the western horizon, a fact which told him that the night was far advanced and Ivar would be off there among the trees somewhere standing the last watch which would soon end at daylight.

Ivar Kristenson. A strange young man and an odd sort, to say the least, the old Viking told himself. He is a rather brilliant young "man of learning" to be sure, but certainly with a bent for unexpected thoughts and actions. Indeed, some of his have of late sorely strained my esteem for the young fellow. Only yesterday at almost exactly this hour before dawn it was, as we waited in the darkness there on the island for what we well knew was to be an attack, he openly defied my order. He suddenly dashed forward alone to what would certainly have been his own destruction.

That and to say nothing of the fact that the odds against us would have been increased to where our chances of survival could have been reduced to naught.

Of course, as things turned out it mattered not, but how were we to discern before the Dark-skin maiden made known her presence, but what a battle to the death was in the making?

And then once again as though he would add insult to injury, Ivar defied my authority. Not in so many words, or actions either, to be sure, but certainly in his own mind.

Certain I am that he sensed the truth that I was about to insist upon his leaving the Skrelling woman behind. And equally certain I am that he would have refused again in open defiance.

I decided that on balance it was better to have Ivar as one more against the Skrellings and let the maiden do as she would. So I relented. And it remains to be seen whether I chose wisely or foolishly.

So ran the old Viking's thoughts as he sat there in the darkness waiting, although hardly expecting, to hear the sound again that he thought must have awakened him.

Finally, again reclining full length, he turned on his left side and pillowed his head on his arm. But the old warrior's right hand did not relinquish its hold upon the trusty sword. But sleep now seemed out of the question. And his resentment provoking thoughts helped matters not in the least. Now he was thoroughly aroused. That young "man of learning" must needs be taken down a peg, friend though he is.

Always have I listened, with at least pretended patience to his constant arguing in defense of those who follow the new Christian God. Arguing which, I must admit, has in the main bested me in the battle of words. But only for the reason that he is a master of words, while I am, but a master of weapons and strategy.

But the next time—or, better I should say when the time is ripe, I shall employ a new weapon. I shall attack him with the sword of truth. I shall challenge him to justify the goings-on in the days when the new religion first invaded the Northland.

'Twas in the time of King Olaf Tryggvason, and 'tis said by some that it was King Olaf himself who brought the New God to our homeland.

The King was determined, so the sagas have it, that his own warriors to the last man should be followers of the New God of the Christians. And in those days, even as in these, there were some who were loath to abandon the ancient gods of our forefathers.

So means of persuasion became the order of the day in the camps of King Olaf's warriors. Means which, to say the least, ill became a champion of this so-called God of Peace and Love.

Eight strong men, two to each arm, and two to each leg, held the unbelieving warrior flat on the ground, while another placed a cooking pot on the fellow's bare belly. Then they would fetch hot embers from the fire and drop them into the pot—in sufficient quantity to finally persuade the warrior to recite the words, and thus renounce his allegiance to Odin, Thor, and the others, and accept King Olaf's New God.

"*Uff da.*"

Yes, when the time is ripe, I shall confront young Kristenson with this shameful bit of history. And he shall have no defense. This time "Torkel" shall win the battle of words.

The petulant old warrior finally dozed off into a fitful sleep. A sleep beset by dreams of constantly and hopelessly fleeing before an overwhelming horde of pursuers.

And when he awoke again, the black forces of night were already retreating before the white warriors of the day. The dawn was at hand.

But the old warrior's right hand still rested upon the haft of the great sword. The much coveted weapon he had salvaged after the massacre on the lakeshore. For some odd reason, he had pretended not to know to which of his fallen comrades it had belonged. But well did he know, as did also the other three survivors, it was none other that the great two-edged sword of Hjalmar the Wild Man.

* * * * * * * * *

Ivar's next awareness was that of a dull throbbing pain; but there was no immediate recollection of the struggle. Only the vague sense of danger and half-conscious realization that his life might well depend upon his rousing mind and body to action.

And then, slowly, the recollection of what had happened. With what seemed a great effort he rolled to one side and raised himself up on one elbow.

Ivar eyed the dark form of his adversary and waited for some movement that would tell him he must once more force himself into action.

And now came the awareness that the struggle was over. As he raised his body to a sitting position, the sky in the east was considerably lighter than it had been but a moment ago—he must have been unconscious for some time.

But what happened to the Skrelling warrior? Ivar staggered to his feet, and retrieved the spear. Then very cautiously, he approached his fallen antagonist. But there was no need for caution. The Skrelling was dead. There was no doubt about it as he lay there on his back, a half-buried arrow standing upright in the warrior's chest.

By a split second, Ivar told himself, had that arrow saved his life. And there was no question as to the direction whence it came. A point-blank shot by a bowman concealed among the leaves and branches of the fallen cottonwood.

Apprehensively he shot a quick glance toward the tree, almost expecting to either see his benefactor step forth, or be the recipient of an arrow himself, but neither happened. Cautiously he approached the tree and peered among the branches but could see nothing.

He stepped back and again looked down at the Skrelling's body. And in the dim light of early dawn something about the arrow shaft caught his eye. Something that seemed familiar and he stooped for a closer look.

Was he imagining things? In the poor light of the coming dawn, the shaft and feathers resembled those of his "Good Luck" arrow that he had given the Skrelling maiden when they met that fateful evening on the shore of the lake before the day of the battle. However, it could hardly have been from the maiden's bow. Surely she was still back at the camp with the others sleeping.

Ivar took hold of the arrow to withdraw it, but it was firmly lodged in the Skrelling's chest. He thought perhaps he could pry the ribs apart so he could retrieve the arrow.

But no, he recalled a Father's instruction held that it was a sin to maltreat the dead, even if they were the enemy. He released his grip on the arrow's shaft. Besides he thought if he removed it, he would find the point to be made of stone, as were all Skrelling arrowheads. Surely the resemblance would prove to be just a coincidence. And indeed, what if it was his "Good Luck" arrow, what then? He decided to forgo trying to find the answer and say nothing to the others.

Then having no means to bury the dead Skrelling, he strode to the water's edge where lay the dead man's canoe. He then dragged it alongside the warrior's body and tipped it on its side and then respectfully eased the body into the canoe. He dragged the canoe back to the water and floated it. Then, he shoved the canoe with all his strength in the direction of the opposite shore.

Returning, he picked up the Skrelling's axe, hefted it thoughtfully and then tossed it into the water.

Raising his hand to his temple, he gingerly ran his fingers over the swollen area. He looked at his hand, expecting to see blood, but there was none. Luckily, he told himself, he must have been struck with the flat of the axe-head, instead of the sharp edge.

Again returning to the river, he stooped and drank deeply of the cool, refreshing water, and bathed his arms and face. And again straightening, the Norseman took a long look across the river, but saw nothing of importance.

Ivar's head was still throbbing severely as an after effect of the injury, and a deep feeling of physical exhaustion came over him. He sat down in the tall grass, and pulling his knees up, folded his arms across them and rested his head upon his arms. It is not yet broad daylight, he reminded himself, and I am yet on duty as sentry. I dare not lie down for fear of going to sleep.

Again he commenced to ponder the matter of the arrow that had saved his life. How could this fortunate act have come about—was the arrow really meant to down him? And why did the bowman leave? Did something nearby suddenly frighten him? Aside from being miraculously in his favor, it made no sense at all.

But the sudden presence of the lone Skrelling plagued him—what was he doing? Strange indeed would it be if he had set out to attack the Norsemen's camp single-handedly. Certainly he must have companions across the river. There was no doubt, it now seemed, that the glow he had seen in the darkness was from a campfire across, and some little distance down the river.

The unfortunate Skrelling warrior must have been a scout for the very band from whom the Norsemen were now fleeing for their lives. In that event, Ivar told himself, the matter could not be dismissed simply by disposing of the Skrelling's body. He was now troubled by this thought and his earlier conviction ... .

Then with a start, Ivar jerked his head upright as he recalled that it had been in the early morning hours that the Skrellings had made their previous attacks.

Again he scanned the river and the opposite shore. Surely anything between him and the river's bend downstream should now be clearly visible. But he saw nothing, as his gaze swept over the scene, not even the dead Skrelling's canoe, which the current by now should have carried to a point about where the strange glow had appeared. Rather odd, he thought, that it should have drifted out of sight so quickly. No, there was no longer any doubt about it. It was there about where that tall tree stands. Now he was certain that the momentary glow of light, campfire, or otherwise, had not existed only in his imagination.

It was becoming lighter and he saw something move on the far side of the river—almost exactly in the direction in which he was now looking. The dead warrior's canoe, he thought. But no—he was mistaken. A canoe it was, but now, plainly enough he could see, it was occupied by two warriors. And as he gazed another canoe appeared, and then another.

Leaping to his feet, and instinctively crouching low as he ran, he dashed for the cover of the fallen tree in the direction of their camp. He dove in among the branches, and turned for another cautious look. A fourth canoe had now joined the others.

He did not wait to determine whether or not there were more. Scrambling through the tangle of the fallen tree, his foot slipped, and caught in the crotch of a branch, and as he fell he wrenched his ankle severely. But in the next instant he had freed himself and was running for his life and the lives of his comrades.

Wisely, he refrained from calling out to his companions as he neared the camp. His voice could very well carry across the water to the ears of the Skrellings. But there was no need for a shouted warning. Torkel and the others saw him coming, and guessed the meaning of his great haste.

"Armor and weapons," Torkel commanded calmly, as Ivar approached. Though there was no need for the order: Lars and Sigurd were already donning helmets and armor, almost eagerly, it seemed.

"They come," Ivar announced, rather unnecessarily. "Four light canoes with two warriors each I counted. I waited not to observe further."

Torkel commenced at once to outline his plan. Very likely it was that he had formed it in his mind well beforehand. He spoke calmly, but quickly and precisely, "We shall conceal ourselves in the bushes at the very edge of the wood—bows and arrows first to fell as many as possible as they beach their canoes and cross the open ground at the rivers edge. Then your heavier weapons as they close in upon us.

"And mind you, Ivar—no wild spear thrusts—a short jab just below the ribs. What good your spear if it jams between ribs, and you break the shaft as he falls? To you, Lars and Sigurd, I need say but one word—FIGHT. And may Odin, the god of battles, be with us."

The Skrelling maiden, of course, knew nothing of the spoken words, but well did she understand the meaning of the sudden excitement.

As Ivar's three companions set out toward the river, he turned to the girl and, although he had not intended to do so, he yielded to the urge to again take her in his arms for a moment. And as he released her, forgetting that she could not understand, said, "You must remain here. We will return when we have finished our task."

The girl took two reluctant steps backward, as though to assure him that she understood. And Ivar turned to hurry after the others. But he had scarcely covered a dozen paces when he heard a half-suppressed little cry of anguish. And in a moment she was again at his side, this time with bow and arrow in hand.

She was not smiling when she looked up at him. But Ivar could very well read the expression on her face. This young girl, this stout-hearted little daughter of the wilderness, would fight and she would kill, if need be, in defense of a friend.

Well ahead of the two young people, Torkel and the other two reached the margin of the wooded area where it yielded to the narrow grassy slope along the river. They crouched and crept into the edge of the bushes and tall grass to peer out and survey the situation.

Ivar and the girl hurried to join them, and as they drew near, they were startled to see all three of their comrades suddenly rise up in plain sight.

"They are retreating," Torkel shouted, half joyfully and half in disbelief. "I understand it not. See, they move downstream with great haste. They will soon be out of sight around the bend—six ... eight ... ten light canoes I count, if my sight fails me not at the distance. And I would say there are two warriors in each."

"So it appears," Ivar replied, as he strove to make another count before losing sight of the Skrelling canoes. And almost certain he was, though he said nothing to his companions, that one of them had an empty canoe in tow.

"What think you, Ivar?" Torkel asked but did not wait for a reply. "Do you suppose," he went on, "that they took counsel among themselves, and concluded we were of greater strength than they had expected?"

"It could very well be," the younger man agreed, "Strange things can happen, and sometimes we know not the reason." But if he had any conjectures, he kept them to himself.

But the old Viking, now in a jovial and talkative mood went on, "Or could it be, this is foolish, I ask only in jest: could it be that the gods carried the message to them that we were ready to fight to the finish, so that our very determination struck fear into their hearts?"

Ivar and the other two smiled at Torkel's joke but said nothing, their minds occupied with their own thoughts.

"Now I ask you, Ivar," he went on, as though with a sudden inspiration," do you not agree—it was Odin, the god of battles, who came to our aid and not your Christian God of Peace?"

But Ivar though sharing the old warrior's exultation, somehow was not at the moment in the mood for joking.

"No, I would not agree," he said, forcing a smile, "but yet, I presume we should give Odin his due."

Torkel gave a short laugh as though to indicate that he had meant no offense by the question. Lars and Sigurd grinned. And Ivar felt rather pleased with his answer.

The Norsemen and the Skrelling maiden turned to retrace their steps back to the camp.

"Well, that was a rather strange turn of events, to say the least." Torkel reflected, "For several days have we fled before them, and now when they overtake us they turn tail as though fearing to attack.

"But we shall take no chances; they could be pretending flight as a ruse. Out of sight around the bend, they could circle back on foot to attack by stealth.

"It is best," he continued, "we move our camp back across the river—and upstream a short distance. There we will wait, and watch.

"But what ails you, Ivar? I observe you limping as you walk. And you have a bad bruise on one side of your head."

"It is nothing," Ivar replied. "In my haste I slipped on a wet branch and fell as I scrambled through that fallen tree back yonder."

For a moment he thought Torkel was about to question him further, and he felt relieved when the subject of conversation was changed back to moving the camp.

"Yes, we must move back across the river," Torkel repeated, "but it will be no simple matter of crossing directly. The Skrellings could, at this moment be watching from the cover of the trees at the bend downriver expecting such a move, and thus to determine the number of our party, counting us as we cross the river.

"But we shall outwit them. We shall carry the boats by land around the upstream bend—and there cross at a point out of their sight."

And so the camp was moved. And all day the Norsemen and their guide rested in camp. And waited—and watched.

And all day Ivar pondered the puzzle of the strange death of the lone Skrelling warrior. All day he waited, hoping that Torkel, Lars, or Sigurd would make some remark which might supply a clue to the answer, but there was none.

Again he contemplated the strangely familiar arrow shaft, and rued his decision not to examine the point. At the time, it had seemed a proper Christian choice—but now his curiosity was starting to get the better of him.

Toward evening, as Ivar went to take up his next shift at sentry duty, the maiden and his other companions were busying themselves with preparing the evening meal. On his way to the river he casually walked in the direction of the tree against which leaned the Skrelling maiden's bow and quiver of arrows. Stooping, he quickly examined the arrow shafts looking for the familiar blue-and-white-striped shaft of the "Good Luck" arrow, but it was gone—he had been saved by the "One-in-the-Center."

Yet how could she have been at the right place at the right time? Surely she had not kept watch with him the whole time—perhaps she had heard the commotion and came to investigate. Then again, if so, why had she not come to his aid after she had downed his assailant? —or perhaps his "Good Luck" arrow was still back in her lodge, wherever that is. No—the mystery was not yet solved.

13

A CHANGE OF PLANS

Once again the evening meal was finished. And once again
Torkel sat whittling a twig. But this time it was not the
likeness of a spearhead. First, he squared the twig neatly
and then split it lengthwise. Then, holding the two halves
between his fingers, he split the twig again making four
small sticks, about half the length of his hand.

Whether or not there was any connection between the
whittled design and the workings of the old warrior's subconscious mind, he could not have told even had he been
asked. Lost in thought, his mind was paying no heed to
what his hands were doing.

Quite in contrast with the joviality that followed last
evening's meal, a strange silence had settled over the camp.

Lars and Sigurd were both whetting the blades of their
battle-axes. Not that there was any great need for a high
quality of keenness for weapons of that heft. It was something of a ritual with them, something to be done in those
rather rare intervals when there was naught else but
waiting to do—much as a woman polishes a utensil while
waiting for the cooking fire to come alive. And then, too,
was not a keen edged weapon always more pleasing to
Odin, the god of battles.

Ivar had not yet completed his next shift at sentry duty.
Sigurd had spelled him while he made his way back to
camp to partake belatedly of the food for which he had little
appetite. In truth, he had told himself, it would scarcely

have been worth while except that it afforded the opportunity to exchange a smile with the young woman before he
again hurried away.

Torkel had insisted upon a watch throughout the day,
and this time Ivar's would end at nightfall.

And very likely, because of the young man's absence,
the Skrelling maiden simply sat as though deep in thought
and waited.

The Norsemen had all been of one mind: it would not
be wise to move until they could take advantage of the
cover of darkness. Too great was the possibility of an
ambush to risk moving in daylight. There remained an even
chance of the Skrelling band having been attempting a
clever bit of strategy by pretending flight.

Always there were the possibilities—the uncertainties—and the ever-present need for the utmost vigilance.

No. The joviality of the previous evening was no more.
Last evening Torkel, in calling his followers to counsel, had
said, "I like it not to put an end to your merriment." But
this evening, the meal had been eaten almost in silence and
there was no merriment afterwards.

True, early that morning, there had been the elation at
seeing the Skrelling band take flight, pretended or otherwise. But later, sitting idly through the long hours of the
day, the old Viking had taken to calculating and recited,
"You say, Ivar, that we had journeyed for fourteen days
when we were attacked on the lake? Very well then, let me
think. The fifteenth day we fled southward and the greater
part of the night too, so far as that matters. Then the day
we rested on the island, the day you engraved the message
on the stone, would be the sixteenth. Yesterday we followed
the Skrelling maiden westward, the seventeenth day. And
this day, it is eighteen days since we left the Knorr and our
comrades on the shore of the Salt Sea. And my orders to

Erling were these words: 'You are to allow us fifteen days to journey inland, and fifteen days to return. If we have returned not when thirty days have passed you may well give us up for dead.'

"And well do I know—Erling already appeared anxious lest the foul weather of autumn overtake us before we could reach our winter camp at Vinland.

"No, comrades," Torkel bluntly announced. "It is obvious that we shall never reach the Salt Sea before the Knorr weighs anchor."

And so they sat and waited. Waited for darkness, and for what next? Indeed, what next?

And now the old warrior, absently toying with the four sticks he had whittled, finally held one of them upright on the ground, and with his knife handle, tapped it lightly, leaving it standing erect. About a hand's breadth away, he placed another—then the third and fourth. Then he again tapped each stick in turn, one—two—three—four, and said, "Four. Four men we are. Four—all that remains of my band of valiant warriors. Sixteen good men—all gone. And what has been gained? Nothing. Absolutely nothing. There was the King's order; well do I remember his very words: 'Find the lost Greenland Colony.'

"And we have failed. We? No, it is I, Torkel the Wise Warrior. Wise?—HA. I have failed, and have failed miserably. Sixteen good warriors. The best. There was Black Botolf, the first to go down—caught a Skrelling arrow in the first onslaught. And then there was young Thorwald, Oskar, and Hjalmar—the 'wild man.' I know not why, but I grieve over the loss of my cantankerous friend Hjalmar more than the others. And then there was—"

The old Viking's sad reminiscences were suddenly interrupted by a little sound from the Skrelling maiden as she rose to her feet. Her ear had caught the welcome sound of familiar footsteps long before the Norsemen were aware of someone's approach. And in a moment, Ivar appeared coming from the direction of the river.

But not in haste Torkel observed to himself, by way of contrast with this morning's happenings. And he did not inquire, as Ivar came forward, as to whether he had observed any signs of the Skrellings.

And now the twilight had given away to dusk. And the dusk was fast deepening into the dark of night.

"We must be moving, comrades," Torkel announced. "The moon, rising as it does, later each evening, should not arrive to betray us until well toward midnight, if my reckoning is correct. We must be moving, though I know not in what direction. And now that I ponder the question—what matters it?

"Thus far, we have trusted the Skrelling maiden and the gods to guide us. And I see no reason now to do otherwise."

And now, once more they were afloat on the river. And none of the Norsemen were surprised when their young guide turned northward downstream as had the Skrelling band early that morning.

In a few moments they passed the point of land—the narrow little wooded peninsula where they had camped the previous night. And in another moment or two, they were passing the fallen cottonwood which marked the sight of Ivar's life-and-death struggle with the lone Skrelling the previous night.

It was about here, Ivar recalled, that he had flung the Skrelling's axe into the water. And over on the shore, alongside the fallen tree, he imagined he could even see, despite the growing darkness, the trampled grass where they had struggled.

Ivar felt something akin to a pang of guilt as he recalled his decision to say nothing to his comrades regarding his personal battle with the lone warrior. Perhaps it was wrong. Yet ... .

But soon the scene of the encounter, and also the disturbing thought, were left far behind.

"Observe, comrades," Torkel said, "the North Star as it rides ever ahead of us. Certain I am, that this is the great river we followed on our journey southward from the great Salt Sea."

And then, after a moment's hesitation, and with what seemed an unusual burst of enthusiasm, he said, "Do you suppose, comrades, that it could be possible by manning the oars night and day, and in shifts, that we might yet reach the Knorr before Erling sets sail?

"But no," he sadly answered his own question. "The days are but twelve in number. Two men to a shift at the oars instead of four would reduce our headway almost in half, and naught would be gained.

"If only we had a boat of greater size—and a sail. If only we could have saved one of the long-boats.

"*Ja Vel.* 'Tis but idle talk."

No one replied. There seemed no point in making any comment upon these observations. They were reconciled to the fact that even though they might yet escape death at the hands of the Skrellings, they, in all probability, would spend the remaining years of their lives in this hostile land.

And the four Norsemen bent to their task with eagerness. It was as though they were glad, at least, to again be on the move. What matters the direction. Night progressed, and they continued to row with swift but silent strokes northward on the river, moving with the current.

And as the moon appeared over the wooded horizon to the east, the old Viking and his companions were suddenly startled to a renewed alertness. There was a strange sound off in the darkness to the left and downriver ahead of them. A sound that caused four oars to instantly hang poised above the surface of the water while the four men listened intently. A long drawn out, and mournful wail it was, not unlike a familiar night sound often heard in their homeland, as of a dog baying at the moon.

But no, this was more of a high-pitched yap–yapping, rather than a deep-throated howl. And almost at once the call had been answered, it seemed, from a point far downstream, the second sound almost identical with the first.

A signal of some sort no doubt, Torkel had immediately guessed. A Skrelling signal, disguised as though it were the howling of a dog, yet not well enough disguised to deceive us.

The Skrelling maiden sensing their alarm had looked back and beckoned them onward, and then made two or three quick paddle strokes with odd little vigorous motions as though to suggest impatience.

Half expecting their guide to pause and turn toward the right bank of the river and a hiding place, the puzzled Norsemen had again applied their oars. And Torkel had muttered under his breath—he liked it not.

And throughout the greater part of the night at intervals of perhaps an hour they had heard the strange sounds repeated, always coming from the west bank of the river—now from nearby, and again from far in the distance. But their young guide pushed onward. And the Norsemen followed—weapons ever in readiness, but nothing seemed to occur that would suggest a need for their use.

And now, in the first faint light of the coming of another dawn, there appeared dimly in the near darkness yet plainly enough it was, the mouth of a small stream joining the great river from the eastward.

The young woman turned to her followers and motioned "silence." Then, laying her paddle across the canoe, she pointed with her arm in the direction of the smaller stream.

Immediately, the Norsemen nodded to one another as they recognized this as the point where they had left the great river several days past—yet it seemed like weeks ago. Yes, there were the bleaching trunks of the two great trees uprooted by storms of other summers, lying almost across the mouth of the smaller stream. No, there could be no mistaking these landmarks.

But why should their guide call their attention to this particular spot? It hardly seemed possible that she could be aware of their having passed this point before. Nor could it have any bearing upon their present flight. And certainly the Norsemen had no intention of ever traveling that disastrous route again.

Torkel recalling that here, at the junction of the two streams, had been their last camp site before leaving the river and now ruefully remembered Black Botolf's objections. Perhaps he should have taken heed. Perhaps it was that his quarrelsome friend had some sort of premonition of the tragedy soon to come. But now, it no longer mattered. Botolf was dead. The expedition was a failure. And there was no turning back what the gods had ordained.

For what seemed a long time, the girl sat there silently, looking and listening. And then, suddenly, she turned her canoe westward toward the opposite shore. And although puzzled, Torkel and his companions followed.

In silence and with extreme caution she beached her canoe and dragged it to a place of concealment in the trees and underbrush along the shore. The young woman now took the two deer-skin bags from the canoe and laid them on the ground. Then taking her hunting bow, she fastened the bags, one to each end, and raised it to her shoulder. She slung the quiver of arrows across the other shoulder. There was no mistaking her meaning: it was as though she had said, "Here must we abandon our boats—and walk."

Torkel and his comrades gathered up what supplies and weapons they could conveniently carry and followed her as she led the way cautiously into the thickly wooded area along the river.

For what seemed like a long time to the Norsemen, the Skrelling maiden led them, with the stealth of a wild animal Ivar thought, through the darkness of the sheltering trees.

No one spoke. In single file they walked in the footsteps of their young guide: Torkel first, then Ivar, Lars, and finally Sigurd, who seemed to possess a more acute sense of alertness, followed in the rear.

Only once did the Skrelling maiden hesitate, as though uncertain of her direction. At a small opening in the trees it was. She stopped to gaze at the stars for a moment, and the Norsemen, familiar with setting a course at sea by night, understood full well the meaning of her hesitation.

Finally, and almost abruptly, the trees and under-growth were becoming more and more sparse, and now, at last, the dark forest was behind them. And the fugitives suddenly found themselves at the margin of what at once appeared to be a vast, rolling expanse of tall, dry grasses.

And far ahead of them, scarcely audible in the distance, yet distinctly enough, Torkel and his companions heard, for the last time, the mysterious Skrelling signal as of a dog howling at the moon.

Fully expecting her to again hesitate or change the di-rection of their flight, the Norsemen were surprised when their guide now led them boldly out into the grasslands and on westward. And so, the fugitives turned their backs to the crimson tint that tempered the darkness of the eastern sky.

The early morning that followed was clear and crisp, and the Norsemen, despite certain unspoken misgivings, welcomed the opportunity for a change in their mode of travel—for a time at least.

And now their guide was pacing them with a certain air of urgency. Not as though in desperation but rather with a strong desire to put distance between them and the river.

So onward strode the old Warrior and his three companions; the dry grass crunching beneath their boots where it grew shorter across the ridges and waving higher than their heads where they skirted the marshes.

Finally, shortly after sunrise it was, atop a low ridge, their guide stopped and turned, indicating in sign language: "It is time to rest."

They all sat down rather gratefully while looking questioningly at one another but saying nothing. And then after a few moments the Skrelling maiden, speaking for the first time rather freely in her own strange language and gesturing made the others to understand that it was now safe to speak aloud.

Torkel was the first to speak, "I like not this sort of thing. We know not where we are going, nor why. What think you, Ivar?"

But he waited not for an answer, and in a tone which clearly indicated a growing petulance, Torkel continued, "It is plain enough to observe, Ivar, that this Dark-skin maiden has taken a serious liking toward you, otherwise would I be inclined to suspect that her plan could be to lead us into an ambush. "I understand not," he continued, "and I like not, this leaving the river to tramp westward through these endless grasslands."

"Nor do I understand it, comrade Torkel," the younger man replied with a trace of irritation. "Yet I say, and this is also plain enough to observe, she is fully as anxious as we ourselves, to put distance between us and the Skrellings who killed our companions."

"So it appears," Torkel agreed rather cautiously and looked at the ground as though not entirely satisfied with his own reply.

And now Ivar could scarcely help but sense a new feeling of resentment on the part to the old warrior. He had touched a sensitive spot in reminding Torkel of the massacre. Instantly he regretted having mentioned the death of their comrades and attempted to make amends for his indiscreet reply. "Or, better I should say, no doubt the maiden deems it prudent that we hasten to leave far behind us the place where the gods chose not to come to our aid."

Torkel dug the heel of his boot into the turf with a sudden motion that told his companions that words of displeasure were forthcoming.

"'The gods'—you say. You speak, of course, of our warrior gods. Very well then, what of your Christian God? To the aid of whom did he come—the Skrellings?"

Ivar, resenting the unreasonableness of the older man's question, attempted vainly to form a reply as the outburst continued. "Well, what think you, Ivar? Twenty men we were but a few days ago. And now we are four. I say—what think you now of the New God of the Christians?"

Ivar's face reddened anew as Lars and Sigurd looked at him, their glances seeming to echo Torkel's question. Finding his voice at last, and scarcely concealing his own indignation, he replied rather heatedly, "The four of us are yet alive. What think *you*?"

The old warrior felt the sting of the rebuke, and again looked at the ground as though forming an angry retort—

"Comrades—look."

It was a suppressed call of alarm from Sigurd as he rose to his knees and pointed westward.

And there was no mistaking the cause of his apprehension. Two Skrelling warriors were approaching from
the west. Almost running they were, but coming at a slight
angle, as though they might miss by a rather wide margin
the spot where the Norsemen reclined.

"Keep down, and lay hold of you weapons," Torkel
commanded. "Possible it is that they will pass by without
seeing us. If not, an easy task it will be to dispatch these
two to Odin. But he had no more than spoken when the
girl, suddenly rising to her feet, waved and shouted to the
approaching Skrellings.

"Down, you fool," Torkel snapped, as he floundered
forward on his knees and moved as if he would seize her.
But the Dark-skins had already changed their course, and
were heading directly toward the fugitives.

"Very well then, Ivar—" the old Viking growled, half
threateningly, but left the remark unfinished.

And then he continued, "I doubt they will dare attack,
what with only two of them. But be ready to fight. We know
not the workings of their evil minds." The Norsemen arose,
weapons in hand, the early-morning sun reflecting spears
of light from the burnished blades as the two approached.

The girl spoke a few words to the pair and they stopped
at a respectful distance. Almost at once, the newcomers laid
their weapons upon the ground, possibly at the urging of
the young woman, but just as likely at the realization that
they were outnumbered two to one.

They came forward several paces and again stopped
making signs of friendship but otherwise paying little heed
to the Norsemen. They talked in what appeared to be a tone
of excitement rather than hostility, and for a longer time
than seemed necessary to explain their presence.

Handsome young warriors they both were. And Ivar,
eyeing them narrowly as they stood there talking with the

maiden, was aware of that strange feeling again coming over him.

But it soon passed as the Skrellings suddenly turned and went back to pick up their weapons. Then, nodding at the Norsemen—but still giving them a wide berth—the pair hurried on in the direction of the river.

"Messengers, runners no doubt," Torkel commented. "But for what purpose? If only we could understand their language."

"Give us time, comrade Torkel, and one of us shall learn their language," Ivar said with a short laugh. But the others failed to see any amusement in the attempt at a joke.

And again did the Skrelling girl take the lead setting a brisk pace toward the west.

There seemed no longer a need for silence, and they began talking freely. Lars and Sigurd limited their conversation to a violent cursing of Skrellings in general, but carefully avoiding, however, any reference to the young woman who was serving as their guide.

Torkel strode on for a while in thoughtful silence, and then said, "I am now fairly certain that the maiden is attempting to lead us away from the hostiles and to more friendly territory."

"Of that, I have been certain from the outset," Ivar replied. "But I chose to mention it not."

"Well do I understand your choice, Ivar," responded Torkel, "assuming that to be her intent. Had not the gods of good fortune brought you to a chance meeting with the Skrelling maiden who took a liking to you, she would not now be guiding us. Should evil come of it, you will blame yourself for the result. "But let it not trouble you, Ivar," he went on. "Certain it is that we are in no worse position than we were three days ago. And besides, good may yet come of it."

Ivar said no more on the subject. The old warrior had finally ended on a cheerful note. Better to leave it that way.

And so they trudged onward, now and again skirting the edge of a marsh, now crossing a low ridge, or occasionally fording a small, almost dry steam. But always trudging westward. And always ahead of them lay the tall, dry grass as far as the eye could see.

High noon and the sun's heat added to their discomfort. And now, they came upon another little stream. Along its banks they found a few small cottonwood trees. They sat in the little patch of shade to rest and to again eat sparingly of their provisions.

"A follower of the sea soon wearies of walking on land," Torkel observed. The others nodded but said nothing.

"I am hoping we soon reach our destination if, indeed we have one. Do you suppose, Ivar, the maiden has become confused, and knows not where she is leading us?"

"That I doubt," replied Ivar. "Do you not observe just beyond that tree the trampled grass where we have not yet walked? She is backtracking the two Skrellings we met this morning. Though for what reason I know not."

"Right you are, Ivar. Right you are. At least, we can be certain that we are not wandering blindly," Torkel agreed. "But see, she is telling us it is time to move on."

They arose, rather wearily this time, and trudged onward, ever westward.

And now, as the fugitives topped another low rise of ground, their guide suddenly stopped, hesitated a moment, and then hurried on. At the same time, the Norsemen observed what appeared to be a Skrelling village on the plain just ahead. Fully expecting to circle the village at a safe distance, they looked at one-another with puzzled glances when the young woman led them directly toward it.

Instinctively they readied their weapons as they drew near. But there was no need. The village was deserted.

"What do you make of it, comrades?" Torkel asked, and noted further, "Observe: their fires still smolder. And there a woman has been preparing food in what was this morning's shade. She left the task unfinished.

"Certain I am," he continued, "that they hurriedly abandoned their homes no earlier than this morning."

Then, not waiting for possible suggestions, he concluded, "They left in haste and in fear of something. Of that I am also certain."

"Possibly," Ivar suggested, "they learned of our coming, and fled in fear.

"Unlikely," Torkel replied, "surely they would have known we were but four strangers guided by a young Skrelling woman. Hardly would that panic the village."

But their guide seemed not greatly interested in the deserted village. Almost at once she was saying in sign language: "We must go. We must not waste time here."

And, as the four somewhat perplexed Norsemen continued on their journey, at least one question in their minds was answered: the direction in which the villagers had fled. A broad path of trampled grass led away to the westward.

For a time they trudged on in silence, their young guide ever in the lead, striding forward with an air of undiminished determination.

And as the day wore on, and despite their growing weariness, the Norsemen's attitude toward the westward trek seemed to improve somewhat. Especially since Torkel, having apparently forgotten his early-morning petulance, now assumed a slightly more cheerful outlook.

Finally, Torkel spoke again, "I have been turning it over in my mind, comrades. Certain it is that the villagers could not have fled in fear of us. But equally certain it is that their flight was from some cause or other.

"'Tis best that we assume the most reasonable possibility, namely that they fled before a war party from other hostile tribes. Very well then, if that be the situation, does it not appear that we are following in the footsteps of both the pursued and the pursuers?

"And does it not follow, that the war party will either overtake and vanquish the villagers, or abandon the pursuit and perhaps retrace their steps? And could they not have already sighted us at a distance and be lying in ambush just over the next ridge?

"No, comrades, we have by no means yet reached the more friendly territory to which we assume the maiden is guiding us.

"We must be on the alert for an ambush," Torkel concluded, "but not by the warriors from the deserted village of that we may be certain. Again I say, we must be ever on the alert—keep your weapons in readiness."

Torkel's three companions nodded in agreement but said nothing. Ivar wanted to raise the question as to why, if they were in truth following a path made by the inhabitants of the deserted village, and also of a supposed pursuing war party, why did not their guide think of the same possibility, and alter their course to avoid meeting with hostilities. But, for some reason or other, he remained silent.

And still they tramped onward. But, there was a feeling of improvement; the wearisome crunching sound of the dry grass underfoot had lessened somewhat, now that they were walking a path well trampled by the fleeing villagers and possibly by a war party from whom they may have fled.

* * * * * * * *

And now, about midafternoon it was, and once again had the Norsemen and their young guide sat down to rest. But this time, there was no stream. And there was no shade. And there was nothing to break the monotony of the scene but a small, almost dry marsh—a marsh with only a little patch of open water, now and then reflecting a flash of sunlight through the rushes.

And this time, the Dark-skin maiden seemed not nearly so anxious to again resume their journey—and likewise the Norsemen. All last night had they fled northward on the river. And, for the greater part of this day they had tramped westward through the grasslands. A great weariness had of a sudden possessed them. For the moment they were content merely to sit and rest.

Ivar feeling rather depressed along with the tiredness, had sat down near the young woman as was his custom. But this time he took care not to recline as close to her as usual. He had the feeling she was growing weary of the venture she had undertaken—that she might even regret having commenced it. But the feeling soon vanished as she stole a glance in his direction, uttered a few rather tranquil-sounding words in her own strange language, and smiled. He understood nothing of the spoken words, but the smile ... well did he understand the language of a smile.

Lars sat, head bowed and arms folded across his knees breathing deeply. Well could he agree with Torkel's remembered remark from earlier in the day: "A follower of the sea soon wearies of walking on land."

Sigurd sat as though unconsciously imitating the position of Lars—but with one exception. Now and again he would raise his head, squinting in the sunlight and splaying his nostrils, like a hunting hound sniffing the air as though in an attempt to identify some faint, almost imperceptible odor being wafted on the breeze.

Torkel was unhappy. But no, it was not merely a recurrence of the peevishness he had felt early this morning. Now he, the leader of the King's expedition, was thoroughly displeased with himself. He, who in years gone by had earned for himself the title, The Wise Warrior. He, whose very life's environment had always been on the water, the trees, and the rugged country of their homeland, had allowed himself, and he knew not how, to become beguiled by a strange young woman—by this young Skrelling maiden. He had been beguiled into leaving his boat and the river to trudge away into this endless nowhere of rolling grasslands.

How, indeed, would one find cover in such terrain if threatened with an attack by an enemy far superior in number? How, indeed, could one maneuver out of sight of such an enemy in order to avoid combat with a hostile force of overwhelming strength? He cursed his stupidity.

And so the decision was made. Torkel would have no more of this nonsense. He and his comrades would set camp here, beside the marsh, for a night's rest. With the coming of dawn they would retrace their steps toward the river. Then they would journey northward on the river traveling by night and hiding by day, if need be, to avoid further trouble with the Dark-skins. They would journey northward toward the Salt Sea where they had left their ship and their other companions.

True enough, the Knorr would be gone before they could reach the sea. But what matter? If it so pleases the gods that they must spend the remaining years of their lives in this evil land, then let their abode be established beside the sea. Let them at least possess something of the way of life they had chosen. And let them leave far behind this endless dry prairie over which they now found themselves trudging.

Yes, with the coming of tomorrow's dawn, Torkel told himself firmly, he, Lars, and Sigurd would retrace their steps toward the river. Let there be an end to this nonsense of trudging across a barren land.

But for some reason he decided, for the moment, not to announce his intentions.

And so the little group of fugitives sat in silence. There seemed to be no point in making conversation. It was as though everything that required saying had already been said. At the moment nothing mattered but rest.

But little did the Norsemen and their guide realize that their rest was to be so short-lived.

Suddenly Sigurd, the ever alert one, cupped his hand to his ear, as though listening intently. He slowly turned his head one way, then the other. And then, sprawling flat in the grass, he held his ear to the ground. His companions looked at him, first in amusement, and then in alarm as they realized the significance of his movements. But only for a moment did the Norseman hold his ear to the ground. In the next instant, he sprang to his feet and looked in all directions almost at once. And even before the others were on their feet he was pointing to the west.

And then they saw it.

But for a long time no one spoke. Then, Ivar remarked, almost as though intending it to be a joke, "Well, comrade Torkel, there is your ambush."

Torkel made no reply.

Coming toward them over the brow of a long, low ridge they beheld an alarming sight. But no, it was not an ambush party from the little deserted village. Nor was it a larger war party. It was an army of at least two thousand.

Almost like an ocean wave it seemed, as it flooded down the slope and out onto the flat prairie.

And there was nowhere, absolutely nowhere, the Norsemen could take cover. There was not even a small hillock that might serve as a vantage point from which to attempt a defense—a defense which in any event could have only proven futile against such odds.

And no one so much as thought about taking flight. A useless attempt indeed it would have been. A hundred fleet-footed warriors would have run down the weary travelers before they could cover five hundred paces. No, escape was impossible.

"We shall attempt first to make council," Torkel announced with his usual calmness, "but unless it pleases the gods that they be friendly then must we do our best for Odin. We must do our best, here and now, for this shall be the last battle for 'Torkel the Wise Warrior.'"

Lars put his right hand to the blade of his trusty battle-axe and tested its sharpness with his thumbnail. "*Djevelen koke meg* (The devil boil me)," he swore softly.

Ivar strove desperately to calm his wits to where he could think rationally. They could be friendly. But supposing they were not. What then of the Skrelling maiden? They may well consider her a traitor and kill her.

But hold on—we can pretend she is our captive. Let them rescue her from captivity. But, how to make them believe we hold her as captive? Ah, simple enough. Bind her hands; this bow string will do very nicely.

But the maiden, wide-eyed with perplexity and bewilderment more than fear, Ivar thought, would have no part in the deception. She understands not the purpose, he told himself.

For a moment he considered calling upon his companions to aid him in seizing and binding her by force. But if she struggled, the ruse would likely fail, and he abandoned the idea.

And again the little group of fugitives stood in silence, and waited. Watched and waited while the Skrelling horde approached. Watched and waited with mixed emotions of helplessness and amazement.

Finally, at what seemed a greater distance than the circumstances called for, the great army came to a halt. Then came the sound of shouted commands, and immediately four, or perhaps five dozen of the warriors, detached themselves from the center of the main body and marched forward. The one in the lead, no doubt their war chief, strode toward the Norsemen with what seemed, an attitude more of curiosity than hostility.

Torkel, sword sheathed as a gesture of friendship, but with his right hand open and in readiness to seize his weapon stepped forward to meet them as they approached. Seven long strides he took and then stopped, as though he had turned to stone. And in the same instant their chief did likewise at a distance of perhaps thirty paces.

It was more than astonishment—it was something bordering on utter disbelief on the faces of both leaders as they stood staring at each other.

And then, "These are not Skrellings." The thought struck Torkel like a staggering blow. "They look more like people from our homeland."

His mouth opened, but for a moment he was unable to form the words. Then he shouted, "*Kan du snakke Norsk* (Do you speak Norwegian)?"

"*Ja visst* (Of course)," came the startled reply. "But who, in the Devil's name are you?"

"Paul Knutson," Torkel responded, "my name is—better known as 'Torkel the Warrior.'"—omitting the word 'Wise'— We are from the court of King Magnus. We seek the Lost

Greenland Colony. The Skrellings killed all but the four of us. But who from Hell are you?"

"I am called Johan Byrnjolfson," he replied. "You say you seek the Greenlanders? Well, my friend you need seek them no further you have found them. We are your Lost Greenland Colony."

And at this rather unusual introduction, both men ran forward to grasp each-other's hands.

14

REUNION ON THE PRAIRIE

To Paul Knutson, now known as "Torkel the Warrior" the realization that the failure of his expedition had, suddenly and surprisingly, changed to an astonishing success, brought no great exaltation as might be expected. To him, however, there seemed little cause for rejoicing. Perhaps it was the fact that the accomplishment had cost him the lives of sixteen of his comrades—a feeling that such a loss far outweighed the gain.

And in addition, it was the fact that the achievement was no success at all. True, he had found the lost Greenlanders. But it was too late. Now, by all odds, the chances were that the news would never reach King Magnus. As Torkel himself had announced to his companions only yesterday, "We shall never reach the Salt Sea before the Knorr weighs anchor."

And now this startling but friendly encounter with an army on the march told him there was, indeed, something of a new problem at hand—a problem in which he and his comrades were very likely to become involved in some way or another. He must gain knowledge of its terms, and so he asked, "But tell me, my friend. You are leading a great army. Against whom are you marching?"

"We are marching against no one," the other leader replied, "We are but preparing to form a line of defense. Have you not heard? The Skrellings east of the river, the Ojibwahs, they are marching against us.

"Or, better I should say, they plan to attack the Dakotahs, and their friends the Mandans. And we ourselves, the Norse Colony, we have no choice but to join forces with our allies.

"The Ojibwahs had planned a surprise attack so we learned by sheer chance. And so, by great good fortune, have we been given a measure of time in which to prepare.

"Their plan, as I understand it, was to conquer the Dakotahs before the Mandans could come to their aid.

"As for our colony, for twenty years have we dwelt in the land of the Mandans to the westward from the hunting grounds of the Dakotahs. But I am inclined to doubt that the Ojibwahs even know of our existence.

"In truth," he went on, as though discerning a need to acquaint the newcomers with the situation, "the Norse Colony is part of the Mandan nation.

"Several of the younger Norse warriors are half Mandan, or half Dakotah, as is my son here." He gestured toward a young warrior who had sauntered forward from a group that appeared to be the leader's bodyguard and stood by in silence.

"'Byrnjolf Johansson,' as he is called. He speaks both Norse and Skrelling. Myself, I had neither the aptitude nor patience to learn their language.

"And indeed," he went on, "what need? The younger people have always been willing and eager to interpret. But Byrnjolf's mother, she was a Dakotah maiden—HAH—she has learned to 'snakke Norsk' as well as me."

At this point the younger man as though considering his father's remarks a sufficient introduction stepped briskly forward, where there then followed a general shaking of hands. Then the older man continued, "We, the Norse warriors, numbering scarcely half a hundred, and about three hundred Mandans, are here in the center. Our north and south flanks are both from Dakotah tribes," he explained, "and all in all, we are close to two thousand.

"Yes indeed, I venture to say, this time we shall give the Ojibwahs a 'welcome' they shall never forget.

"And yet, I like it not. We, the Norse colonists that is, are followers of the new Christian God. We wish only to live in peace among the friendly Mandans. We like not the thoughts of fighting and killing. And the war will be but a useless slaughter—on both sides."

Torkel was struck with a sudden uneasy feeling. Under the circumstances should they not be considering preparation for the forthcoming battle rather then thus wasting time with what seemed like unnecessary talk?

He was still perplexed when the other man who had introduced himself as Johan Byrnjolfson addressed his next words to the young warrior.

"Byrnjolf, pass the word and return here as quickly as possible—pass the word: here will we rest, but only for a half-hour.

"And you, yourself carry this message to *Songetaha* (The strong one): Good fortune has brought us four warriors from my homeland. Warriors, who I'll wager, have no love for the Ojibwahs east of the river.

"And ask him to come here that we may make council and lay our plans."

But Johan Byrnjolfson, rather oddly, Torkel thought, seemed in no haste to settle down to the matter of making plans for a stand against the invaders.

"Nor is this the first time there has been trouble with the Ojibwahs," he went on, as though eager to outline the events of the past before attacking the problem of the immediate future.

"There was the 'Great War of fifteen years ago' as the Mandans and Dakotahs call it. The Ojibwahs, a great horde of them, it seemed, crossed the river and beat their way well into Dakotah territory before help from the Mandans finally arrived. There were several days of the most desperate fighting before they could be forced back across the river."

He hesitated as though choosing words to describe a sad experience. And then said, "By chance it was, that my family and some kinsmen had traveled eastward to the river on a hunting expedition. A band of Ojibwah scouts moving southward from the main encounter came upon our camp.

"We were outnumbered—there were six to eight of them, and we were but four, not counting the women, yet we finally drove them off killing two of them."

"But when it was over, my two children, 'twas all I had at the time were missing. The boy, Byrnjolf, he was about five years old turned up two days later, frightened within an inch of his wit's end, and half starved. The Ojibwahs had him, and to this day he remembers not how he escaped. He remembers nothing but running—running and hiding."

The Norseman lowered his gaze to the ground and subconsciously caressed a little tuft of grass with the toe of his boot, and then added, "But his younger sister—we never found."

There was a short silence. Then, as though having thrust the sad recollection from his mind, Johan straightened to again face the newcomers.

"And so, I trust you may well understand we have reason to hate the Ojibwahs and the desire to seek revenge. But yet, I like not to think of tomorrow."

Here Torkel manages to interrupt. "But tell me, these 'Ojibwahs', as you call these Skrellings east of the river? You are quite certain they intend to attack? You mentioned a warning—"

"Ah yes, excuse me, I meant to explain at the outset. Three young boys from a hunting camp only two days ago, it was, far to the south from where we expect the attackers to cross the river. And there was an Ojibwah maiden in a canoe alone. She had companions in another canoe on the far side of the river, so the story goes, but they kept their distance.

"But let us sit down. You and your comrades are tired, and we ourselves could do with rest.

"Well," Johan continued as they seated themselves, "the Ojibwah maiden probably at the risk of her own life gave these boys the warning, even told them where and when their warriors were to cross the Great North River—it was to be this morning at sunrise, where the River of Pezheekee the Bison enters the larger river."

And then, as though suddenly seized by a deep feeling of frustration. "If only we could have had more time. If only we could have reached the river to have fallen upon them at the crossing as they beached their canoes. We were, however, fortunate in that we had already assembled our warriors for parading before the villages and thus were able to reach this far without delay."

Torkel, weighing the other man's story as it progressed, was struck with a possibility, nay, almost a certainty—three boys, far south on the river, a maiden in a canoe with companions in another canoe.

He was about to interrupt with a suggestion born of this train of thought but decided against it and remarked instead, "But supposing—you surely have of course already thought of this—supposing these boys only made up this wild tale merely for the excitement it might bring?"

"That, I have not overlooked, my friend," the other leader replied. "But what could I do? There was no time for making certain. There was naught else to do but prepare for battle. If they come, we are ready for them. If they do not come; someone has made fools of us. It will be one way or the other—and that very soon.

"I had hoped," he went on, "that we would have had word before now. Last night, about midnight it was, I dispatched two runners to the river—"

"Ah yes," Torkel interrupted, "the two Skrellings we met. About sunrise, or shortly after, it was. They spoke a few words to our guide, but we, of course, understood not what they were saying."

"About sunrise? Hmm, that is not good," Byrnjolfson said with a frown. "Almost certain I was that they would have reached the river well before sunrise. But tell me, when did your party leave the river?"

"About the first light of dawn, it was," Torkel explained, "and we traveled briskly, walked, that is, yet we did not run. We were well away from the river by sunrise."

"Well, the distance is likely greater than I thought," Byrnjolfson admitted. "But I am hoping they return soon.

"But tell me, what happened east of the river? You say your party took rough treatment from the Ojibwahs? Well, I am not surprised, after what they did to us fifteen years ago." He did not wait for Torkel to answer but rose to his feet and gestured in the direction of where the main body of his army sat or sprawled in the grass, all grateful for the half-hour's rest their leader had ordered.

"Here comes Byrnjolf with old *Songetaha*," he announced, as Torkel and his companions arose also. "The old warrior is Great Chief of the Dakotah nation," he went on rather hurriedly as though eager to supply a short explanation before the arrival of the two.

"It is said that in the Great War of fifteen years ago he killed a dozen Ojibwahs with his own axe." Lowering his voice, he continued, "Friendly enough, the old chief is, but with a considerable distrust of strangers, as you will no doubt soon observe."

As the two drew near, the older man whom, Byrnjolfson had referred to as *Songetaha*, raised his hand in what the Norsemen recognized as a gesture of greeting.

They returned the salutation as young Byrnjolf spoke a few words in the Skrelling language and then in Norse. "This is *Songetaha*, Great Chief of all the Dakotah tribes."

Torkel, smiling, stepped forward and moved as though to extend his hand. But the old chief made no move to do likewise, and instead, folded his arms across his chest his face expressionless.

"He means no offense." Johan hurriedly explained. "It is but the difference between their customs and ours."

But the smile vanished from Torkel's face.

"Tell him, Byrnjolf," Johan began, "that these men are friends from the Northland. They came seeking our colony and that the Ojibwahs killed most of their party."

The younger man translated the words for the old chief and then his reply. He says, "'Tis well. We welcome the friends of our friends." But there was still no change of facial expression.

Once again the old Skrelling spoke, this time at quite some length, and Ivar, assuming that their young guide understood, glanced in her direction. She was blushing deeply as she lowered her gaze to the ground. Ivar gathered that she was the subject of the old chief's remarks, though he seemed to be speaking directly to young Byrnjolf rather than to the maiden, and an uncomfortable feeling came over him.

He felt somewhat relieved when Byrnjolf commenced his translation, but the feeling soon returned to one of resentment as the interpretation continued, "He addresses his words to you, father. He says, 'Do you not know the precept which has guided our warriors on the war-path since the beginning of time?' Do you not know that it is not wise having a woman with your warriors?' He declares it can bring nothing but bad luck. And he likes it not."

Johan at a loss for words made no direct reply, but turned to Torkel's group and said, rather lamely, "Well, the chief is of course aware that this young woman here is your guide, but no doubt she is from east of the river—and surely an Ojibwah, our enemy."

It was not the question that caused Ivar's face to flush with anger. It was the way the man spoke the name, Ojibwah, as though attaching a stigma to the very word.

"Well, you may tell him this—" he began. But Torkel interrupted, "Tell the old Skrelling that the matter of the maiden is of no concern to anyone but us."

"No," Johan protested, "let us be prudent in this.

"Tell him," he went on, "that the maiden is their guide, and that she has aided them in escaping death at the hands of her own people. Now she fears for her life, should she attempt to return."

Torkel remarked to himself that Johan's words were essentially correct, although neither he nor his companions had verbally conveyed any such ideas since their arrival. But at least this would make an astute answer to the old chief's objections. And, in truth, a more prudent one than he himself had suggested.

At any rate, he could see no reason for questioning the validity of the proposed reply and nodded his head in agreement.

Their interpreter relayed his father's reply to the old chief, who in turn uttered a sound which the Norsemen took to have a meaning approximating, "Very well then," even before Byrnjolf repeated the word in their language.

Johan smiled as though highly pleased with his diplomacy. Torkel's companions were all aware of something like a feeling of relief. But Torkel himself could well agree with Johan's earlier observation that *Songetaha*, Great Chief of the Dakotah nation, was indeed possessed with a distrust of strangers.

But Johan Byrnjolfson, leader of the Norse-Mandan-Dakotah allied warriors, was also an impatient sort of man. "Now," he said with an air of having satisfactorily settled one matter and of approaching another with eagerness. "Now let us discuss plans for 'welcoming' those Ojibwahs. The young maiden here, possible it is that she may know something of their designs."

It was evident that he had not thought of the same possibility that had entered Torkel's mind but a short time before; this girl and the "maiden in the canoe" who had warned the three Dakotah boys could be one and the same.

"Perhaps we should question her," he continued. "'Twill do no harm to make the attempt at least.

"Here, Byrnjolf," he addressed the young man who had acted as interpreter between the Norsemen and the old Dakotah chief. "Speak to the young woman. But be careful, as already has she likely been offended by *Songetaha's* remarks. Do not arouse her anger, or likely she will tell us nothing. First, ask her if it is true her people's warriors are marching against us."

Ivar scowled with disapproval. It seemed to him that the stranger, despite the urgency of the occasion, should have asked permission before questioning their guide. But the scowl went unnoticed and soon vanished, as prudence dictated.

Byrnjolf stepped forward and addressed the Skrelling maiden in her own language. "My father wishes me to ask you: Is it true that the Ojibwahs plan to attack us?"

She answered with a few crisp words that gave her listeners the impression that the girl was trying to mimic Johan's impatient manner of speaking.

Byrnjolf translated. "She says yes, that she knows it to be the truth."

"Now ask her—" Johan began.

But already she was again speaking, and again the younger man translated. "She says there are 'many, many warriors.' She says all summer they have been gathering at a secret war camp near a lake some distance east of the river." He then added, "In Norse that could mean as many as two thousand or more."

"That could very well mean the lake where they attacked us," Torkel guessed, ignoring the estimate of the number of warriors.

"It begins to sound reasonable," Johan admitted. "But how would a young girl know of the plans of their war chiefs? Ask her how she learned that her people's warriors were about to make war upon us. But be careful now, mind you. She could well be displeased at this question."

But if the question was resented there was no indication. The girl spoke at considerable length this time. And young Byrnjolf, having now gained confidence in his role as interpreter, attempted to more-or-less translate as she spoke.

She says, "Her father is Grey Hawk, Great Chief of all the Ojibwah tribes. He is a kindly old man who would harm no one. It is his nephew and foster son, Black Eagle their war chief, who is causing all the trouble.

"Black Eagle seeks revenge for the death of his father in the Great War of fifteen summers ago. She has heard them talk and heard her father attempting to prevent the attack. But Black Eagle is a headstrong young man—a madman. He will not listen to reason. He says this time his warriors shall conquer the Dakotah nation, and he shall have his revenge."

Here there was a pause as the girl choked with emotion but soon regained her composure sufficiently to continue. And when she had finished, Byrnjolf turned to his father with an expression of abhorrence mixed with disbelief and said, "She says to tell you this; she heard Black Eagle declare that this time they would take no captives, and even kill the enemy's women and children."

There followed a few moments of shocked silence. Finally, Johan spoke, "This, of course, could be an idle threat; yet we can only assume it to be the truth. And I would say the maiden speaks the truth, but for one thing. This Grey Hawk, it was said fifteen years ago that even then he was no longer a young man. Strange it would seem that he should have so young a daughter."

"Strange indeed, yet not impossible," Torkel replied. "And the boy could have misunderstood. Perhaps we should have him ask her to repeat what she told us of her relationship to Grey Hawk."

Johan nodded to his son, and the boy, softening his tone, again addressed the girl. "Excuse me, but my father wants to be sure he understood you correctly that you said Chief Grey Hawk is your father?"

And this time Byrnjolf waited until he was sure she had finished before commencing his interpretation. "She says yes. As far back as she can remember, Chief Grey Hawk has called her 'Daughter,' and she has called him 'Father.' But she adds this: only a few days ago had she learned that she is, in truth, only his foster-daughter."

"Well, that seems to answer my question," Johan said.

Byrnjolf continued, "She also told me this Black Eagle is Grey Hawk's foster-son. Do you suppose then, that Black Eagle and the girl could be brother and sister?"

"No," Johan replied, "I would say, if I judge this young woman correctly, 'twould be unlikely for her to have a brother like that wild dog; assuming it is true what she says of him, and I doubt not her words. Do not question her further on this. It could very well arouse her anger, and all efforts to discern their plans could be brought to naught."

And immediately, Ivar was aware of a changing attitude toward this man Byrnjolfson, whose demeanor up to now had engendered a feeling of dislike.

"But did you say," Johan went on, "or, did you understand her to say their war chief is the old great chief's nephew? Ask her again, to make sure. Not that it matters now, but this Black Eagle, if such is the case, could very likely become 'heir-to-the-throne' when the old chief dies."

"Well," young Byrnjolf agreed, "she seems not at all displeased with our questioning her."

Again he addressed the girl in the language of the Skrellings. And once again he interpreted. "She says yes, Black Eagle's father was Grey Hawk's brother. Of her own parents she knows nothing; she repeats that she is Chief Grey Hawk's foster-daughter. But listen to this, father. She is not Ojibwah at all. She has learned only a few days ago that she was taken captive, as a little child, in the Great War of fifteen years ago."

"She was ... what? Do you suppose, Byrnjolf—could it be possible? But no—no, they took so many Dakotah children as captives. No, the odds against it are far too great," he ended with a note of sadness.

And then, suddenly, Johan's face lightened as though with a great new hope.

"But well do I remember, the child was barely three years old, but she could speak a few words in her mother's language. And she could repeat her name. Ask her name, son. Ask her name."

Byrnjolf asked her name and she replied that her father called her "*Memengwaa* (Butterfly)."

Johan's disappointment was obvious, but he remained silent.

"But wait," Byrnjolf exclaimed, "she speaks further. She said she also has a name that she sometimes called herself when alone, though she knows not what it means."

"Well, what is it?" abruptly asked Johan feigning interest while still trying to hide his disappointment.

This time the answer needed no interpretation. The girl simply said, "Mah-ree-ah."

"Mother of Christ," Johan exclaimed. "Then indeed she could be our Maria. How else for Heaven's sake? It would be almost impossible for a Skrelling child to be given a Christian name. Yes, she could be—she must be."

Ivar who had sat listening—first with growing interest but now with open-mouthed astonishment started as though to make a suggestion, "Perhaps we should ask—"

But Johan interrupted. "But wait," he almost shouted. "Something else do I remember. A little copper armband she wore. If only she still had it, then there would be no doubting. Ask her is she remembers an armband."

But now it was obvious that the young woman was becoming bewildered with all this questioning, but it must have seemed to her that the excited meaningless chatter between questions had some importance.

So Byrnjolf, indeed a man of more patience than his father, strove more or less successfully to calm his own excitement to where he could quietly explain the present possibilities before questioning her further.

And, as he concluded his explanation, the maiden's eyes were ablaze with excitement. Then he mentioned the armband. And the young woman almost screamed with delight as she reached for the deer-skin bag. Long since had the trinket become too small for her arm, but always had it been cherished as a curiosity, something bordering on magic. When burnished bright with a polish of dampened ashes, its color would change to that of the clouds in the evening sky when a midsummer storm was approaching.

There was yet no word in her language for copper, so as a child she had called it her "piece-of-the-sky band." It was one of her most prized possessions.

And there was the lettering Johan Byrnjolfson himself had inscribed on it—well worn, but still legible: "MARIA JOHANSDATTER."

But instead of the expected wild shout of joy, the father suddenly lowered his voice, and gazing at the inscription through tears, said quietly and calmly, "Ah, but wait until her mother learns of this ... ."

Ivar stole a glance toward where the old Dakotah chief was standing. *Songetaha* was smiling.

Byrnjolf, red-faced with embarrassment at his father's unexpected show of emotion, turned toward his new-found sister and commenced to say something. But at that instant a shout from Sigurd brought the touching scene to an end.

They all sprang to their feet. Johan's two Mandan scouts were approaching. In great haste they came, but with their gait slowed almost to a walk by fatigue.

Four warriors dashed out to meet them and each grasping an arm practically supported the whole weight of the weary runners for the last three hundred or so paces.

The two sank to the ground exhausted and, impatient though he was to hear their report, their leader did not ask his son to question them at once, but waited a few moments until they breathed more easily.

They took turns speaking, while Byrnjolf interpreted. "They say the sun was two hands high when they reached the river. Already had most of the Ojibwahs crossed to our shore. They guessed their number to be at least two thousand—perhaps more.

"They say hundreds of canoes filled the river, and lined both shores. Fearful of encountering enemy scouts upon their return, they waited not to see all of them cross, nor to determine closely their number."

"Well, it is about as I had expected," the older man said rather gravely. "Except I now judge they are closer upon us than I had estimated. But we shall be ready for them. They shall not take us by surprise."

Then a sudden burst of impatience. "But I like it not. This cursed war; it could last for weeks. And I should be taking Maria to her mother."

But just as suddenly, his thoughts turned back to the task at hand. "What think you, my friend? You have fought these Ojibwahs before. It is now late afternoon; I judge they will arrive by nightfall, or shortly after. What think you? Will they launch their attack this day, or will they await the morning?"

"I would say," Torkel replied, "that they will await the coming of dawn. Yet, of this we cannot be certain.

"If they have not already done so," he continued, "they will soon be overrunning the deserted village we passed through earlier in the day as it is directly in their path. This will tell them your people have been forewarned, and their plan for a surprise attack has miscarried. But yet, we can by no means assume that this would discourage them to abandoning their plan."

The impatient Johan now seemed ready to listen as Torkel continued, "And having discerned the meaning of the abandoned village, they will send out scouts to locate our defense line. Perhaps, even now, their runners observe us. During the night, if I mistake not, they will move as closely as possible and strike at the first light of dawn."

"And if I were in command," Torkel added, "I would leave your lines as they are for the time being thus to delude the enemy scouts. Later, under the cover of darkness, draw back to the top of that ridge, allowing your flanks to join your center in a sort of bow-shaped line.

"Thus will your enemy be put to a great disadvantage in an uphill attack. Your bowmen should be in the forefront—to take on the first assault—loosing their arrows on a downhill slant, with much less effort and greater accuracy of aim. And likewise it will be an advantage to those who wield the spears and battle-axes.

"And above all," the old warrior concluded, "do not overlook the possibility of an assault on one or both of your flanks. Draw them in so as to double your strength on your extreme left and right. And here again: your bowmen in the front supported to the rear by your heavier weapons. And then let them come."

Johan extended his hand, "I am most grateful, my friend, for your wise counsel. Now must I have Byrnjolf convey your words to Chief *Songetaha*. Certain I am that they will meet with his approval. Hah—observe how his mood has changed in the last half-hour." The two men turned again toward Torkel's group, where the old Dakotah chief stood silently aside, arms still folded, and with a facial expression still closely resembling a smile while Ivar and Maria, with the aid of young Byrnjolf the interpreter carried on an animated conversation. It was a rather lighthearted one indeed, as though they were all but unmindful of the coming struggle.

Turning, Torkel addressed Ivar. "Well," he began, almost reproachfully caring not if the others heard, "what think you of the happenings of this day, and of those which we can well imagine shall take place tomorrow. For myself, I have reason, as you may well know, to seek revenge against the Skrellings east of the river. And tomorrow shall furnish the opportunity. But yet, I like it not. Too much of this sort of thing have I seen. Perhaps it is that the years have commenced to quench my thirst for battle. Perhaps it is that I am growing too old to be a warrior."

The old Norseman studied the ground at his feet for a moment, and Ivar sensed an argument in the making. "You and I have talked, Ivar, and we have even quarreled, in a friendly way of course, about this thing of the 'New God of the Christians.' And now, today, have we observed what I will grant you, can be no other than his doings, this young maiden restored as by a miracle to her parents.

"But what of tomorrow? I have said, and again I say, there is no room for him among Norse warriors. Either he must go, or so must the Vikings.

"Tomorrow's doings shall be those of Odin and Thor. Tomorrow, at dawn, comes the fighting, the bleeding, and the dying. Now then," he concluded rather sharply, "do you not understand this? That if your Christian God were so much more powerful than the ancient gods, do you not understand that certainly he would provide a better way?"

Torkel did not wait for Ivar to make a reply. It was as though he expected none. He turned and strode rather slowly away towards the north, hands clasped behind his back and with his eyes lowered to the ground. Seven long paces he took. And turning abruptly, he returned, seven paces to the south. Ivar fully expected a continuation of the Torkel's outburst. However without a word, the old Norseman again turned abruptly away, and for the first three paces, once more studied the ground in his path. Then he straightened to gaze skyward to where a lone vulture soared and wheeled, wings motionless on a high air current.

Ivar, following Torkel's gaze, could well imagine that the evil-looking bird possessed some prescience of the coming battle. It was as though the soaring scavenger looked down with eager anticipation as it contemplated tomorrow's carnage.

No doubt Torkel was, at this very moment, cursing the bird under his breath. But Ivar did not overlook the possibility, unlikely though it seemed, that the old warrior could have been looking far beyond the circling vulture, and that he could have been gazing heavenward as though seeking guidance from above.

Once again Ivar counted Torkel's seven measured strides toward the north. And once again the warrior halted as though to again retrace his steps.

As he turned, a breeze rising from the west wind caught the old Viking full in the face, and in that instant the thought crashed through his mind like a thunderbolt. "FIRE," he shouted. "We shall turn them back with fire. The west wind—see, it is rising. We shall let the west wind serve us.

"Quick, Johan. Let me have forty of your men who speak Norse, if you have that many. Send half of them at once. The other twenty, let them stand in readiness. Have them stack their weapons, but let them keep their knives."

A few sharp orders and forty-some warriors advanced, all anxious for whatever new venture was being planned. Another order and twenty eagerly surrounded Torkel.

"Now," Torkel commanded, "each of you cut a good armful of grass and fashion it into a long twist, about the length of your body, or longer, and about the size of your arm. That will make a firebrand; here, let me show you—there now this is what is needed.

"Now, Johan ... the other twenty men—see that each has a garment or something that can be wetted in the marsh over yonder, and tell them to make haste and return quickly."

Johan sent them on the run and then turned to the old Viking. "My friend, plain it is that your plan is to set fire to the prairie. Yet I understand not the need for—"

"No time now to explain," Torkel interrupted. "You shall understand it a moment. We must hurry while the wind is in our favor. Wait ... let me go fetch my flint and fire steel."

A dozen quick strides to where he had laid his pack of personal belongings—and he was back in a flash. "Here, Johan, you strike a blaze while I tell the men what they must do.

"Now hear these words, all of you," he commanded. "Form a line—you with the firebrands, ten to my right and ten to the left. Number one man in each group—that is you, and you here closest to me. You will light your brands, but hold on, await my signal and then run twenty paces, you to the north, and you to the south.

"Every twenty paces you will stop and set fire to the grass and continue thusly until you have covered one hundred paces.

"Your companions will run ahead of you, each man in turn, stopping so as to leave a man at every one hundred ... you understand? Again, number one man will carry fire to number two, and so on.

"Now, you with the wetted garments—each of you will follow one of the fire bearers to beat out the flames that burn back toward our lines. It should not be difficult, as the wind will be carrying the flames swiftly away from you to the east."

Already Johan had a small blaze, about the size of his hand. Another handful or two of dry grass, and the flames leaped up.

Torkel shouted, "Ready now, on the left, number-one-man to the north, and on the right number-one-man south ... light your firebrands and run."

And as each group dashed away, the old warrior took to reviewing his calculations aloud. "Let me think now ... each man should set five fires before his brand burns out. At twenty paces between fires ... yes, that is one hundred paces for each man. Twenty men that should be sufficient, more than sufficient ... a fire line two thousand paces in length. And it will grow in length as the wind sweeps it forward."

And the dry grass, high as a man's head in places, waist-high on the average, made excellent fuel as the flames leaped and crackled before the rising west wind, while the dense cloud of smoke rolled skyward and eastward.

The two men stood and watched in silence for a few moments. Then Torkel said, "If the Ojibwahs are as close upon us as I reckon they are, they have already observed our smoke. I hope they do not tarry too long. I would rather not see the devils burned to death."

"They would do the same to us," Johan said, with a hardness in his voice. "Do not forget. Maria told us Black Eagle would even kill our women and children."

"Well," Torkel replied, "certain I am, that your women and children can rest easy this night. Now, if only the west wind will hold. Very likely it will diminish somewhat after nightfall, but I would wager that the dawn will find the Ojibwah army forced all the way back to the river.

"However," he continued, "we shall take no chances. We shall follow them— Excuse me, Johan. I should say if, I were in command, I would follow them on the very first light of dawn and with the full strength of your army."

"Thank you, my friend. Thank you for your wise counsel again," Johan said. He again grasped Torkel's hand, shook it warmly, and added, "And yet I know not how by mere words to thank you for the return of my long-lost daughter. My mind staggers with the task of accepting the truth that she is indeed the child we lost so many years ago."

"Do not thank me," Torkel said with a smile. "It was not my doings. It was the doings of the New God of the Christians and a certain young man." He nodded in the direction of Ivar, who was still busily engaged in a three-way conversation with Maria and her newly discovered brother.

Johan smiled broadly and was about to reply but on second thought, checked his words and changed the subject of the conversation.

"There is a camp," he said, "behind our lines on the far side of the ridge; you can see it from the top. The women and children and the old men who fled the village, the one you passed through and another farther to the south, are camped there. My wife's sister is also there. Let my son and your young companion take Maria to her. The men can return by nightfall, if they tarry not too long."

* * * * * * * * *

Never—neither before nor since—has the sod of the great Dakotah grasslands been trod by a happier trio: Maria Johansdatter, her brother Byrnjolf Johansson, and Ivar Kristenson—"The Fair-haired-One."

Refreshed by a light, yet ample meal from the stores of Johan's provisioners, they had set out in high spirits, in the direction of the refugee camp far to the rear of the Norse-Mandan-Dakotah army.

"There it is," Byrnjolf announced as they reached the top of the ridge. He spoke in the language of the Skrellings, "You can see it if you look slightly to the south of the setting sun."

The words, of course, were strange to Ivar's ears, but well did he comprehend their meaning. There, far in the distance lay the camp silhouetted against the sunset—the rather crude and hastily erected shelters of the women, children, and old men who had fled before the invading Ojibwah army.

The Skrelling maiden, whom Ivar in his mind had named, "The One-in-the-Center"—though now it was beginning to seem natural enough to think of her as Maria gave a little cry of delight and chattered excitedly.

And this time, with something akin to a thrill of joy, he recognized one, but only one of her words, his own name, Ivar, with an accent oddly transposed, yet spoken plainly enough.

Byrnjolf grinned. "She says to tell you she can scarcely wait; she is so excited—says we must hurry."

Fatigue from last night's journey on the river and from today's arduous trek westward as the three strode onward with youthful enthusiasm was now pressing on Ivar. Yet Ivar was suddenly aware of a strange feeling, as though he could go on like this off across the far edge of the world and onward into the sunset.

But now, there came the sudden recollection of another evening. Long ago and in another world, it almost seemed. But hold on, Ivar. Are you losing your wits? In truth, it was but a few days ago. But yet, how is this? The days, each day, certainly must have been longer that the usual span of so many hours.

There was the *very* long day of the battle on the lake, the long day of the massacre, and the flight of the survivors. The day spent in hiding on the island, and the engraving of the message on the stone. The day of the long journey westward to the river with their pursuers they knew not how far behind them.

And then there was the day of the desperate struggle with the lone warrior. The day that could well have been his last had it not been for a mysterious and miraculous flight of an arrow.

And then another day spent in hiding, and the all-night journey northward on the river following their guide, this strange young Skrelling woman. Following her they knew not to where nor why.

But what matter the days, their coming and their going, and their happenings? What matter the other days? This day, this is the one to be long remembered—a day, and now an evening, not even to be surpassed by that other evening, the evening of the lakeshore, and the "One-in-the-Center," and the "Good Luck" arrow. And strangely enough, he could almost hear again the mischievous taunt from one of his comrades: "*Ho, Ivar, Hvordan går det* (How is it going)?"

* * * * * * * *

And now there had taken place another joyful reunion—Maria Johansdatter and her aunt, her mother's sister whom the girl, of course, remembered not at all.

"Widow Olufson" the older woman was now called, while she dwelt among the Norse colonists—another younger sister of *Songetaha*.

She had fled westward with her friends and neighbors at the warning that the Ojibwahs were on the warpath; the warning that came, though of course she knew it not at the time, from this young woman the daughter of her sister, who she remembered only as the child who had been carried away by the hostile tribes "East of the River."

And finally. "It grows late," Byrnjolf said, speaking in Norse. "Even now it will be well after darkness has fallen will we return to my father's camp." And then, in the language of the Dakotahs. "We must bid you farewell for now, Aunt White Flower, and ... and Maria, my sister. Strange it yet seems to be speaking again to my little sister, as I well remember I did so many years ago."

He turned to Ivar with another translation. "Maria says you must not forget to return," he said with a grin.

Ivar said, "Tell her the strength of all the gods shall not be sufficient to hinder me."

Byrnjolf, with a mischievous little laugh, relayed the message, whereupon there burst forth a wave of gleeful chatter among the other three. And Ivar suspected that his remark had been enlarged upon in the process of translation. He grinned in return and wanted to say something but could think of no words to fit the situation. Instead he shuffled his feet in a subconscious manner as though attempting to cover his embarrassment,

Still smiling, Byrnjolf turned abruptly and strode off in the direction whence they had come.

And, still somewhat embarrassed, young Ivar, extended a hand to the Widow Olufson, who was now acquainted with the Norsemen's customs. He then took the younger woman in his arms for just a moment, and then hurried to join his companion.

In silence the women stood gazing after the two young men as they tramped briskly away to disappear into the growing dusk of evening. Then they turned to one another and smiled, both faces aglow with happiness, albeit each with a happiness somewhat dissimilar to that of the other.

The older woman made a slight gesture in the direction of her shelter, as though she was about to speak, but her train of thought was interrupted by the sound of approaching voices—voices which she recognized as those of friends and neighbors.

From a respectful distance had they observed the coming of the two men and the strange young woman, coming they well knew, from the direction of what they assumed was now, or must soon become, the field of battle. And now, having observed the departure of the men, they were driven by curiosity to the temporary home of the Widow Olufson.

Maria again turned to her newly discovered aunt, and with something akin to an air of urgency, as though there were words which needed saying before the approaching delegation came within the sound of her voice.

The faintest suspicion of a blush tinted her cheeks. "Tell me please, Aunt White Flower—how would they say ... I mean, in the language of the strangers from the north, how would they say, '*Gi zah gin?*' (I love you?)."

"I can scarcely imagine why you ask," the older woman said with a smile. "But well did I myself learn those words long years ago. In the language of the Northmen you would say, '*Jeg elsker deg.*'"

The girl's lips moved as she repeated the sentence to herself. But she did not pronounce the works aloud. It was as though she were awaiting her first attempt to speak them for some very special occasion.

JOHAN'S REMINISCENCES

Johan Byrnjolfson, the leader of the Norse-Mandan-Dakotah allied warriors, retired early that evening. He was weary to the point of exhaustion.

But sleep seemed out of the question. He was fully awake long after nightfall when he heard the voices of his son, Byrnjolf, and the young newcomer, Ivar Kristenson, at a distance as they were challenged by a sentry, and the chiding questions with evasive replies. And finally, their lowered voices as they neared the sleeping camp.

The three other strangers, the one who called himself Torkel, and the two younger men—already had he forgotten their names, were bedded down near the campfire.

And his thoughts now turned to a critical appraisal of the newcomers ... a rather odd sort, that man Torkel. What was the eke-name by which he had referred to himself? Ah yes, "Torkel the Warrior." He claims to have led an expedition sent out by King Magnus of Norway. But under a different name, Knutson he had said. Rather odd indeed.

Yet, perhaps there is no reason to doubt his story. Twenty years have passed since we left Greenland, yet it seems such a short time ago. Very likely no attempt was made to leave any record of our going. After all, what need to leave any message for possible adventurers from the Eastern Settlement. Little help indeed had we received in recent times from that direction.

Nor was there any plan to ever return. We would hopefully establish a new settlement somewhere in the Great New Land to the West. A settlement which would, one day, far outshine the East Greenland Colony.

So, perhaps it was natural enough for them to call us the "Lost Colony" when they came upon our deserted dwellings in Greenland. But why would the King, or anyone else, for that matter, be concerned of our whereabouts after all these years? Was it for religious fervor, tithes, or taxes?

And then too, he mulled, this Torkel fellow, a pagan warrior in the service of the Christian King Magnus. Yes, very odd.

But yet, what were the words he used? Ah yes, he had said, "It was the doings of the New God of the Christians, and a certain young man." Rather strange words for a follower of Odin and the other gods of our ancestors.

And of course, the "certain young man" is the one he called Ivar. He seemed to be a fairly decent sort, for a warrior. But plain it is that the young man is interested in Maria. And I like not the idea of a wandering warrior as a future son-in-law. No, I seem to have taken a sort of dislike to the fellow—although perhaps it is more a natural rather than logical feeling.

And so rambled on his jumbled thoughts—as do the thoughts of one whose mind has become weary of its burden, and then, of a sudden, is intoxicated with a great new happiness.

And uppermost in his mind, of course, was this latter emotion, the joyous, and yet almost unbelievable truth of the return of his lost child.

He remembered countless other nights over the span of fifteen long years when he had also lain awake, thinking, planning, hoping ... and despairing.

To begin with, there had been the ill-fated hunting expedition eastward to the Great North River. A three-day's journey it had been. But always well worth the effort was the annual trip to the river—where fish and game were to be found in abundance.

There were the two brothers-in-law, Vrål Olufson and himself, and their two Dakotah wives, Morning Star and White Flower—sisters they were—and also my two small children, Byrnjolf, a boy of five years, and Maria, barely over three. Accompanying the party were two experienced Mandan guides that were well acquainted with the famous hunting and fishing grounds.

And there was the camp in a shady, little, wooded area not far from the river's bank—a sort of opening among the denser trees and thickets that fringed the river for some distance back from its margin.

The first morning in camp, the men had gone forth at daybreak with hunting bows and a goodly supply of arrows to seek the feeding grounds of waterfowl. And shortly thereafter the two sisters set out to gather wild berries in a thicket not more than a stone's throw from the camp. The two children, weary from the long journey, were allowed to continue sleeping.

There was no hazard, so it seemed, in leaving them unattended for an hour or so; true though it was that east of the river lay the land of their quarrelsome and hostile neighbors, the Ojibwahs.

But there seemed to be no need to be anxious this time of the year. Never had the Ojibwahs been known to encroach upon the hunting lands of the Dakotahs except in the late fall of the year, when for some reason known only to The Great Spirit, the vast herds of bison moved eastward out of the grasslands, preparing to winter along the river.

No, surely there was no danger in leaving the children alone for a short time when they were easily within calling distance.

The two Norsemen and their guides had scarcely arrived at the marsh some distance to the southward from the camp when they heard a scream. Fifteen years had passed since the Great War, but he would never live long enough to forget the scream that reached his ears through the stillness of the early morning air.

Immediately the hunting party was running in the direction of the sound.

A band of Ojibwah warriors, a scouting party, it proved to be, had by chance come upon the sleeping children, and moments later the two women in the berry thicket. Although not known at the time, the main body of the Ojibwah invaders had crossed the river quite a distance to the north from where our camp lay.

And, like a bird instinctively striving to lead a predatory animal away from its nest, the young mother and her sister fled southward in the direction taken by the hunters.

And now, fifteen sad years later, lying out here in the great grasslands under the late summer stars, once again did Johan relive the tragedy.

At the sound of the women's screams, the two brothers-in-law and the Mandan guides instantly commenced retracing their steps, arrows drawn in readiness as they ran.

Bursting through a clump of dense undergrowth, they almost met five of the Ojibwahs head-on. And taking the women's attackers by surprise, they loosed a flight of arrows at close range almost at the same instant. But with less effect than one would expect at such close quarters.

Three of the Ojibwahs instantly halted, turned, and fled. The fourth staggered and fell, but caught himself on one hand as he went down and instantly regained his footing, only to run a half-dozen steps and again fall never to rise. And the fifth, intent on capturing the two women had, in the same instant, seized Vrål's wife and thrown her to the ground before the warning cries of his companions reached his ears.

Too late was his attempt to leap to his feet. Vrål's left fist crashed into the Skrelling's face, the force of the blow rolling him backward and to the ground. In a flash, the Norseman drew his knife with his right hand and, leaping astride the Ojibwah, raised it high for the avenging thrust.

But a shout from Johan stayed his hand. "*Hold*, be not in haste. No doubt they have carried the children away. Let him live, and we will force him to lead us to the children."

Vrål grudgingly lowered the weapon, and growled, "Very well, but had you sung out an instant later ... ."

And almost at once the procession was hurrying in the direction of the camp with the Ojibwah scout in the lead, followed two paces behind by Vrål and flanked on either side by the Mandan guides, all with arrows set and bows drawn. And with the angry Vrål almost hoping, it seemed, his wife's attacker would make some sudden move toward escape.

The two women, white-faced and weak from the anticipation of reaching the camp and finding the children gone, brought up the rear assisted by Johan.

But there was no outcry—and no tears as they came upon the empty sleeping places. Their anguish had carried them beyond the point of weeping.

"Very well, '*Hest*'," Vrål commanded, his voice rasping with emotion, as he addressed one of the young Mandan guides whose size and strength had earned him the Norse nickname which meant "Horse," and who had acquired a fair understanding of the Norsemen's language. "Very well, now. I think you understand our plan. Speak up if you do not. All right—now tell this sour herring we will spare his life, if he will lead us to the children."

The Mandan nodded to indicate understanding, and then turned to the Ojibwah, speaking with firmness in the language of the Skrellings.

The Ojibwah straightened in an attitude of defiance as he replied, speaking at what seemed more length than was necessary.

The guide translated, "He says, 'very well, that he will lead us to the children.' But he also says, 'no good will come of it. His warriors will kill their captives before they will give them up. He says—'"

"Then tell him ... ," Vrål broke in with a curse, "tell him we may as well kill him here and now."

"But hold on," Johan interrupted, "tell him that, but also tell him this, that we have made him an offer, and we hold ourselves bound by it."

"It could be," he turned to Vrål and added by way of explanation, "that if he leads us to the children's captors, we might well rescue them by stealth, if in truth the use of force seems imprudent. It is a gamble we must accept."

"Agreed," said Vrål, "but let us see that he understands this." He turned to the Mandan guide, and said, "Tell him if the children are harmed, it will also mean his death—and a slow one at that—we will no longer be bound to spare his life—and death can come in many ways."

There was a rather lengthy exchange of words between the Mandan and the still defiant Ojibwah, the delay causing Johan concern lest his hot tempered brother-in-law should lose patience and fly into a rage and end the exchange by slaying the Ojibwah on the spot. Nor did he feel less concerned when Vrål suddenly slacked his bowstring and lowered the weapon only to again unsheathe his knife.

Again the interpreter spoke, "He says he fears us not, but that he accepts our offer, by which he too holds himself bound. Says we need not hold our weapons in readiness for he has given us his word. Then he says this, that it is best for us and best for the children if we let him go in peace. Also that he is a *storkarr* (important person), and is head of the Ojibwah scouts. His name is *Makuatah*, (Sleeps awake) brother of Grey Hawk, chief of the Ojibwah nation.

"He says if we do not let him go, his brother's warriors will seek you out and kill you after the war is over. He doubts not that the fighting has already begun scarce a half-day's journey from where we stand—"

"Tell him," Olufson angrily interrupted, "we know nothing of any war, and that we shall not release him until he leads us to the children. That he can then go and tell his brother to *Kommer til Helvete* (Come [go] to Hell)."

Again the Mandan addressed the Ojibwah, who now replied, first with a puzzled glance as though he comprehended not the meaning of the curse when translated into the Skrelling language, and then he spoke to the Mandan. And once again the guide relayed his words. "He repeats, his brother's warriors will kill you if we do not let him go in peace."

The Norseman raised his knife menacingly. "Tell him we care nothing about his brother's warriors. Tell him to commence walking and lead us to the children *now*."

There was another short exchange of words between the two Skrellings, the Ojibwah, meantime proceeding rather slowly across the little grassy clearing that was the campsite, the Norsemen and the two Mandans following closely. It was as though the Ojibwah scout feared the wrath of the Norsemen, should he further forestall the beginning of the quest for the missing children, yet seemingly unwilling to forgo an opportunity for delay.

As he reached the North border of the enclosure, where the decaying trunk of a fallen tree formed a sort of barrier between the camp and the dense thicket beyond, he halted and turned, beseechingly, to the Mandan guide.

Vrål's lips moved as though he were attempting to force words suitable to express his exasperation. "Tell him—" he began, but already the brief exchange of words was finished, and the Mandan guide interrupted the Norseman's order.

"Now he says to tell you it will be a half-day's journey. Says he is hungry, has not eaten since yesterday, and begs for food and drink."

Vrål, now almost at the end of his patience, uttered a curse under his breath, tossed his knife in the direction of their food supply, and said, "White Flower, cut him a chunk of dried venison and fetch him some water."

The Ojibwah moved as though to recline on a fallen tree trunk in anticipation of the food.

Johan, perhaps no less impatient than his impetuous brother-in-law, strode briskly in the direction indicated by the toss of the other's knife, and said, "We had best carry with us some provisions, if the Ojibwah speaks the truth, it may well be after nightfall before we return. Here, let me—"

A sharp cry from one of the Mandan guides brought him to a halt. He whirled around in time to catch a glimpse of the Skrelling, who, instead of taking a sitting position, had suddenly, and with lightning-like movement, stooped, snatched something from the ground, and almost in a flash, he belted into the thicket and disappeared.

The two Mandan guides managed to loose their arrows at the fleeing prisoner in the instant he fled. But the Ojibwah instinctively crouched low and allowed them to sing harmlessly over his head.

With a cry of rage, Vrål leaped over the tree trunk and crashed headlong into the thicket in hot pursuit with Johan not a dozen paces behind him.

The two guides instantly took stock of the situation and refrained from joining in the chase realizing that the women would be thus left unprotected against the possibility that the three other Ojibwahs scouts could be lurking nearby.

As Vrål plunged through the thicket, a stout branch caught in the angle formed by the bow and bowstring, and the weapon was torn from his grasp. He waited not to retrieve it. The Skrelling, now perhaps fifteen paces in the lead, burst out the far side of the thicket, and thus freed from the hindrance of bush and branch, set an arrow to the bowstring as he ran. It was not until then that the Norseman realized that the object he had snatched from the ground behind the tree trunk was a bow and arrow quiver, left there, no doubt, when the raiding scouts first came upon the camp and the sleeping children.

The fleeing Ojibwah suddenly halted, turned about, and loosed the arrow at almost point blank range at Vrål. A miracle it would have been, had he missed at such close quarters. With a sickening thud the arrowhead sank in the Norseman's chest. But it fazed him not in the least in his mad pursuit of the Skrelling.

Again the Ojibwah turned and fled, while setting another arrow as he ran.

And again he halted, even at a more deadly range than before, drawing the bowstring as he turned. But this time, in turning, he pivoted on his left foot, taking a half-step backward with the other to brace himself for the second shot. By some freak of fortune, his right foot sank in the edge of a fox's burrow and he stumbled backward in the instant he loosed the arrow, and it hissed through the air a full arms length above Olufson's head, and with a terrible roar of pain and rage the berserk Norseman was upon him.

With his left hand he seized the Skrelling by the throat. With his right hand, he grasped the arrow's shaft and wrenched it from the wound in his chest. Gripping the shaft as one would the haft of a dagger, he raised it for a thrust.

"HOLD," cried Johan Byrnjolfson.

But too late—in that very instant Vrål plunged the arrow into the Skrelling's treacherous heart.

And so perished *Makuatah*, headman of the Ojibwah scouts, and brother of Grey Hawk, Chief of the Ojibwah nation. Unfortunately with him perished also was the one and only possibility of rescuing the Byrnjolfsons' children.

But two days later the anguished parents were cheered, to some extent at least. They came upon the boy, frightened, bewildered, and half-starved.

Byrnjolf, however, could recall but little of the abduction. He had been roused from sleep by his sister's muffled cry, and opened his eyes in time to catch a glimpse of her being carried away, bundled in her blankets, over the shoulder of a tall Skrelling.

He had opened his mouth to cry out, but the sound never came. Instead, he had heard, rather than felt, it seemed, the blow that silenced him. A blow obviously intended to render him unconscious rather than to kill.

And he remembered walking, being led behind his captor like an animal. And he remembered being tired, very tired. But that was about all.

The boy knew nothing of how he had escaped. His hands had been bound with a leather thong. Another lengthy thong was fastened, securely, though loosely, about his neck as a leash. That leash, so they soon discovered, had been severed by burning.

It was supposed that the boy in his first night in captivity had managed to draw the rather lengthy thong across the embers of a camp fire. And, once free, he had managed somehow to loose his hands, stolen away, and fled in the general direction from whence his captors had taken him.

Maria, the younger child, was never found. Long before the fighting was over, she had no doubt, been carried by an Ojibwah far into their territory east of the river.

There had been many other captives during the war, of course, but chiefly from among Dakotah families who chanced to be in the path of the invaders. And there was talk, and there were well laid plans for following the Ojibwahs across the river in a rescue attempt.

But *Songetaha* the Chief of the Dakotah Nation counseled against such a move. Only too well did he know the strange workings of the heart and mind of the Ojibwahs.

"*Makuatah* spoke the truth," he cautioned, "when he declared the Ojibwahs would kill their captives out of spite before they would give them up.

"Better it is by far to leave be. Indeed, it has been said, that they treat their captives not badly, especially children, that even they take them into their families as their own.

"And again, in truth has it been said, that many of the Ojibwahs dwell in stout and comfortable lodges far from the Great North River, far to the east, among the headwaters of another great stream. Some call it 'The Great South River,' others call it 'Mississippi, Father of Waters.'

"There will our lost children grow to manhood and womanhood, well treated, for the most part we hope, if that be of any comfort to you. Yes, though it grieves your hearts, better by far to leave matters be as they are."

So spoke *Songetaha* the chief of the Dakotah Nation. After fifteen years Johan clearly remembered every word.

* * * * * * * *

Vrål recovered from his wound, though it was generally thought it would shorten his life. Some even believed the stoical Norseman's death would be hastened by an overwhelming burden of remorse for having destroyed the chance, slim though it may have been, of making use of the Ojibwah scout in the search for the missing child.

As the day of the tragedy had receded into the past, and the late autumn mornings had commenced to become tempered with that old tang which presages the coming of cooler weather, Vrål's usual cheerfulness had finally faded into a deep despondency. He grew irritable and quarrelsome, preferring to remain by himself and resenting any attempt at friendliness on the part of his neighbors.

He could scarcely have helped but recall that it was he himself who had scoffed at Johan's misgivings, when it had been finally decided that the wives and children should accompany them on the ill-fated hunting expedition close to the Great North River.

Johan deeply concerned with his brother-in-law's distressing change of attitude, had called at his hut one evening for the purpose of making one more attempt at convincing him that this could not go on—that there must be an end to this self-reproach, lest he drive himself insane.

But the attempt availed him nothing. Vrål would not be comforted, and finally had flown into a rage and threatened him, should he ever dare mention the matter again.

16

VRÅL'S MISADVENTURE

The next morning Vrål Olufson was gone. He had taken his hunting bow and a quiver of arrows. Also a buffalo robe and a packet of food and had vanished into the night.

And now there was no doubt about it. The sturdy Norseman had certainly lost his wits entirely. Now his friends had discovered that his skis were also missing. No sane person would strike out over the dry grass on skis.

But Vrål was not insane. He was unreasonable, stubborn, and fearless to the point of foolhardiness. But he had by no means lost his mind.

The season of the year was that which was to be known by settlers hundreds of years later as "Indian Summer." The sky was a deep blue, and from midday until sundown there was a smooth warmth in the air. And the almost unnoticeable breeze from the west left strands of white cobwebs floating horizontally in the sunlight.

But the breeze also brought with it a feeling of approaching winter—and the darker days ahead with increasing winds out of the northwest signaling colder days and snows which were sure to follow.

That was likely the reason Olufson had strapped the skis to his back. And it was well that he did. That was the year the snow and deep cold came a whole month early.

The next night he made camp among the dry rushes near the shore of a small marsh. But no, he could not risk a campfire's smoke; he had not yet left the territory peopled by the friendly Mandans and Dakotahs. He must at all costs, avoid contact with friends as well as enemies.

Trudging eastward at a steady and stubborn gait, the Norseman reached the Great North River at sundown of the following day. He would again establish an overnight camp, and in the morning he would devise some means of crossing. He had hoped to find an abandoned canoe, but there was none.

Vrål roused himself with the dawn and, with renewed determination set about the next task. First, he must gather dry branches from fallen trees and driftwood from the river's bank. These he would lash together for a raft.

But search as he would, Olufson soon discovered that he could not assemble sufficient material. In the end he was forced to settle for a raft the size only to float his weapons, skis, and his pack.

There was no other choice. He removed his garments, placed them atop the heap and waded into the stream pushing the raft ahead of him.

The water was cold. And the depth in midstream required several yards of strenuous swimming before he again found footing on the soft earth of the river's bottom. Wading ashore and shivering with cold he hurriedly replaced his garments. Then he straightened and stood for a moment to gaze toward the trackless wilderness east of the river.

Now, there was a need for the utmost caution—Vrål was now in the land of hostile Ojibwahs.

He struck out at a brisk pace, but despite the exertion it was almost midday before he felt the chill of the river leave his body. But then came a feeling of uncomfortable warmth and the need to rest. Unburdening himself of the pack, he stretched out on the grass and soon fell asleep. On awaking he again had the feeling of chill and discomfort.

That night the Norseman again rolled himself in his buffalo robe and slept, albeit rather fitfully. The morning came with heavy clouds and a wind from the northwest. Great flocks of waterfowl were winging their way southward, an unfailing sign of colder weather to come. The sign which he deliberately chose to ignore.

Vrål found a secluded spot and kindled a small fire. He prepared his morning meal but found little desire for food. He had to force himself to eat.

When he again set forth, there was a feeling of a painful tightness through his chest. He was reminded of the time when, as a young boy in Greenland, he had fallen into the fjord in midwinter. He had been ill for three weeks afterwards. "*Lungebetennelse*," (burning of the lungs), his parents had called it.

But there was no thought of turning back. The stubborn Norseman had set his mind to a task. For three more days, under darkened skies and increasing cold he tramped eastward through grassy meadows and pine forests. He now commenced to observe with apprehension, that already the marshes were covered with a thin coating of ice. But certainly, so he told himself, the extreme cold of winter was yet several weeks away. Time enough, he assured himself, to accomplish the task and return to the Norse settlement.

Then, late one day, it came—the first snowfall—a few scattered flakes to commence with, then a swirling whiteness that soon covered the ground. No doubt, Vrål reasoned, the weather would turn mild, and the snow would turn to rain by morning.

But his prediction failed to materialize. The following day the snow had reached a sufficient depth to permit use of the skis. And the snowfall continued steadily throughout the day. Now the depth was such that making progress without skis would be difficult.

Late in the afternoon it was, when the Norseman came upon the first sign that he might be nearing an area of human habitation. The moccasin tracks of two Skrellings. But there was no great need for alarm he told himself. They appeared to be headed in the same general direction he was taking. Probably an hour or two ahead, so he judged by the depth of the new snow that had fallen into the tracks.

But one thing now seemed certain: the Skrellings, no doubt seeking wild game, could hardly be expected to wander more than a day's journey from their homes in this sort of weather. And this being the case, so he reasoned, he must now be nearing his destination.

The wind was rising and with it increasing coldness. Finally, topping a rise of ground, he stopped to rest and to seek a suitable spot for an overnight camp. A casual glance ahead and down the slope disclosed nothing of particular note except for a small lake in the near distance, its surface already white with snow-covered ice.

But a second glance brought a thrill of excitement; there on a flat, tree-covered area near the lakeshore were lodges.

Now, at last—and what were the words old *Songetaha* had used? Ah yes: "'Tis said they dwell in stout lodges, far to the east near the headwaters of a great stream."

There indeed stood the lodges of an Ojibwah village. And stoutly built they appeared—even at a distance. Very likely, he told himself, they would be of double-walled construction with cedar bark on the exterior and with an inner wall of woven withes from the willows. The space between the walls would be filled with dry grass and rushes for added warmth in winter.

Yes. This could very well be the place. The lake itself could very well be the "headwaters of a great stream."

With quickened heartbeat the Norseman suppressed an immediate urge to attempt to steal closer to the village. Instead, he settled down to the task of preparing what he well knew would be an uncomfortable sleeping place in the snow.

Vrål roused himself before dawn the next morning, beating a heavy covering of snow from the buffalo robe as he arose to his feet. He had slept scarcely at all. There was a bitterness in the cold. He felt as though he were chilled to the bone.

There had been another heavy snowfall, drifting with the wind late in the night—turning to a deep cold stillness toward morning.

And now, with the utmost caution, he must approach the Skrelling village. He had the night before observed a thick clump of bushes within a stone's throw of the largest lodge—a lodge which, judging from its size, could have been some sort of meeting place for the tribe. He must reach it before daylight. He must conceal himself there in the bushes and wait and watch throughout the day. There was of course the chance that his hiding place might be accidentally discovered. He would take the chance; there was no other way.

But no—he could not use the skis. The first Ojibwah to venture outside would certainly come upon his path, and would naturally follow the odd-looking track.

He cut strips from the buffalo robe and bound them around his feet—thus to imitate the track of Skrelling moccasins. He must remember to walk with feet pointed straight ahead, or toed-in slightly, as the Skrellings do.

But moving down the slope proved difficult. The drifting snow had formed a slight hardness in the upper two inches of its depth. Ideal it would have been for the skis. But unfortunately, the firmness was not sufficient to bear one's weight without them. The result was a plodding gait through the almost knee deep snow. At each step it gave the Norseman the feeling that on the next the surface might support his weight. But no, the going improved not in the least as he warily made his way down the slope. The upper firmness of the drifts continued to give way between steps, as his full weight bore upon it.

'Tis just as well, he thought, at least it would hardly seem reasonable that any of the inhabitants would be out and abroad in this sort of footing and early hour of semi-darkness.

Yet, Vrål made ready with bow and arrow. Though certainly, he again assured himself, he would have no immediate need for the weapon.

But such was not the case. He had covered less than half the distance between his sleeping place atop the ridge and the Skrelling village below, when suddenly in the half-light of the early dawn from out of nowhere, it seemed, a young Ojibwah appeared directly in his path. No doubt the two observed one-another at the same moment.

Instantly the Norseman took note of the fact that the Ojibwah carried no weapon except for the knife at his belt. And obviously the Skrelling made a similar observation, realizing that he was out-weaponed, he turned and fled.

In a flash Vrål determined what must be done. Silence the Skrelling before he can sound the alarm. Fell him with an arrow to the spine. Finish him with your knife before he can cry out for help. Planting his feet firmly, the Norseman raised the bow and arrow to make the draw. But something was amiss. There was an odd feeling of brittleness to his weapon's action. The deep cold had produced some strange effect upon the yew-wood bow. It would certainly snap under the strain of a full draw.

He sent the arrow on its flight at not much more than half-draw. And the result bore no resemblance to the dexterity ordinarily attributed to the use of any weapon in the hands of Vrål. The arrow's flight was slow. Traversing a down-curving arc, it caught the fleeing Ojibwah before he could cover a dozen paces. The arrowhead barely pierced his leathern breechcloth, but sufficient indeed it was to send the Skrelling down the slope with redoubled effort and with howls of pain and fear.

Such a sight would ordinarily have evoked a roar of laughter from the Norseman. But now there was no time for laughter. Almost at once there was the sound of excited voices from the Skrelling village. And now it was Vrål's turn to take flight.

With great haste, yet with what seemed slow progress he made his way back up the slope. Halfway there he halted and turned to observe a dozen or more Ojibwahs in eager pursuit.

But even as the depth of the snow impeded his own flight, so did it hamper his pursuers. Reaching the place where he had left his pack, the Norseman tore the track-disguising strips from his boots and had barely straightened from the binding on the skis when the jabbering and shouting Skrellings came within weapons' distance.

An arrow, narrowly missing his right thigh, slanted downward and buried itself in the snow some yards ahead. As Olufson grasped his pack and not waiting to sling it to his shoulders lunged into the first ski stroke. Another missed his head by slightly wider margin as the next succeeding lunge put his body into full motion. A dozen more vigorous strokes of the skis and the Skrellings, hindered by the snow that now proved to be a boon to the Norseman, soon were left far behind him.

And so Vrål fled westward. But no, he assured himself, his quest had not proven a complete failure. Now, at least he was familiar with the lay of the land. With the coming of spring he would return.

A great weariness came over him and the burning in the chest increased as midday drew near. Yet there was no other choice but to push onward. Another night as cold as had been the last and the snow drifts would firm to where moccasin clad feet of the Skrelling warriors would not break through.

Should they persist in the pursuit they could by walking and running over the drifts make almost as good progress as could he himself with the skis. His margin of safety and his chance for survival now depended entirely upon his advantage of the several hour's lead he might gain this day. He must put distance between himself and his pursuers.

And the cold grew more intense as the day wore on. Halting only long enough to undo his pack, he hurriedly ate a few handfuls of food and with a handful of snow managed to slake his thirst. And again he pushed onward; the rhythmic swish-swish of the skis over the frozen drifts the only sound to reach his ears in the stillness of the great, white, endless landscape.

As the day drew to a close, a biting wind sprang up from the northwest. The burning in the chest became a sharp pain with each breath. Now he must cover his face with a fold of his tunic and breathe through the fabric to keep his face from freezing.

A dizziness seized him but soon passed as he halted to briefly rest. When he again set forth, his feet seemed no longer a part of his body. They were a part of his skis—wooden. And the pain in the chest, it commenced again the moment he put his body in motion.

Now he realized he could not go on. He must seek a spot to build a fire. Certainly he must now be more than a half-day's lead ahead of his pursuers. Yes, he must take time to build a fire or perish.

There ... in that clump of young pines just ahead. There will be some protection against the wind. And here near the center of the thicket lay a fallen tree. Its dry branches and foliage will do very well for kindling.

Quickly now, he thought—undo the skis' bindings. Kick the snow into a looseness that will permit scooping away to reach bare ground for the fire. But what is this? Hands so stiff with the cold he could barely loosen the bindings.

Now to undo the pack, get the flint and fire-steel, and the tinder box. *Ja vel*, but first sit down ... rest a bit. Put the hands inside the garments and warm them against my body.

Now there, that should be sufficient. But no—why hasten. Rest a little longer. Lie down. The pain in the chest is almost gone. There is a great weariness ... and the irresistible need for sleep.

Ja vel. A short nap—then back to the task of kindling the fire. Ah, I feel a strange ... deep feeling of comfort. And it grows dark so early ... .

The wind abated during the night, but there was another heavy snowfall. In the morning there was no trace of the telltale ski track leading into the thicket. Neither was there a track leading out the opposite side.

A jay-bird, one of those hardy species not to be driven southward by cold weather, perched on a low branch and scolded loudly at a little snowshoe rabbit that hopped leisurely into the clump of pines. The animal, no doubt following a familiar route in its morning's quest for food paid no heed to the quarrelsome jay.

But the rabbit shied abruptly aside at the unfamiliar sight of an odd-looking mound of new snow—a mound about the size and shape of a large deer.

17

EXODUS AND A PREDICTION

The people of the Norse-Greenlander colony knew nothing, of course, of what had befallen Byrnjolfson's unfortunate brother-in-law. He had mysteriously vanished from the settlement and finally had been given up for dead. It was the winter following the "Great War" between the Ojibwahs and the Dakotahs—the winter when the snow and the deep cold came a whole month early.

And now, after fourteen more years had passed, time had accomplished that which Vrål had given his life in attempting.

Johan turned on his pallet for the hundredth time it seemed—to gaze at the moon, hanging low in the western sky. Hanging, so he imagined, directly above the Norse settlement with his home and fireside and Maria's mother.

He smiled, and it seemed odd. Never before had he lain awake and relived that terrible day of fifteen years ago and ended the reminiscence with anything like a smile.

He yawned and breathed deeply of the cool night air. Like the great waves of tall prairie grasses, caressed by the west wind, the events of the day drifted across his consciousness to vanish, one after another into a soft black curtain of drowsiness that was finally closing in upon his mind.

Vanishing were the long march of the warriors—the strange meeting of the four adventurers from the homeland of his forefathers—and their guide ... Maria, his daughter.

And their leader who conceived the plan for sending fire against the invaders. A pagan, yet speaking words one might expect from a Christian, "The doings of the New God of the Christians, and a certain young man ... ."

He slept.

* * * * * * * *

And so the dawn found Byrnjolfson's Norse-Mandan-Dakotah warriors again on the march. Across the blackened prairie they tramped, eastward toward the Great North River.

In the lead strode Johan and Byrnjolf. Abreast of them, right and left, were Torkel and his three companions and *Songetaha,* all keenly anxious to observe the results of the old Viking's grand scheme. A scheme which now seemed so startling in its simplicity and ease of execution that Johan could scarcely resist a feeling of disappointment that he himself had not thought of it.

They assumed a brisk, yet unhurried, gait. After all, there seemed to be no great need for haste. There was, of course, the possibility that the invaders had not been forced to retreat all the way to the river and that a battle might yet be in the making. But yet, so long as the advance lay across the burned prairie which afforded the Ojibwahs little opportunity to conceal themselves, there was scarcely a chance of their having attempted to set an ambush.

And Johan, in high spirits and a talkative mood, now recounted, for the benefit of Torkel and his companions, the reason behind the so-called "Lost Greenland Colony."

"Well, in truth, let me say, we are not a 'lost colony' at all. We came here, to the Great New Land of the West, of our own free will twenty years ago. We came simply to seek a better way of life than that which we had in Greenland.

"First there was the severity of the Greenland winters, the shortness of the growing season, and then, the ever present annoyance of the natives. Seldom, to be sure, did they venture to attack us, but their raids against our live-stock drove us to exasperation.

"And for one reason and then another, the trading ships from Norway and the Eastern Settlement began avoiding us. That I would venture to say was the final blow to our Western Settlement.

"And so it was at last, the decision was made at our *Storting*, (Great Council of the Settlement). We could at least be scarcely worse off in an attempt to launch a new colony in the New Land of the West. We knew of Leif Erikson's expedition finding grapes, and we wanted to travel far enough to the south where we could also expect growing conditions mild enough to support grapes and similar crops. However, we did not want to make the long sea voyage south along the coast line and decided to try our luck by heading to the west instead.

"A dozen good ships carried us safely. We lost not a single ship on the journey. Three hundred and twenty-nine men, women, and children we were. With us we carried sufficient goats and sheep with which to commence build-ing herds in the new land.

"The bulk of our livestock, of course, we were forced to leave behind. We simply freed them to forage for them-selves. But for how long, we knew not. Certain it is that the natives were well supplied with meat, for a time at least.

"After considerable searching we came to this New Land of the West where we have found contentment. Our settlement is in the land of the Mandans which lies to the westward from the land of the Dakotahs. And they too, are friendly toward us. If only we could say the same of the Ojibwahs east of the Great North River.

"The Great War of fifteen years ago, of course, brought tragedy to many of the Dakotah families, especially those who dwelt in the path of the invaders.

"As it so happened, we, the Norse-Greenland colonists, were scarcely aware of the war until it was almost over, except of course the events encountered by our hunting party. I have already told you the Ojibwah scouts overran our camp, and you know the rest, that is, if you can imagine the grief of losing our child and the long years of sorrow and regret. Thankfully that has ended, finally and happily, by the coming of your party.

"But out of that war there came a great determination sweeping the tribes of the Mandans and Dakotahs, and yes, the Norse colony as well. The decision was made that we must build an army; the tragic loss of so many captives must not happen again.

"And so it was that I, who have never been known as a warrior—I am but a tiller of the soil, yet I was the one to be chosen for some odd reason to organize the warriors. And proud I am of my army.

"And a warning system we had. Every man and every boy over the age of ten must learn the signal and its meaning. A signal to be passed from person-to-person, from hunting camp to hunting camp, and from village to village.

"The cry of the wild dog, it was, with the sound changed slightly as to not be mistaken by our own people for the barking and howls of domesticated dogs, of which there are many in this land. And ... Hah .... I doubt not but what you and your comrades heard the call two nights ago and perhaps imagined the land to be overrun with wild dogs.

"It was the call of the *Vilde hund* (wild dog) that sent the villagers fleeing westward in the dark early hours yesterday morning, the men to take their places in my army, and the women, children, and old men to seek safety behind our lines.

"But hold on. In my haste, I find myself far ahead of my story. I have yet to tell you: we left Greenland and sailed westward braving the fearsome waters of *Ginungagap* (Hudson Strait) and onward into the Great Salt Sea of the north. You yourselves have not told me, but well do I imagine you followed the same course.

"And almost certain it is that you followed the same waterway southward, though likely you covered the distance in perhaps fifteen or twenty days.

"For ourselves, we established a winter camp on the shore of the Salt Sea ... and it took the greater part of the following summer for the journey southward, what with our women and children and livestock—to say nothing of the task of moving our other belongings.

"Almost at once did we meet and make friends with the Dakotahs and Mandans soon thereafter. And ... speaking of the livestock reminds me; our Skrelling friends, at first could not understand our keeping goats for their milk and sheep for their wool. So far as the Dakotahs and Mandans were concerned, an animal was good only for its meat and its skin. And for the first year or so. until the natives could be taught otherwise, a goodly number of our animals mysteriously disappeared. You may well imagine, however, it was really no great mystery. And a strange thing it was; the Skrellings seemed to consider the thievery no wrongdoing.

"And thus it went, a few troubles here and there over the years but nothing of great consequence, except of course, the Great War of fifteen years ago, and now ... the present trouble with the Ojibwahs.

"Our colony has thrived, and now after twenty years, we are, for the most part, content with our lot.

"In truth, one might say, the 'Lost Greenland Colony' as you call us, is indeed a part of the Mandan Nation. Actually, one might say we are part of both the Mandan and Dakotah Nations.

"But ever does a thought keep coming to plague my mind. And a disturbing thought it is, to say the least. And this it is: the Norse-Greenlanders' colony is doomed to be conquered peacefully by its own friends.

"I have reckoned up, and it is almost as though we are a mountain stream descending as a waterfall into the Great Salt Sea of the Mandans and Dakotahs. And even as the fresh water of the stream clings to itself for a moment, and then, of a sudden it is no more, so shall the Norse colony be swallowed up.

"And thus will it happen, as have I told you, many of us who were young men twenty years ago have chosen Skrelling women as wives. Thus our children are half Norse and half Skrelling.

"Now supposing our children when grown marry either Mandans or Dakotahs. Their offspring will be but one-fourth Norse.

"And ponder this, if you will. Say, on an average, a new generation every twenty-five years. Now, take the same span of years as is reckoned from the settlement in Greenland in the days of Herjulf Bardson and Erik Thorwaldson, who was called 'Erik the Red,' until the exodus of the West Greenland Colony, meaning of course ourselves. About three hundred years it measures.

"Now, say three hundred years hence, that would make twelve generations in the new land. But, let us say, so as not to over-paint the picture, in one generation out of two husband and wife are of like ancestry, blood mixture or call-it-what-you-will. Thus may we count six generations in which the Norse in the blood-mixture will be further divided in half over the span of three hundred years.

"You will observe then; the children of the next which we will count as second generation will be but one-fourth Norse. The fourth, I am counting but one generation out of two, will be one-eighth. The sixth, one part in sixteen. The eighth: one part in thirty-two. The next, one in sixty-four. And finally, the twelfth, the Norse ancestry will be but one part in one hundred twenty-eight.

"Of this we may be also certain, with the thinning of the Norse with Skrelling, there will come a thinning of the Norse language and customs until at last the Norse Colony shall be no more.

"Those have been my thoughts. And the thoughts have saddened me. But now, now am I cheered by your coming, by the coming of my countrymen.

"When we have finished with the Ojibwahs, you will be journeying back to the homeland, now that you have found the Lost Colony. You will be spreading the word among our countrymen: word of the Great New Land of the West.

"And more colonists will come. Of that too we may be certain. And I doubt not but what the very grasslands we now tread upon will one day be the New Home of the Norsemen."

Abruptly, Johan fell silent as though awaiting the effect that the impact of his words may have left upon his listeners. He strode onward, head uplifted and smiling as does a man who has lofty visions for the future, albeit a very dismal distant future for the present Norsemen.

But neither Torkel nor any of his three companions made reply or comment. The old Viking's gaze seemed ever fixed upon the ground immediately ahead as they walked. And there was no smile upon his face.

18

AT THE GREAT NORTH RIVER

And so advanced Johan Byrnjolfson's army eastward, across the blackened grasslands of the prairie.

"Oh ho—what have we here?" he suddenly exclaimed, as his son Byrnjolf, now striding a half-dozen paces in the lead, stooped to pick up an abandoned Ojibwah spear.

"And there lies another, and another. Here, indeed, must the flames have pressed hard upon their heels that they were casting off their weapons."

And so it went—an abandoned spear here and a stone-headed axe there. And now and again in scattered groups of perhaps from three to a dozen or more, bows and quivers of arrows, feathers burned off and shafts badly scorched. Such was the mute evidence of the desperation with which the enemy had retreated, abandoning every ounce of weight that might hamper them in their flight.

And as the distance shortened between them and the river, the march of the Norse-Mandan-Dakota warriors assumed the air of a triumphal procession.

Finally, Torkel spoke. "I would wager," he exulted, "that with such abandonment of their weapons, they will put up little, if any, resistance to our advance."

"A strange thing," Johan meditated aloud ignoring the other's remarks. "Two days ago under these same conditions would I indeed have welcomed an opportunity to see them attempt to resist us. In my heart there dwelt a strange thirst for revenge. And that in spite of what I have already said, that we are followers of the Christian God. "Do you suppose," he went on, "could it be possible that the ancient gods, Thor and Odin, the god of battles, yet hold sway over us?

"Or, could it be this: that over the span of twenty years we have dwelt among the Skrellings, and with their god, whom they call 'The Great Spirit,' that the thing I mentioned has already commenced, the thinning of our Norse customs and beliefs?

"But no, that cannot be possible. I shall cast that thought from my mind. The New God of the Christians has restored our lost child to us, and my thirst for revenge has been quenched. I shall think no more upon the matter."

Torkel smiled one of his rare smiles but made no reply. No longer did he lower his gaze to the ground. Far ahead he was gazing toward the eastern horizon where he could barely make out the dim outline of the fringe of trees along the river. Their destination was now in sight.

And now, as the end of their march was at hand, not one dead Ojibwah body had they found. The invaders had raced for their lives and won—although, plainly enough they had won but by a narrow margin.

Already wearied by their invasion march westward, they had been forced to turn and retrace their steps. Forced to run until they sank to the ground from exhaustion, and forced to rise and run again, as the approaching wall of flame had given them no choice—except death by fire.

As they were forced to breathe the smoke that rolled ahead of the flames, they became at last a choking, struggling mob, fighting desperately among themselves for possession of the canoes along the river's bank. Thus was the end of Black Eagle's march against the Dakotahs.

Johan and his warriors reached the river by early evening. On the opposite shore where it was joined by the smaller River of Pezheekee the Bison, smoke rose peacefully from a hundred or so small campfires. Like a hundred white flags of truce, it spiraled upward into the blue of the late summer evening.

A strange silence hovered over the scene.

"What think you now, friend Torkel?" Johan asked as the two men stood gazing across the water.

"I would say," the old Viking replied rather dryly, "that the Ojibwahs have had their fling at invading the land of the Dakotahs. And, this I would wager, that they have gotten their bellies full of it.

"But yet ... observe. A canoe puts out from the bushes along the shore. Be on your guard, lest there be trickery. It could be a ruse to hold our attention. Pass the word to your warriors."

Johan spoke a few sharp words to his son, who, in turn, addressed the nearest warriors in the language of the Dakotahs. And what seemed to be an accurate repetition of the words echoed quietly left and right along the line.

But there was no need for the warning; the canoe came on alone. A rather sturdy craft it was and manned by four warriors, two in each end, while a fifth sat in the center. Their movement was deliberate, but unhurried, and they uttered no sound until they were within about four boat-lengths from where Johan and his comrades stood.

The oarsman reversed their strokes to halt the forward course of the canoe, then swung it broadside to the shore and held steady, their paddles moving with only sufficient force to avoid drifting with the current.

Torkel and the other three survivors of his ill-fated expedition recognized at once the one seated in the center as the old warrior who had attempted in vain that fateful morning before the battle on the lake to persuade them to turn back.

Now he rose to his feet, and steadied himself with the shaft of a spear against the uneasy motion of the boat and raised his hand in the Skrelling token of friendship.

Then the old Skrelling spoke slowly and deliberately.

A nod from his father, and young Byrnjolf stepped forward to act as interpreter. "He is saying," Byrnjolf began, "he is saying something which means about the same as 'greetings to the victors, from the defeated.'

"Now he says, 'I am Grey Hawk, Great Chief of all the Ojibwahs.'"

There was an uneasy pause, and then Byrnjolf continued, "And now ... and now he says, 'We are beaten ... we have no heart to fight. Our war chief Black Eagle is dead. We have found his body floating on the river in a canoe—an arrow through his heart—an arrow from the bow of one of those strange men from the North.'"

Ivar gasped as the undeniable truth about his life and death struggle with the lone Skrelling came to him. He had fought with the Ojibwah *war chief* and lived. Lived—yes, but yet not by his doing. It was no longer a mystery—he was convinced that it was indeed Maria who had brought down his assailant. But afterwards why had she not come to him? Then came the thought: Maria had killed Black Eagle with whom she had lived as brother and sister most of her life. Although it was not yet light, perhaps she had known she had killed her brother, and having been overcome by mixed emotions—she fled the scene. It seemed strange, however, that when Ivar returned from his sentry duty she had appeared just as he had left her. Ivar concluded it would be best to say nothing of Chief Grey Hawk's announcement, and let the others assume Black Eagle had died during the battle on the lake.

The old chief again spoke, and their interpreter continued. "And now he is saying, 'We have held a council with the chiefs of all the Ojibwah tribes. I now speak for them. I speak for all Ojibwahs. I speak to all the Dakotahs and to all the Mandans.

'We ask for peace, though we have no right to ask it. We ask peace and friendship, forever, with the Dakotahs and the Mandans—and with the Strange Men from the North.

'In truth do I speak—thirty women will we send to you as hostages that you may have faith in our words—that our words will not deceive you.'"

The old chief suddenly ceased speaking but remained standing, as though awaiting a reply.

And now it was *Songetaha's* turn to speak.

"Grey Hawk," he began, firmly but without anger, "we want not your women as hostages. Already have we faith in your words, even as we had faith in our abilities and weapons. We accept your offer of peace.

"Send the chiefs of all your tribes to our shore," he continues, "and let us smoke the pipe-of-peace together that there may be friendship between our nations, and that the Great North River shall no longer be a dividing line between us, and that there shall be peace between our nations forever."

And so, there was peace once more along the Great North River—a peace that was to be forever. And for four days did the warriors from both sides of the river join in the wild celebration. The jubilation was joined heartily by Torkel and his three companions who gladly embraced the end of hostilities.

JOHAN'S BOLD ATTEMPT

"But this truth must I tell you," Torkel was saying to Johan, "though loathe I am to bring you this disappointment.

"You have said you are gladdened that my companions and I will be carrying the story of this New Land back to the Homeland—that your colony might be strengthened by the coming of more and more of our countrymen.

"And the truth of the matter is," he continued, "that was our plan, and the plan of King Magnus, to find the lost Greenlanders that he might send aid to their colony.

"But the 'Ojibwahs,' as you call them, upset our well laid plans.

"Ten of our men had we left to look after our ship by the Great Salt Sea to the north. And twenty of us journeyed southward in two long-boats with both sails and oars.

"The Skrellings fell upon us, first in open battle upon a lake, and again by stealth as we slept. We lost the long-boats and four of us barely escaped with our lives.

"Fifteen days had we allotted ourselves to journey inland, and fifteen for our return to the ship. Fourteen days had we covered when they attacked us. And this day is numbered nineteen, no, twenty since we left the Salt Sea.

"Another twenty ... more likely thirty days would now be our need for the return to the ship—what with the loss of our long-boats and with nothing but canoes and paddles to carry us.

"And long before we could reach the sea, our companions there will have given us up for dead and sailed without us. They dare not tarry, if they are to reach our Vinland camp ahead of the autumn storms.

"Possible it is," Torkel continued, as though seeking to temper the other man's disappointment with a slim hope, "that the King may send another search expedition, so determined is he to find the Lost Colony.

"But, if he does not, and in this I join with you in your disappointment, the failure of our expedition could well delay the coming of the Norse colonists by several hundred years.

"But when they come, and certain it is that they will come, and if, perchance they follow the waterways we ourselves have followed they may find our mark: the stone upon which Ivar engraved his runes.

"'We were eight Swedes and twenty-two Norwegians, on a journey of exploration,' it began. But in truth, never have I questioned the scribe as to the rest of the message.

"And so have we placed our mark upon this land—this land which, as you yourself has said, shall one day be the new home of the Norsemen."

For a long time the two men sat in silence. In the old Viking's words there was something of a grim finality. It was as though there was nothing further to be said.

But finally, Johan spoke. "Saddened indeed I am, and this in spite of the great joy your coming has brought us.

"If as you say, the failure of your party to return to the homeland does in truth delay the coming of the Norse colonists by several hundred years, then indeed is our small colony doomed to extinction. Doomed to be swallowed up, as I have said, by our own friends, the Mandans and Dakotahs.

"It grieves me to think," he went on, "that these sad truths came not to my mind ten or twelve years ago. Very possible it is that had I sent a work party to the Salt Sea, they would have found at least one of the old ships worthy of an attempt to repair it to seaworthiness—but now, after another ten years of neglect ... ?

"Do you suppose, friend Torkel," he continued after another long pause, "... could it be possible that ... you have said twenty days would be your need to reach the Salt Sea, so ... ?"

"More likely thirty," Torkel replied.

But Johan was a man of persistence as well as impatience.

"Very well then, say thirty days. But supposing," he urged, "supposing that for some reason or other your comrades were to be delayed in sailing for... let us say, ten or twelve days. That would make their sailing, say twenty or twenty-two days hence instead of ten."

"True, yet I doubt very much—" Torkel began, but the other Norseman interrupted.

"And, and supposing we were to send a canoe downriver manned by a crew of young and vigorous oarsmen with orders to make all haste. To make all possible haste to reach your comrades before they set sail ... reach them with our message—a message which must be carried to the Homeland, lest our colony perish.

"Do you think it possible, friend Torkel?"

But the old Viking seemed not to share the other man's enthusiasm.

"Possible," he added, "but unlikely. The Knorr must sail ten days hence unless they dare heed not my orders. And, should they choose to heed them not, they shall answer to me for disobedience." "Although," he added, "in truth I must say, I know not when nor where."

But Johan was not to be dissuaded. "A war-canoe with six good oarsmen," he reflected, ignoring Torkel's remarks, "and with a seventh, to spell the others in turn. Certain I am that *Songetaha* would be glad to see that we are furnished with both boat and oarsmen. What think you, friend Torkel, do you think it could be successful?"

"I doubt it," Torkel bluntly replied. And then he continued, "Far too great are the odds against its success. Yet, if you are a mind to set a crew to the task, certainly 'twould be no harm in trying.

"But now, in truth must I say, my bones are wearied to where my wits serve me not well. Let me lie here on the soft grass and rest." And the old Viking stretched out on the ground—pillowing his head on one arm.

Then, as though an afterthought, he said, "But take care that you send at least one man who speaks Norse if you value the lives of your boatmen. Actually, it could well be best if Lars or Sigurd, or better yet both, could be convinced to join the attempt, since they would be instantly recognized."

And so Torkel rested and slept, but not so with Johan. He had set forth, with giant strides, in the direction of *Songetaha's* campfire.

* * * * * * * *

Johan, Byrnjolf and the Norse newcomers waited not for the finish of the great celebration—the jubilation that marked the peace between the Skrelling Mandan and Dakotah and Ojibwah nations.

The day following their triumphant march to the river found them again traveling westward, the younger members of the party now taking the lead followed, at a more leisurely gait, by the older men.

"I can scarcely wait, friend Torkel," Johan was saying, "for the happy moment when Maria meets her mother."

There was a thoughtful pause, and then, "If there only could be some means by which I might reward you for bringing such great happiness to us. If only I could—"

"Let not your mind be troubled, my friend," Torkel interrupted. "Be not troubled about rewarding me. I have said, and I say again, and in truth do I believe the deed was by the Hand of One who stands head-and-shoulders above our ancient gods.

"Yet, if indeed you must reward me, allow me but to join you in your happiness, and I shall have my reward."

Johan made no reply, but smiled as though pleased at the old Viking's remarks. His mind, so it seemed, had taken up another train of thought. And when he spoke again, it was with a note of sadness.

"Ever does the thought return. Ever does it return to plague my mind your words of yesterday, friend Torkel. If the coming of our countrymen to the Great New Land of the West is, in truth, delayed by several hundred years, they shall find no trace of the Lost Greenland Colony. They shall find no trace of the Norsemen, except as you say, 'our mark,' our runes engraved on a stone we can only hope will be found."

Johan squared his shoulders as though in a vigorous effort to cast aside a distressing thought and changed his stride with a few energetic paces which caused the other man to quicken his step accordingly.

"But let us not be troubled with matters hundreds of years hence," he said, and his tone carried a distinct trace of impatience. "A few days from now we shall reach the dwellings of the people you have called 'The Lost Colony.'

And you, and your comrades, shall see a welcome such as you can scarcely imagine.

"There shall be food, and rest—and *ves heil, øl, og vin* (wassail, beer, and wine). With this will I wager: you will find little time to yearn for your homes in the Northland."

Torkel again smiled but made no reply. He seemed lost in deep meditation.

And again the two Norsemen strode along, side-by-side in silence. There was no sound, save for the crunching of their boots over the charred stubble of the grasslands.

Finally—once more, Torkel spoke.

"I have been turning things over in my mind, friend Johan. And thus do run my thoughts: Since I no longer have my ship, I am, in truth, no longer a Viking, either as warrior or explorer. And, since I am no longer a Viking, it shall please me to cast off my Viking name.

"No longer shall it be 'Torkel the Warrior.' It shall be 'Paul Knutson,' the Christian name given me at birth.

"And indeed it shall well please me, but be so kind as to mention this not to young Kristenson, it shall well please me to spend the rest of my days as one of His followers ... as a follower of the New God of the Christians."

Both men halted and looked at one another, Johan with a look of surprise, and Paul Knutson with another rare smile. They grasped one another's hands warmly, and then, without a word, turned their steps westward toward the setting sun and the Norseman's "Land of Peace and Contentment," beyond the land of the Dakotahs in the land of the friendly Mandans, the chosen home of the Lost Greenland Colony.

ERLING NJALSON ON THE SALT SEA

Far to the north on the shore of the Great Salt Sea, Erling Njalson, second-in-command of the Knorr, was roused from sleep by the level rays of the rising sun, sat up and vigorously rubbed his bearded face with both hands.

As usual, his next act was to glance seaward to where the ship lay at anchor. All seemed to be in order.

He had overslept. His nine comrades, always hungry, were already stirring about with the task of preparing the morning meal.

And as always, he glanced at the campfire's smoke. It was rising straight upward. This was good; it meant another day of fair weather.

His next act was to grasp his trusty spear, the Norsemen's constant companion night or day. Then, before rising to his feet, he reached for his knife, buried to the hilt in the soft sand that was his bed, and carved a notch, small and neat, in the spear's shaft.

And again as always he counted the notches—now twenty.

Twenty days had now come and gone since that morning when Torkel, the Knorr's commander, took two long-boats and nineteen companions and had set forth up the river, southward into the heart of the Great New Land of the West in search of the Lost Greenland Colony.

"Ten more days," Erling said aloud. But, in truth, he needed no reminder. Well did he remember the exact words of Torkel's order: "If we have returned not when thirty days have passed ... ." But he liked not to dwell upon the remaining words of the order.

Of course, he promptly assured himself, there was no reason to suppose that the journey inland and return would require the full thirty days. Very possible it was that now, after twenty days had passed, Torkel could well be expected to arrive any day—perhaps even today.

But they arrived not that day—nor the next day—nor the next.

The Norsemen busied themselves with the ever present task of providing food—chiefly through hunting of wild game for their present needs, as well as for provisions for the homeward journey. Smoked venison, dried fish, and such edible wild roots as the nearby marshes might afford, made up the bulk of their stores.

And another task, more tedious, to be sure than the hunt for game, was the rather arduous task of moving the supplies out to the ship which due to the shallowness near the beach was anchored some distance offshore.

A rather tiresome task it was. Torkel had, of course, taken both of the long-boats for the journey inland, and as Sofus Åsen complained, the meager load capacity of the small-boat made the labor seem like "eating soup with a sharpened stick." But the work served, in a measure at least, to break the monotony of waiting that seemed to increase as the days passed.

And the Norsemen may as well have been encamped on another world, in so far as other human habitation was concerned. They saw no signs of the Skrellings, those sometimes hostile, though not too troublesome natives they had encountered back at their Vinland camp.

Their one-and-only intruder was an old bull moose, perhaps attracted to the camp by the smell of salt or simply curiosity. Seldom did he fail to put in his appearance each day shortly after the evening meal was finished.

Too old and tough for meat so the seafarers reasoned, and the antics of the old fellow served the men as an amusement of sorts. And so, though sorely tempted at times, they had refrained from slaying the inquisitive, old beast.

But now, as the days wore on and tempers commenced to show signs of fraying, the old bull was fast becoming more and more of a nuisance it seemed. And finally his persistence, along with other characteristics, had earned him an eke-name. Hans Håkon it was, who first called the ancient moose "Old Torkel's Ghost."

No disrespect toward their commander, The Wise Warrior, was intended—the name seemed simply to fit the old bull's individuality. To most of the men, it seemed humorous, if not strangely appropriate. And the time was now at hand when a bit of humor was sorely needed.

And so, for several days following the christening, "Old Torkel's Ghost" had been alternately befriended and again driven out of camp with a hail of pebbles and mild curses.

But then for some reason which he chose not to explain, Erling took a dislike to the old bull-moose's name and forbade its use. And he also gave the order in terms which left no room for doubt that the animal was not to be harmed.

And so the days passed, slowly yet somehow all too swiftly. And finally, another sunrise, another awakening, and another notch on the spear—thirty he now counted.

This day the stoical Norseman partook of the morning meal without appetite and in silence. Then rising to his feet without a word, and again taking up his spear he strode silently away along the sandy beach toward the west.

For more than an hour he walked aimlessly and seemingly without purpose, turning over in his mind again and again the sad truth that Torkel had used his self allotted thirty days.

And again the old Viking's orders: "If we have returned not when thirty days have passed, you are to give us up for dead and sail without us."

No. There was no escaping the truth. Torkel and his nineteen companions were dead. No doubt killed by hostile natives.

And Erling uttered a violent curse directed at nothing in particular. But certain it was, that the words would have bode ill for any stranger who might have chanced to cross his path at that moment.

A feeling of helplessness came over him as he strode onward. Let me ponder now—so ran his thoughts—I could name every man, should I choose to set my mind to the task. There was Hjalmar the Wild Man and Oskar the Tall One. And there was Sigurd—and another sturdy one called Lars. And that quarrelsome one we called Black Botolf. Then there was that young fellow, Ivar, the maker of charts. I knew his father in Bjørgvin (Bergen). A merchant named Khristen Ivarson, he was.

So began what was to have been a series of sad recollections as he remembered, one by one, the names and faces of his lost comrades.

But it ended abruptly as he rounded a little rocky point of land and suddenly came upon a small somewhat sheltered cove, and an astonishing sight to say the least. There lay at least a dozen Dragon-ships. But hold on. What is this? They have been beached, but certainly not by a storm. In a rather orderly row they lay as though hauled ashore by their crews—each a huge task in itself. Such were his thoughts as he quickened his steps for a few paces and then commenced to run in his eagerness to reach the ships. "Seafarers from the Homeland," he cried aloud.

But he halted abruptly as he neared the scene—there was not a living soul in sight, nor any evidence that anyone had been there recently.

And the ships, yes, an even dozen there were. But no longer could they be called ships. They were total wrecks. Their ruination had been brought about by time and the inexorable action of the elements.

The Dragon-ships had been hauled ashore and deserted by their crews. Of that he could be certain. And twenty years ago, if not longer, the Norseman estimated, as he sank his knife into a rotting timber.

Then suddenly it dawned upon him; here were the vessels of the Lost Greenlanders.

Yes, here was the answer. Too great were the odds against any other solution. They had forsaken the sea, and their ships, to journey inland.

Not a single boat did Erling discover among the ships. Mute evidence, yet almost conclusive, that the Norse-Greenlanders had taken the very route up the river recently followed by Torkel and his men.

But where were they now? They are most likely dead. No doubt killed by the natives of this strange new land. And now, the men who had set out to search for them had probably met the same fate.

And again he vented a violent curse. This time directed against whatever had caused their deaths.

But why had not the crew of the Knorr made this discovery? Why? Simple enough it was. Their quest for game, and for freshwater fish had, invariably, taken them inland up the river and away from the beach.

Yes, here was the end of the journey for the missing Greenland colonists. Here was an interesting find to say the very least. But yet, somehow, it brought no joy to his saddened heart. With a shudder, he turned his back upon the dreary scene, and commenced to retrace his steps back to camp.

He would not mention this to his crew lest it cause dissension among them. He would banish it from his mind. Let the memory of the discovery perish with the dying ships. Let it die with the brave men and women who had wandered too far from the homeland, and let it die with the saga of Torkel and his brave companions.

An empty victory, indeed it would be, to return to the homeland with nothing to report but the loss of twenty men and the unlikely tale of finding a fleet of rotting ships.

The discovery must however, be reported to the King. And then, perhaps ... .

As he neared the campsite he observed, somewhat surprisedly, that it was deserted. The small-boat with a single occupant bobbed through the waves toward the shore. It was Hans Håkon.

He stepped from the boat, and carefully beached it on the sand before turning to the approaching Njalson. "We have been waiting, sire," the younger man announced, with the usual due respect toward his superior.

And then, "Fresh water casks filled and all stores aboard," he added, a little too gleefully, Erling thought.

"*Ja vel*," was the older man's only reply as he shoved the spear into the sand, and then, loosing his grip on the shaft, ran his fingers subconsciously over the thirty neatly carved notches—one for each long day of waiting. "I have been pondering," he finally said, leveling his gaze at Håkon's face, "I have a mind to ... yes I think we shall. We will delay our departure one more day."

"But, sire," came the startled reply, "everything is in readiness. The men are all aboard—ready to weigh anchor. We must ... we cannot ... do you not ... do you not think sire ... ," he stammered.

"Speak clearly man," Erling commanded. "What are you trying to say?"

"I mean to say, sire," he blurted. "Commander Torkel's order ... we were to sail after thirty days," Håkon protested, growing bolder as he found words suited to the occasion. "Recall, sire. It was an order ... lest we run afoul of the autumn storms on the homeward journey."

Erling's face reddened with a sudden, unreasoning anger. "A curse upon the autumn storms, and I will hear no more about Torkel's order," he stormed.

"After thirty days he said we were to give him up for dead. Very well then—if Torkel is dead, who may I ask do you suppose is now in command of the Knorr and this expedition?

"I, Erling Njalson, am in command now. And I say a foul curse upon the storms of autumn."

He glanced seaward toward the ship, and with a sudden motion, pulled the spear from the sand. And then, as though on second thought, thrust it back.

"Go back to the Knorr, and tell your comrades we shall wait for our comrades *ten* more days."

And without a word, Hans turned and strode briskly back to the small-boat.

And so it was, that once more the camp on the shore of the Great Salt Sea of the North was laid out. There was some grumbling at the delay, but for the most part, the men seemed to share Erling's feeling in the matter—that it would be well worth the gamble. Another ten days against the possibility that Torkel and their other companions might yet return.

But the days passed. Relentlessly, yet all too quickly it seemed. They were days of anxiety, days of hope, days of dread, and finally, days of despair. And then once more, the Knorr was in readiness for sailing. And once more, the small-boat bobbed toward the shore and grated on the sand.

But this time, there were no cheerful words from Håkon. He sat silently in the boat with oars in hand while Erling approached in silence and in sadness.

Halfway across the sandy beach, he stopped, turned abruptly, and strode back to the abandoned campsite.

Arriving at the center of what had been their camp, he seized his spear and with both hands, and, raising it aloft over the dead ashes of the campfire, thrust it deeply into the sand and left it there, upright.

Forty neatly carved notches on the shaft.

* * * * * * * *

Once underway, the Knorr hurried before a brisk breeze out of the southwest, the great sail taut and straining at its fastenings. Like a frightened bird it seemed, anxious to be gone from some evil place.

Erling had set the course: Northeast by East. He would head, as nearly as possible in the direction of *Ginungagap*, that rough but one-and-only waterway between the Salt Sea of the North and the great Outer Ocean beyond.

But no, he would not return to their Vinland camp the original headquarters of the ill-fated expedition as Torkel had planned. He would take a shorter route and head for Greenland, bypassing the site of the abandoned Western Colony, to seek comfortable winter quarters in the East Greenland Settlement.

With the coming of spring, he would prepare to journey onward to the homeland. The homeland and the sad report he must carry to King Magnus.

Erling stood in the bow of the Knorr, and watched with a strange feeling of satisfaction despite the gloom that hung over his very soul—the little plumes of sea spray, where the ship cut its way through the protesting waters.

We are making good headway, he told himself with forced enthusiasm. But even as he spoke the words in his mind, he realized that he was merely attempting to thrust aside other and less pleasant thoughts.

And then, another sudden realization—they would soon be out of sight of land. Out of sight of the place where they had set camp on the beach and waited for forty days in vain for the return of their comrades.

Erling knew not why, and, indeed there was no purpose in the thought, but now he must have one last look back toward the campsite before it vanished.

He turned and leveled his gaze toward the shoreline.

His heart leaped in his throat. There on the beach, almost at the edge of the river where it shallows out across the sand. There was a speck in the haze of the distance.

Could it be? Ah, but no, impossible. Certainly the sails of Torkel's long-boats would present a much larger object even at such a distance. But yet, it could be. It must be.

And then, "Ho, comrades. Look sharply to the beach. Can any of you see, or are my wits making a fool of me?

"You, Håkon—younger than mine, your eyes are. What do you make of the small object on the strand near our campsite?" Hans gazed long and intently back over the wake of the Knorr. And at last he turned with an air of finality. "Old Torkel's Ghost," he declared succinctly.

A few of his comrades smiled, but no one laughed aloud as they bent once more, each to his appointed task.

Erling made no reply to the Håkon's observation. Again he turned and faced forward as though pretending to take no notice of the forbidden use of Torkel's name.

He glanced skyward. Scattering clouds were now scudding before the rising wind. He then looked at the great sail's fastenings, and noted with satisfaction that all were in order. And again he faced forward across the water on toward *Ginungagap*.

For a long time he stood motionless and silent. And then, once again, the thought—the object on the shore. It was nothing. Of that he was certain. Nothing but the old bull moose attracted to the abandoned campsite.

And yet—he would have one more look toward the shore. Possibly, but no, another look would reveal that the old animal had now ambled out of sight and nothing more.

He did not look back. And now, of a sudden, his sadness seemed tempered once more with that strange fascination, as he again fixed his gaze upon the faraway line where the sea and sky seemed to meet. To where the Great Salt Sea of the North rolls onward toward *Ginungagap*, and that Great Outer Ocean that stretches away to where it washes the shores of Greenland and Norway far beyond.

But, had Erling taken that last look, he could not have failed to observe that the speck on the beach had now separated into perhaps a least a half-dozen smaller specks moving about the abandoned campsite.

Or, had he bent his gaze in that direction but a short time later, well before the shoreline sank far below the horizon, he would certainly have observed a column of smoke scattered by the wind. The smoke from a signal fire, kindled by Johan's messengers in high hopes, but left to die in disappointment. But Erling did not look back.

EPILOGUE

In due time the Norse-Mandan-Dakotah army passed over the scorched grasslands and reached the Dakotah villages and then the Norse-Mandan villages. And as promised, the returning army and the four newcomers were heartily welcomed—and there was food, rest, and plenty of *ves heil, øl, og vin* (wassail, beer, and wine).

Although it took some time, Johan's attitude toward Ivar mellowed. He recognized that Ivar was indeed more a man of learning than a wandering warrior, and that his knowledge could also be useful to the community. He also realized the inevitability of things to come between Ivar and Maria, and showed Ivar a good location for a Norse-Skrelling style lodge and where to gather material for its construction.

Ivar eagerly bent to the task, and with the help of Byrnjolf and his Skrelling friends was soon completing his lodge—a necessity for a Norseman before taking a wife.

And then in *Binaakwe-Giizis* (the Moon-of the-falling leaves), which the Norsemen call *Oktober*, there was a wedding. A Christian style wedding it was, although complicated by the lack of a priest, and the need for considerable translating. The three days of festivities that followed were distinctly flavored, as one might well imagine with a blending of Christian, Old Norse customs, and traditions of the Skrellings. Although much of what went on was bewildering to the Skrellings, they were content to understand what they could and ignore the rest. And the proudest and happiest of the wedding party, aside from Ivar and Maria of course, was the aged Grey Hawk, Great Chief of the Ojibwahs—foster-father of the bride.

In time the messengers who were sent to the Great Salt Sea returned with the sad news of the failure of their mission and by what a small margin had it failed. Sad indeed was Torkel when Sigurd handed him Erling's spear with its forty notches.

In time Lars and Sigurd took Mandan wives and settled down to become tillers of the soil, but Torkel, or Paul Knutson, as he now preferred to be known, did not marry.

Over the course of the winter, stories were told about traders from western tribes saying that they had heard that somewhere in the great mountains to the west there was a river called the *Ginebig* (Snake River) that flowed south-westerly and ultimately emptied into a great salt sea.

The stories rekindled the explorer nature in Torkel and in the following spring he, together with two Norse-Mandans set forth on an expedition to the West—to where he now envisioned mountains, as in Norway, that stand high above the water like a giant warrior with his head and shoulders in the clouds. Years came and went, and so did traders' stories about people seeing a hairy-faced person with a very long knife and two companions, but neither Torkel, nor his Norse-Mandan companions ever returned.

The Knorr with Erling in command reached Norway the following autumn, and he delivered his report that most likely the Lost Greenland Colony and Paul Knutson's expedition sent to locate it had been killed by hostile natives. King Magnus was saddened by the news of the loss of his people and his counselor. And while he found it interesting that the Lost Greenland Colony had gone deeper into the New Land of the West, he was then being pressed by other matters and concluded that sending another search expedition was not warranted at the time.

And as the passing years became decades, and the decades became centuries, Johan's unhappy prediction that the Norsemen would eventually be conquered by their friends the Mandans and Dakotahs was fulfilled. There would be no trace of the Norsemen, save for the Runestone.

And Torkel's prediction: "And come they [Scandinavian settlers] will of that I am confident—be it in fifty years or be it in five hundred years," also came to pass as evidenced by the large number of Scandinavians in the upper midwestern states by the mid-19th century.

* * *

About the Authors

Iral Conrad Nelson (1900–1994), principal author, was born and raised on a farm near Gordonsville, Minnesota. He attended the local public schools which were limited to Grammar School and two years of High School. Later he learned the accounting business through a correspondence course. He followed banking for some years, and in 1943 he established his own public accounting practice in Eugene, Oregon which he continued until his retirement in 1981.

His paternal grandparents had emigrated from Norway to Minnesota in 1852, and he was always interested in the Norwegian language and culture. He became reasonably fluent in Norwegian through study of the language on Linguaphone audio records. His associates at the Sons of Norway Lodge told him that he would do well speaking with the natives in Norway.

His maternal grandfather emigrated from South Wales to Pennsylvania in about 1820. His maternal grandmother was born in western Pennsylvania and was likely a mix of Scotch-Irish and German, but with a touch of Native American from the 1700's. His grandmother once told his older brother, "You got more Indian in you than you think you have."

During WWI he served in the Minnesota Home Guard and was drafted into the US Army, but was not called.

Iral Clair Nelson (1927–), secondary author, is the son of the principal author. He was born and raised in Oregon and Idaho. He received a Bachelor's Degree in Mathematics in

1951 and a Masters Degree in Physics at the University of Oregon in 1955, married, and went to work in radiation and environmental protection at the Hanford Project in Richland, Washington which he continued in various capacities for nearly 50 years. He became Board Certified in Health Physics in 1962 and now holds emeritus status.

He served in the US Navy during the Korean War and briefly in WWII.

The decision to reconstruct *Viking's Last Voyage* as written on a typewriter to digital form for publication was based on fulfilling his father's desire to have the story made available to the public, encouragement from his neighbor, Alan Aamot, and his having retired and thus having time to devote to the project. In the process of editing the story considerable research was done. The research was made possible because of the 18th and 19th century journals and other information available on the Internet—none of which were available to his father. The more the related aspects were investigated the more plausible such a story became.